EVERYTHING
PALES
IN
COMPARISON

by

Rebecca Swartz

Bella
BOOKS

2012

Bella Books, Inc.
P.O. Box 10543
Tallahassee, FL 32302

Printed in the United States of America on acid-free paper.

Edited by Katherine V. Forrest
Cover designed by Judy Fellows

ISBN: 978-1-59493-289-2

This book is dedicated to my dad, Harry Swartz,
who taught me to love words and to never give up.

Acknowledgments

Thanks go out to many people, too numerous to list here, who were helpful during the creation of this novel. They know who they are. Specifically, I would like to thank Sgt. Sharon Thomas (ret), Winnipeg Police Dept. and Karen Boily, good friend and beta-reader extraordinaire, both of whom were there from the beginning, and without whose help this book could not have been written. A huge thank you to my editor, Katherine V. Forrest, whose expertise helped make this a better book. I would also like to thank Melanie Wall, whose love and support has been unfailing.

~~~

About the Author

Rebecca Swartz was born and raised in the city of Winnipeg, Manitoba. Possessed of a restless nature, she has moved liberally and often throughout that city and most of western and northern Canada, even venturing as far north as Churchill in the dead of winter. She's worked variously as a dental assistant, DJ, pool maintenance worker and dog obedience instructor. A firm believer in the taking of risks, Rebecca will try almost anything once—except jumping out of a plane. That is something she refuses to try.

CHAPTER ONE

The concert hall was sold out. Couples, groups of three, four and more people crowded the lobby, milling about or moving to take their seats, while still more people filed into the venue. The chatter was loud, the laughter louder, as people struggled to make themselves heard over the background music playing through the loudspeaker system. The mood was pervasively upbeat; these people were here to have a good time.

Constable Emma Kirby glanced around the steadily filling hall and wondered yet again what had possessed her to volunteer for this particular shift. It wasn't as if she couldn't have found something better to do, she was sure she could have. And it certainly wasn't a money issue, since she wasn't getting paid for it. The music, and the artists performing it, could hardly be considered a draw either, since she didn't know any of them. Well, that wasn't precisely true. The three opening bands were unknown to her. Daina Buchanan, the headline act, she was vaguely familiar with, or at least a couple of her songs. One of them, a catchy little number called "Take Me, I'm Yours" was fast becoming a favorite of hers. But even so, Daina Buchanan was a country artist, and Emma was not much of a country music fan.

With a slight sigh and a miniscule shake of her head, Emma abandoned the search for her reasons for being there. It was a fundraiser, sponsored in part by the local chapter of PFLAG, Parents and Friends of Lesbians and Gays, the Rainbow Resource Center and several other corporations from the city of Winnipeg, Manitoba. Proceeds were to be donated to PFLAG, to further that organization's growth. A worthy cause, she knew, and a good enough reason for being there.

Emma hooked her thumbs in her service belt and surveyed the scene from her assigned position at the rear southwest exit. From where she stood, she could view the stage and the crowd with ease. It was a mixed bunch, not unlike any other concert. She had been informed during the briefing she and the other five officers had received at seven P.M., that there were three speakers scheduled for the first half hour. They would come on at eight. Which would account for the rather relaxed attitude of the concertgoers. No one was rushing to their seats; the hall was currently less than half full. Plus, she knew that many of the twenty-five hundred or so ticket holders were mainly here to see Daina Buchanan, who wasn't scheduled to come on until approximately ten P.M. So she didn't expect a capacity crowd until nine thirty or so.

She set off on a little tour, more to ease her boredom than because any real crowd control was necessary. Her stride was relaxed and loose as she headed toward the lobby. Her eyes were alert and watchful, though, and she moved with deliberateness. She nodded to a few familiar faces as she made her way up the closest aisle, maintaining a facial expression that was friendly but not inviting. Once in the lobby, she even stopped to have a quick chat with Constable Rick Meyers at his station. As she made her way back to her post, she was mildly surprised to find herself actually beginning to look forward to the evening.

As the night wore on, and the two warm-up acts came and went, the hall continued to fill until, by the end of the second intermission, it was practically full. Emma, making a pass backstage to check on things there just minutes before Daina Buchanan was due to come on, was brought up short by the sight of a woman just beyond her, her back to her, windmilling her arms. She was dressed in black: black boots, black jeans, a flowing black silk shirt tucked into the jeans. She had short, spiky, blonde hair. *Pretty attractive rear view*, Emma thought. As the woman turned toward her, she ceased her windmilling and reached for the guitar a young fresh-faced guy was handing to her. Emma found herself staring. According to the posters and T-shirts she had seen, but not really paid much attention to, this was obviously Daina Buchanan. *This was her?*

The woman looked nothing like what Emma had expected, more like a punk rocker than a country singer. *Damn, she's good looking.* The woman looked up from strapping on her guitar. Her eyes met Emma's stare. She cocked her head to one side, her expression puzzled but friendly, and flashed Emma a crooked little grin. Emma's heart gave a strange little leap in her chest, and she immediately blushed, feeling foolish and oddly uncomfortable. She ducked her head, turned, and without looking back, quickly returned to where she was supposed to be.

She didn't even have time to reflect on the incident. The lights went down, the background music faded and the crowd came to life. Lighters and glow sticks flared up throughout the audience, and the cheers, whistles and applause became a tumult as the curtain rose to the chords of the opening number. As the band, with Daina in the forefront, was revealed, the crowd went wild.

Emma found herself caught up in the excitement. From her position she was able to do her job and enjoy the show. She marveled at the dynamic energy and sheer physical presence of the woman onstage. Halfway through the set, she decided that purchasing a copy of her CD was definitely in order. The band left the stage and Daina Buchanan, in a single spotlight, began a solo.

Emma wanted to watch this performance, but her attention was caught by a scuffle between a security guard and a couple of scrawny rowdy guys up her aisle. She frowned in annoyance, but automatically headed in their direction.

One moment she was striding up the aisle, the next she was knocked off her feet by a huge, concussive shock wave from an explosion somewhere behind her. She hit the ground hard, cracking her left shoulder against one of the seat arms.

What the fuck?

Then, excruciating pain shot through her arm, and debris began to rain down all around her.

Her ears filled with screams and cries of fear and pain, she made an attempt to struggle to her feet, only to be knocked down by a flood of panicked people fleeing the hall. Regaining her feet once more, drawing back into the relative safety of an empty side aisle, she glanced around in confusion. Smoke was filling the hall and the lights were down, making it almost impossible to see. The terrified crowd rushing past her did not help matters. The explosion, she realized, had come from the stage area; from what she could make out, the stage itself was almost completely destroyed, backdrop, lighting, everything was in a shambles. Her instincts took over. She attempted some measure of crowd control, but in such a panicked state, no one paid her the slightest heed. She almost got knocked down again before she decided to abandon her attempt at moving down the aisle and opted to vault over the seats in an effort to get back to the stage area.

What the FUCK?

Suddenly, the hall was filled with light. She saw bodies, she saw blood, she saw people struggling amongst wreckage strewn everywhere. She saw her fellow officers across the way. At her left shoulder, her radio crackled to life. She grabbed it and, over the cacophony surrounding her, spoke into it, uttering reassurances of her well-being, demanding rescue units, backup and fire crews. The smoke seemed to have come from the initial explosion; there was no fire evident now, but she wasn't taking any chances.

The hall continued to empty out and she was able to leave the rows of seats and make her way down the aisle. She noted, almost absently, that no one appeared to have been trampled in the mad rush to escape, which was a miracle. She also noted that, though there was a lot of wreckage, only the stage and those rows closest to it, the first two or three, seemed to have been affected. But that was still a lot of people.

Thank God the house rule for this venue was no rushing the stage. She kept her mind on the rational, refusing to give in to the horror of the whole situation. Otherwise, she would be lost. *The injured, deal with the injured.* She repeated the litany over and over, even as she bent and assessed casualties, reassuring them that help was on the way. She knelt beside a large young fellow with blank, staring eyes. Blood poured from his nose, soaking his white T-shirt, but he seemed oblivious. She looked into his eyes, speaking gently to get a response. As she placed a hand on his shoulder, he reacted violently, cringing away from her and striking out with both hands, a fearful cry escaping him. Emma barely missed being knocked over as she pulled back sharply. The bulky frame of Constable Meyers suddenly loomed in front of her. He took hold of the guy's flailing arms, shouting something at Emma, but for a moment she couldn't make it out, couldn't concentrate. Something about the stage. *What about the stage? There is no stage.* Someone on stage, he was yelling. What? Who? And then it hit her: Daina Buchanan had been on stage, right when the explosion occurred.

Meyers gave her a light shove. Go, she heard him say, I'll take care of this one. Go!

She went, stumbling over debris, her mind spinning, eyes darting everywhere. She was aware of her heart pounding, racing in her chest, her face and hands slick with sweat and grime. *Jesus Christ, how in the hell am I supposed to find her? Just do it!* she told herself sternly. She set her jaw and skirted around and over huge sections of stage material and jutting struts. A thought occurred to her and she latched onto it: If the explosion had been strong enough to knock her off *her* feet, could it have been strong enough, considering the proximity, to throw Daina clear? She had no idea, but it was a start. She headed for the area behind where the backdrop had been.

As she worked her way there, flinging aside what wreckage she could and avoiding what she couldn't, she became aware of others who were obviously involving themselves in the same search. *Finders, keepers,* she thought, and then bit down on her tongue, hard, to hold back the near-hysterical laughter that threatened to pour out of her. She mentally focused on maintaining a tight clamp on her emotions. Hysterics abounded here; she could not afford to join in.

Mere seconds had passed, she knew, before she reached her destination, but time had slowed to a crawl. She took the area in with one glance, and her eyes fell on a jumble of light and sound equipment and backdrop material, balanced precariously on a section of the stage roughly 8'x8', which was itself teetering over what she could only guess was another speaker. Her attention was caught by an extremely distraught, but apparently unharmed woman stumbling around some yards away, yelling a name over and over again. Just as she was looking away, her brain recognized something before her eye could even register it. Was that a boot? A black boot?

She leaped forward, certainty rising within her along with a sense of dread. Reaching the area, she crouched, removing her flashlight from her belt. She shone the beam into the darkness beneath the delicately balanced mess. A wave of triumph, of excitement, washed over her as she recognized those boots, the black jeans. And then, for one awful moment, she felt totally, completely helpless, as the dangerous predicament Daina Buchanan was in hit home. This whole thing could collapse at any moment, crushing the still form beneath it, if it hadn't already.

She could not possibly move any of the obviously heavy equipment or materials. Grabbing her radio, she called for immediate assistance. Then, crouching lower, she called out to the still form, "Ms. Buchanan? Daina? Can you hear me?" Receiving no response, she did the only other thing she could think of, under the circumstances. She reached under, ducking her head, grasped the woman's ankles and gently pulled. The body slid toward her easily, about a foot, and then was brought up short. She tugged again. Nothing. *She must be pinned.* She whipped out her flashlight and shone the beam beneath the wreckage. Everything was brought into sharp relief. And she could see where the hang-up was: Daina's sleeve was caught by a corner of the speaker that was holding this whole mess off of her.

Okay, well, it's just a shirt, she told herself. *She can always buy another.* Pulling a penknife from a pocket of her service belt, she dropped to her hands and knees. She tried not to think of the passage of time, tried not to imagine Daina's condition. She could not hurry this; to hurry could prove disastrous. And yet, the pressing need to hurry was overwhelming. *Damned if I do, damned if I don't.* She clamped the knife between her teeth, lowered herself to her belly, and with the flashlight in one hand, proceeded to wriggle her way forward into the narrow, confining space where Daina Buchanan was trapped.

"Okay, Daina, I'm coming in," Emma said aloud, hoping for a response. "Just hang in there, girl, I'm going to get you out of here."

She inched her way forward on her elbows, the flashlight beam illuminating the length of Daina's body. *Good thing I'm not claustrophobic.* By the time she reached Daina's shoulders, things were getting pretty tight.

"Alrighty then, let's see what we've got here," she breathed.

The singer lay on her stomach, her face turned away. Her right arm was folded beneath her, her left extended beyond and above her head. Here then was the culprit: the voluminous silk shirt with its baggy sleeves, the left sleeve of which was pinned to the floor by the speaker. Emma, taking a quick glance at the close surroundings, could hardly believe the narrow margin by which Daina had escaped being crushed. At the highest point of this little makeshift cavern, there was maybe a foot of space. When she had initially attempted to move Daina, the woman's body had been angled toward the lowest point. Emma thought it amazing she still had a head at all.

She felt for, and found, the carotid pulse. It was weak and thready, and Daina's breathing was terribly shallow. Emma had felt something else as well; when she brought her hand into the beam of the flashlight, she was not surprised to see her fingers covered with blood. So there were injuries whose nature she could not properly assess, or even assess at all, under the current conditions.

"Okay, honey," she murmured, removing the knife from between her teeth, "time to get you out of here."

"*Kirby?*" The voice, belonging to Meyers, came from behind.

"Yeah, here!" she yelled back, continuing her task of cutting through Daina's shirt, but aware of the beam of another flashlight and the sound of scuffling feet.

"What've you got?"

She filled him in on the situation, ending with, "She's caught up, I have to cut her loose, just give me one more second..." Emma paused, and could never afterward explain what caused her to suddenly drop a hand back and check again for a pulse, for breathing. This time she found neither.

"Ah, shit, *SHIT!*" Fear and alarm coursed through her.

"Kirby!"

"She's crashed, man, I have to get her out of here!" Emma yelled. She slashed once, twice, with her puny little blade. "Pull us out on my signal!" Muttering "Come on, fuck, *come on!*" she slashed a third time and the sleeve was free. "Now!" she yelled, and Daina was whisked from her side. A second later, Emma was likewise pulled unceremoniously from beneath the wreckage. As she emerged, she rolled and twisted, righting herself and almost appearing to pounce on the unconscious Daina.

"Where're the medics?" she snapped, even as she was ensuring she had a clear airway before beginning CPR.

Someone shouted assurance the paramedics were on their way. Barely aware of anyone else's presence, Emma could see, with the better lighting, that Daina was critically injured. A nasty-looking laceration extended from the left side of her forehead past her temple to the midpoint of her ear. Another laceration ran down the left side of her ribcage to her waist, and her jeans were torn the length of the left leg from hip to heel. Emma could just see the edges of another wound and the black jeans were sodden from the bleeding. There was a frightening amount of blood covering her face and neck, and her shirt was soaked from blood pooling while she had lain unattended. But her airway was clear and apparently none of the injuries would inhibit CPR.

She had no clear perception of the passage of time or of her surroundings. Her focus was Daina Buchanan, her goal to bring life back into the still form. On the extreme edges of her awareness she sensed activity, a scuffle somewhere beyond her, and her ears registered a keening wail which her mind instantly shut out. Suddenly, right across from her, a woman dropped to her knees at Daina's head. Emma spared a second to glance at her; it was the woman she had seen stumbling around earlier, the one who had been repeating the same person's name over and over again.

The woman, tearful, distraught, made a move toward Daina, as if to gather her up and cradle her.

"Jesus Christ, get her out of here!" Emma snapped.

A pair of uniformed arms appeared to drag the woman away before she could interfere, and then the EMTs arrived. Emma, sweat pouring off her in rivers, moved aside to allow them access. An oxygen bag was placed. After ripping open Daina's shirt in preparation for the defib paddles, Emma continued her ministrations. The medic called "Clear!" and she flung her arms back. A moment or two of tense waiting, and then she was back at it, the first shock having no effect. Again the call, again the paddles were applied. Again, no response.

Emma looked up, eyes blazing. "Do it again!"

The medic actually flinched. Emma felt a hand on her shoulder, as if to restrain her. She shrugged it off with a violent gesture. She resumed CPR, even though her arms were leaden and her shoulders ached.

"She's in there," she said, and glanced up to see that the medic was priming the paddles even as she spoke. "Do it once more, she's in there, I know she is."

For the third and possibly last time, the paddles were applied and Daina's body arched with the charge. Emma, watching the monitor, was rewarded with a renewed sinus rhythm pattern. Her eyes went back to Daina, and she saw her chest heave as she inhaled breath on her own. Emma released her own breath. With shaking hands, she reached to pull Daina's shirt closed, to afford her a measure of decency. Trembling, her muscles burning with fatigue, she sank back onto her heels. In the aftermath of her intense concentration, she could feel herself disassociating. It was almost blissful. She heard words spoken, but paid no heed; she felt hands applied, proffered assistance perhaps, but she pulled away. She watched, blankly, as Daina was transferred to a stretcher and borne away, accompanied by the distraught woman. There was obviously some connection there, but she couldn't be bothered to think about it.

Lowering her head, shoulders sagging, Emma stared at her hands. She turned them over; they were covered with blood, Daina's blood. As she watched, sweat dripped from her face to her upturned palms. It mixed with the blood, creating thin rivulets that ran off between her fingers. She felt a mild alarm at the thought that her self-control was seeping from her in the same way. And that she was helpless to prevent it. For one awful moment, she thought she might either faint, throw up or burst into tears.

"Kirby?"

The voice was familiar and it startled her back into awareness. A warm burly body crouched beside her. She raised her head. Constable Perry Ames, her partner, met her look with eyes filled with concern. He was off-duty and wore jeans, a dusky blue T-shirt with some obscure printing on it, and running shoes. Solid and well-built, he had boyish features complete with sparkling blue eyes and a gap-toothed smile.

"Hey, you," he said softly, moving to drape an arm over her bowed shoulders.

"Hey, yourself," she returned, managing a tired smile. She blinked, glanced around. "Did you just get here?"

"More or less. I heard the radio report, wanted to see if I could help."

"Well, it's too bad you missed the show," she said, in an attempt at levity. A shudder passed through her. She squeezed her eyes shut and lowered her head again; a second, stronger tremor shook her all over.

"Come on, let's get you out of here," Perry said, tightening his hold around her shoulders.

"No, no, I can't," she protested, trying to shrug away from him. "There's too much to do, I have to help—"

"Emma, Emma, it's done," he soothed her, "it's taken care of, you did your part."

Confused, disbelieving, she let her gaze travel around the concert hall. He was right. Order had been more or less restored; there were uniformed officers and EMTs everywhere, and most of the injured had been removed.

"It looked a lot worse than it actually was," he pointed out quietly. "No deaths, no life-threatening injuries. I mean, other than that girl you were working on. You saved her life, you should be proud."

Emma didn't respond. Her eyes fell again on her bloodstained hands.

"You weren't hurt, were you?" Perry asked gently.

She shook her head, curling her hands into fists. She wondered at the ache in her heart and the burning behind her eyes, and felt a sort of half-hearted anger with herself and her current state of emotions. For the moment, though, she was unable to reassert herself.

"Come on," Perry said, "let's go."

As he rose to his feet, Emma rose with him, unresisting. She briefly leaned against his tall frame, grateful for his solidity, his warmth and his compassion. But her dependence only extended so far. As they made their way out to the lobby, she did so without any assistance from him. They had been partners for almost four years; the level of understanding between them was deep. Her need had been met, there was no offense taken at her attempt to regain her equilibrium.

The lobby was a beehive of activity, with uniformed officers busy gathering statements, mingling with firefighters and various business-suited individuals, all speaking earnestly amongst themselves and looking quite harried. Emma could relate and felt a detached sympathy for them. They had a long night ahead of them. She, on the other hand, had only to attend a debriefing before she was allowed to depart. Her eyes picked out the sergeant on duty to whom she was to report, but she wasn't quite ready to do that.

Placing a restraining hand on Perry's arm, she said, "I'm going to head to the washroom, clean up a bit."

He looked down at her, brow furrowed. "You sure you're okay? Do you want me to stick around? I can."

Her smile was small, but grateful. "No, I'll be all right, thanks. You go on." And in truth, she was feeling stronger, more herself. "I'm glad you were here, though," she added.

He gave her a last searching look and seemed to be satisfied with what he saw. He nodded. "I'm glad I could be here. You take care, okay? I'll see you Wednesday."

She nodded as she remembered, watching him turn away, that she had four days off coming to her. *Thank God for that.*

She headed for the women's washroom, where she proceeded to scrub the blood from her hands and splash cold water on her face. Drying herself with paper towels, she studied her reflection in the mirror, searching for something, but not really knowing what it was she was looking for. She felt affected, almost wounded, and the sudden sense of her own vulnerability shocked her. Outwardly, she appeared unchanged, at least to her own eyes, but deep within she felt altered somehow. And it scared her.

An image rose to her mind, unbidden, of Daina Buchanan flashing that grin at her, and the memory of her own ridiculous reaction caused a wave of irritation to surge through her. *Give it up, Kirby.* She impatiently pushed wet strands of hair off her face. *Get a grip, it's over, she's alive, you did a good job.* She balled up the paper towels, slammed them into the refuse container and left the washroom.

An hour later, letting herself into her apartment, she headed directly to the bathroom, dumping her service belt and holster on the dining room table and shedding her uniform as she went. Her earlier exhaustion had been replaced with a tension, a tightness in her body and mind she hoped to alleviate with a long, hot shower.

But the shower did nothing for her. Her muscles ached and her mind burned. She considered going for a run, but she was unwilling to inflict any further punishment on her already tortured physique.

Heading for the kitchen, clad in a burgundy, terry cloth bathrobe, she uncharacteristically fixed herself a stiff shot of Southern Comfort in a glass half-filled with ice. Drink in hand, she strode into the living room, not bothering to turn on any lights, and dropped into her favorite armchair. She sat in the darkness, her only illumination that of the streetlights shining palely through the patio doors. Attempting to sort through the myriad images and thoughts racing through her mind, she absently took a deep swallow from her drink. Sweet liquid fire burned its way down her throat to pool in her belly. She grimaced. *Oh, yeah*, she thought sarcastically, *that feels real good.*

And then, bowing her head, she burst into tears.

She had no idea how long she cried. The drink was placed off to one side, forgotten, as her unnamed sorrow possessed her and drained her. Sobs wracked her body, tears drenched her skin; it seemed they would be never-ending, that she could not stop crying, that she had been crying her whole life. And when she finally did wind down, when the tears ceased flowing, and the sobs no longer tore through her, she felt neither grateful nor that she had reached any level of understanding. All she felt was an overwhelming exhaustion and emptiness. And an overpowering need to sleep. In sleep, she could find escape.

Shakily, she got to her feet and sought her escape.

CHAPTER TWO

"She left? What do you mean, she left?"

Daina stared blankly at her mother, puzzled, not quite sure she had heard right.

Marlene Buchanan, standing to Daina's right at her bedside in the ICU of Winnipeg Memorial Hospital, shrugged slightly. She was of average height, with a slightly rotund build. Her brunette hair was silvered lightly, and her pale blue eyes fairly sparkled in a face etched with smile lines. She was often in good humor, rarely uncomfortable in any situation, but she was uncomfortable now, eyes flicking momentarily away before alighting once again on her daughter's face.

"She just—left," she said, and shrugged again. "She said...

well, she told us that she just couldn't be here, that waiting around to see whether or not you came out of the coma was something she just couldn't do, she couldn't stand it."

Daina gave a mild start as she realized just exactly what it was her mother was saying. "You mean Kendra's *gone*? She left town?"

Marlene nodded.

Daina's mouth fell open. "Holy shit," she muttered. The expletive seemed rather inadequate, but for the moment nothing else came to mind. She sank back onto the pillow, staring blankly at the curtain which encircled her bed to provide a semblance of privacy. *The surprises are just never-ending today.*

She had just been told, for the second time in a few short hours, first by her attending physician and a neurologist, and then by her mother, that she had been in a coma for approximately fifty-six hours. That had been twelve hours ago; it was going on six P.M. now, Monday, the fifteenth of July. She had lost almost two and a half days, which actually bothered her less than she expected.

She had been told how she ended up in the coma in the first place, that she had basically been standing almost right on top of a home-made bomb, which detonated during her performance on Friday night, and for which no one yet had claimed responsibility; also, that she had been thrown back several feet, only to be buried beneath a pile of rubble consisting of various parts of the very stage she had been performing on. She had grinned wryly at that, a half-formed thought occurring to her, something about living and dying on stage. Until she had been gravely informed that she *had* almost died. She'd sobered immediately when told that she had, in fact, arrested and subsequently been revived through the efforts of the paramedic team and one Constable Emma Kirby. In fact, her informers continued, it was this very same Constable Kirby who had found her, facilitated her rescue and then commenced CPR efforts after her heart and breathing stopped. And who had insisted on those efforts continuing, even when the chances for revival seemed nonexistent.

Daina wasn't quite sure how she felt about the fact that, in essence, she owed this Constable Kirby her life. Considering her injuries, the rescue had obviously been timely. The lacerations running almost the complete length of her left side were thought to have been inflicted by a sheared-off stage strut. No doubt she had come into contact with it while she'd been flying through the air with the greatest of ease, she thought ruefully. She also boasted a dislocated left shoulder, a concussion, and a ruptured spleen; she'd needed surgery to remove the latter. Thank God nothing had been broken, though her ribs were badly bruised; when she'd landed, she'd landed *hard*. She had lost a great deal of blood in a short amount of time, had, in fact, almost bled to death, and it was not known for certain how long she had been without oxygen.

Still, it did not appear that she had suffered any permanent damage. Her body was functioning, her faculties intact. She was stitched, bandaged and her arm was in a sling. Her throat hurt from the endotracheal tube and her lungs felt tight and painful as a result of inhaling the acrid fumes which had resulted from the bombing. She was bruised and battered, but she was whole and she was alive. And she owed it all to this Constable Kirby. The thought made her distinctly uncomfortable. She didn't like owing anybody anything, let alone her life. *How do you return that favor?* she wondered.

Hastily, she shied away from the whole concept, and instead latched onto the latest tidbit of news, that her lover and manager had, without ceremony, apparently jumped ship. She coughed and cleared her throat.

"When did she leave?" she asked her mother levelly.

"Yesterday afternoon," was her mother's immediate reply. "All plans were canceled initially because none of them wanted to leave. I mean, *nobody* in your band or crew wanted to leave until they knew for sure that you were okay."

Daina smiled at this, inordinately touched. Her band members and her road and stage crew were, for the most part, a very warm, fun and caring bunch, but such a show of loyalty was unexpected and deeply affecting.

"Kendra came to us and said it was ridiculous," her mother continued, "she couldn't afford to have umpteen number of people moping around the city of Winnipeg, waiting for God only knows how long until you came out of the coma. So she packed them all off and then came to us again, and said that she would be leaving as well, that she just couldn't handle it."

Daina shook her head slightly, mindful of strained muscles. She was pissed off, she realized, *very* pissed off. Not hurt, not devastated, not even disappointed. Just very pissed off. The woman who had professed her love for her had deked out of the picture when her own lover's life lay in the balance. Now didn't *that* speak volumes? *Couldn't handle it, my ass,* she thought snidely.

"Daina, are you okay?" her mother asked, breaking into her reverie.

"Huh?" Daina looked up and gave her mother a poorly attempted smile of reassurance. "Oh, yeah, Ma, just thinking."

Nodding, Marlene eyed her carefully for a moment, then said, "May I ask you something?"

"Sure."

After a brief hesitation, her mother said, "I realize that this is none of my business but...do you have...a good relationship with this woman?"

Daina blinked, drawing back ever so slightly with mild surprise. Before she could even form a response, her mother hurried on, saying, "I mean, do you trust her, honey? If she's in charge of your career, Daina, it seems odd that she would just walk out on you like this."

And the issue that Daina had been avoiding for some time now was, very neatly, dropped into her lap by her own mother. She quirked up one corner of her mouth in a rueful grin and sighed heavily.

"Well, Ma," she said, "I guess that's what this is all about." She took a deep breath, coughed again. "Kendra is, to all intents and purposes, my manager, and as such she manages my career. She takes care of all the little things that I just don't have time for. What she *wants* is to take care of everything, to be in full control. And I won't let her. And she doesn't like that, not one little bit."

"I see," was all her mother said.

"Do I have a good relationship with her?" Daina continued thoughtfully. "Well, I didn't think it was...bad. Now, well, I really don't know." She paused as she contemplated that thought. She realized that she really *didn't* know how to quantify her relationship with Kendra, and that startled her and brought her up short.

She had met Kendra Morrow three years ago, shortly after she had first arrived in Nashville. Prior to that she had nurtured her budding career as a country singer/songwriter for almost ten years while living in Winnipeg. She had left her hometown under less than favorable circumstances, having to do with a married woman, an absent husband and a lack of information. Once in Nashville, intent on furthering her career in the epicenter of country music, she had known she would need a manager, and an acquaintance had recommended Kendra Morrow. Kendra, she discovered, was a fair-haired Southern beauty of average height and weight, who sported green ice picks for eyes, and brooked no bullshit from anyone when it came to business.

Their first meeting was all business and mutual evaluation, and continued in the same vein for six months afterward, neither of them acknowledging the growing sparks of physical attraction between them. Daina finally realized that if it were left up to Kendra, the attraction would never be acted upon. So one night, after a sold-out concert at a smaller hall, both of them on an adrenaline high, she had pushed the envelope, with a bit of help from a celebratory bottle of their favorite Shiraz. Kendra, it turned out, had required very little seduction, and from that point on their relationship was personal as well. The delicate balancing act that such a relationship required was largely ignored by both of them. Daina preferred to concentrate on her music, Kendra on all things business-oriented. It was not an easy relationship, but it had seemed to work for a couple of years.

It was only lately that Daina had become aware of a subtle shifting. Kendra wanted more control of her career, more say in the decisions being made, more power than the autonomous Daina would grant her. She was not blatant about her desire, but she dropped hints, made insinuations, and suggested courses of action which struck Daina as totally inappropriate with regard to her musical direction. Daina found herself becoming more and more annoyed with Kendra and less enamored. There were warning bells going off in her head all too frequently. And yet Kendra just seemed to take it all in stride, as if her behavior, her attitude, were completely reasonable. Daina was unwilling to deal with the problem, if problem it was, head-on. She did not want to become sidetracked by what could turn out to be petty issues. And so, as was her wont, she thrust her concerns to the side, to be dealt with later, if they were dealt with at all.

Daina was now troubled to realize that her lack of attention to the matter had, quite possibly, caught up with her. With an effort, she mentally shifted tracks and answered her mother's second question. "Do I trust her?"

She sighed and shook her head again. Swallowing, she licked her dry lips and wished her voice were stronger. It was now a sort of throaty rasp, which she found annoying, compared to her usual voice, once described by a magazine critic as a "honeyed growl."

Clearing her throat, she said, "No, I guess I don't trust her." And as those words, and the truth behind them, sunk in, she bit her lower lip and frowned.

"Well, dear," her mother said gently, "that's a difficult thing to come to terms with, especially when you're close to someone. But," and here Marlene rubbed her daughter's arm briskly, her tone lightening, "it's probably better that you realize it now, now that she's out of your life. I didn't really think she was right for you, anyway."

A startled laugh escaped Daina as her mother uttered those words. Marlene Buchanan had already dismissed Kendra from Daina's life, before Daina herself had even done so. Granted, her parents had only just met Kendra two days ago, when Daina had flown into Winnipeg after being invited by PFLAG almost six months ago to headline the benefit concert. Still, she thought with wry amusement, it was too bad the whole situation couldn't be dealt with so easily.

"The reason I was asking," her mother continued carefully, "is because she asked that we contact her should you regain consciousness." She paused for a beat, then added, "And that we not tell you of her request."

Daina stared, puzzled and a little dumbfounded. "Are you serious? She said that?"

Her mother nodded. "She did."

"Jesus Christ." *What the hell is going on here?* And then, another thought occurred to her. "I take it you haven't called her yet."

"No, of course not. Your dad and I thought we should discuss it with you first, to see how you felt about it."

Daina inhaled deeply and then exhaled, a guttural purr sounding at the back of her throat. It was a sound of frustration, of exasperation.

"Well, Ma, I don't know how I feel," she said truthfully. "I really don't. I mean, it's like I should be feeling one way, you know, hurt or whatever, but I'm not. I'm angry. I have no idea what's going on, why she would do this, and that really pisses me off. But it's not like I can do anything about it, lying here in a hospital bed and her in Nashville." She paused, considering, then said gently, "So, as much as I know you don't want to, will you call her, please? Since that was the arrangement?"

Her mother looked pained. "Are you sure, Daina? That's what you want?"

"Ma, I *have* to get this cleared up. I mean, this is my career we're talking about, it's not even so much the personal issue, you know? If she's playing at some game here, then I might as well play along for a bit, don't you think? Who knows?" Daina shrugged. "Maybe she really couldn't handle…this." She waved a hand to indicate herself and her surroundings. "Right at this moment, I don't feel like I know her at all. If someone came up to me right now and said 'Hey, your girlfriend planted that bomb,' I'd be like 'Wow, she must have *really* wanted to break up with me.' "

"Daina, that's not funny," her mother said shortly. "Regardless of what happened to you personally, a lot of other people were injured by that bomb."

Daina was instantly contrite, her grin evaporating. "You're

right, Ma, I'm sorry. That was tasteless. It's just…I really don't know what to think or feel. I need you to call her and I need to get this cleared up, as soon as possible."

"Then I'll call her, sweetheart, tonight." Marlene rubbed her arm gently. "One more thing, honey. That police officer, the one who rescued you? Would you be interested in meeting her?" The question was asked with polite interest.

Daina grinned, recalling memories of a childhood spent being constantly dragged back by her mother or being verbally reminded to thank each and every person for a gift, for their kindness, for their time. Her mother was much more subtle about it now, but it was nice to know that some things never really changed.

"I don't have a way of getting hold of her," Daina said, wondering how she would go about doing so. "Do you know what station she's—"

"Oh, don't worry, honey," her mother interrupted, making a dismissive gesture with one hand, "I can take care of that, if you like."

"Well, there's no rush, but that'd be great, Ma, thanks. Oh, and Ma? Could we keep this quiet? I don't know about *her*, but I don't want any media involved at all." Her parents had already told her that the press had been requesting pictures and interviews, a statement, especially since she had come out of the coma. She knew she would have to release a statement soon, especially in light of what her mother had so succinctly pointed out, those innocent individuals who had been injured. She needed to reach out to the public, and to her fans. But that would have to wait at least another day.

"I believe she feels the same way, honey," her mother said reassuringly. "She's been 'unavailable for comment' since this whole thing happened. I'm sure she'd be willing to speak privately to you, though."

With a wry grin, Daina said, "Especially if *you're* the one doing the asking."

"Well, dear, there's a right way and a wrong way to say and do certain things. You know I believe in doing things the right way."

Daina didn't miss the twinkle in her mother's eyes as she blithely uttered these words, but all she said in return was a polite, "Yes, Ma, I know."

Marlene Buchanan bent to hug her then, rather awkwardly due to the setup. They both came perilously close to tears as her mother took her leave.

A nurse peeked in, and then eased the dividing curtain back. Daina was grateful to see her; she had never been so uncomfortable, physically and mentally, in her whole life. Moving was agony, thinking, torture.

"How are you feeling?" the nurse asked.

Daina managed a wan smile. "I'm trying not to."

"Well, let's help you get some sleep then. You're still on morphine, doctor's orders, but it sounds like you need it."

"You won't get any complaints from me."

As the nurse took her vital signs, preparatory to administering the drug, Daina sighed. "So, I assume I'm missing some beautiful summer weather."

"You are," the nurse confirmed, unwrapping the BP cuff and lowering Daina's arm. "And you'll probably miss some more, but look on the bright side." She smiled and winked. "You will live to see another day."

Daina gave her a perfunctory smile in return, wondering how many more times she'd be reminded of that fact, and if being annoyed by it meant she was ungrateful. Before she could follow that line of thought, the nurse fiddled with the little dial on her IV line. A second or two later, Daina felt the lulling affects of the drug, and willingly let herself drop off to sleep.

CHAPTER THREE

Clad in shorts and a loose T-shirt, Emma was just heading out the door for an evening run when the phone rang. She hesitated, leaning against the opened door and staring back at the phone on the coffee table. The press and TV stations had basically given up trying to get an interview with her. She had refused each and every request extended, politely but firmly.

Police protocol in saving an individual's life involved certain regulations. First and foremost was that the identity of the officer involved was not disclosed, due to the possibility of lawsuits. If a request for the identity was made, by family members for instance, such a request had to go through the chief of police's office for verification. It would then be brought to the attention of the individual officer(s) involved, who could then choose, based on their own comfort levels, whether or not to grant the request. In this particular case, however, someone had leaked Emma's name to the press. Emma could not possibly know who had done so, but she knew the leak was responsible for the media attention being currently directed her way.

From what she knew of Daina Buchanan, the woman was not a huge star. She couldn't really even be called famous. She was only just making a name for herself across North America, though she was definitely well known in her hometown. Winnipeggers, however, were generally not in the habit of hounding their stars, and that held true for the media, as well. People were generally respectful of other people's privacy.

For the last two days Emma had been pestered with occasional phone calls and the odd reporter and camera crew hanging around outside her building. She did not avoid any of these situations; the callers were told she wasn't interested in granting any interviews and could they please not call again. Any phone messages she received she simply did not return. The individuals hanging around her apartment building were approached calmly and told the same thing, and then asked to leave the premises. She remained relaxed in these situations, but no one made the mistake of overlooking the intensity of her gaze or the edge to her voice.

She hadn't had to deal with any more bothersome calls since Sunday evening, almost twenty-four hours ago. On the third ring, she bit her lower lip, frowned and then shrugged. *Ah, what the hell.* She stepped away from the door to answer the phone.

The caller sighed, almost as if in relief. "Constable Kirby? I'm terribly sorry to intrude, but my name is Marlene Buchanan."

Emma gave a start at the mention of the name.

"I realize you don't know me," the woman went on, "but— you rescued my daughter, Daina, at the concert hall Friday night." Her voice rose slightly at the end of her statement.

"Mrs. Buchanan, yes, hello," Emma greeted her. And then asked, a bit tightly, "Has—something happened?"

"Oh, no, dear, no," Marlene Buchanan replied immediately. "Everything is fine, everything is wonderful, didn't you know? Daina came out of the coma this morning, she's fine."

Emma sagged with relief and sat on the arm of the sofa. "Oh, wow, that's great," she said, with heartfelt sincerity, "I'm glad to hear that. I was wondering how your daughter was doing."

"Well, yes, and that's why I'm calling. She asked that I call you."

"She did?" Emma asked carefully.

"Constable Kirby, Daina would not even be here right now if not for you. And she would like to thank you, personally, for what you did."

Emma said nothing; she couldn't think of anything to say. She knew, of course, that what Marlene Buchanan was saying was true. That what *everyone* was saying was true. She, Emma Kirby, had played a major part in saving Daina's life. Were it not for Emma's intervention, Daina would not *be* alive right now. But she did not seek recognition; she did not want any publicity. She had been doing her job; anyone else could have done the same thing. She was being hailed a "reluctant hero" by the media, which was almost laughable. She wasn't reluctant at all. She knew what she had done. She was willing to leave it at that.

"Would it be possible for you to meet with her?" Marlene Buchanan was asking.

"Um…sure, I suppose," she said slowly, knowing she couldn't very well refuse. "If that's what she wants. When would you—well, when would *she* like to do this?"

"Well, we're quite certain she'll be in the ICU for a short while yet, but I'm sure we could get you in, if we specifically asked. How about tomorrow afternoon?"

Trying to get her thoughts in some sort of order, Emma automatically answered, "Okay, sure. I still have a couple of days off, and the afternoon is better for me, anyway." And then, taking the bull by the horns, she added, "Uh, let's say around three, would that be okay?"

"I think that would be fine," was the immediate reply, to which was hastily added, "Oh, and Daina mentioned she would like this to be private, so this will be just between the two of you."

"Oh." Emma was unsure of what that meant, exactly.

"In other words, there won't be any media."

"Oh, okay, well that's my preference, as well." Emma was grateful that Daina Buchanan was not a media hound. *Chalk one up for her.*

"Constable Kirby," Marlene Buchanan said carefully, her tone suddenly solemn and serious, "if it wasn't for you, my husband and I wouldn't have a daughter right now. We're eternally grateful to you. I'm sitting here right now, holding Steve's hand, he's my husband and Daina's father, and we both want to thank you right now if we don't get to do so in person. If there's anything we can ever do for you, you just let us know, dear, is that clear?"

"Thank you, Mrs. Buchanan," she said, swallowing, "and thank your husband for me as well. I appreciate that. I'm glad I was able to make a difference. Your daughter is very talented and seems like a fine person."

"Well, we love her dearly," Marlene said thickly.

"Mrs. Buchanan, I'll be at the hospital at three tomorrow, and I hope I do get to meet you. You take care now, ma'am."

Afterward, Emma sat there staring at the phone, aware of her heartbeat, and of her sweaty palms. She hadn't realized just how much the singer's condition had been weighing on her mind. The coma had alarmed her. To know that Daina was alive and well relieved her immeasurably.

As a police officer, she had saved lives in less dramatic circumstances, and she had also had to witness death once, in a gang-related knifing incident where she had been utterly powerless to save the young man whose life had bled from him while she held him. It had been over in seconds; there was nothing she could have done, and she had accepted that. She had never taken a life, but she knew her actions as a police officer could certainly cause that to happen. She supposed that such a time might come and she believed herself capable of dealing with it.

With Daina Buchanan, the whole scenario had taken on an almost surreal aspect. The bombing, the ensuing panic, the rescue of the woman had been so overwhelming, she had immediately switched to autopilot. Nothing had really registered until afterward. And then the belated realization of her sense of responsibility had all come crashing down on her.

She knew now why she'd broken down that night: to know that she was unequivocally responsible for saving someone's life, that had she made even the slightest mistake that life would have been lost, was a very heavy weight, and she could not possibly remain unaffected by it. Nor could others remain unaffected by her actions, specifically Daina herself and Daina's family.

But was she comfortable with the thought of this impending meeting? Well, she had agreed to it. And besides, it *felt* like the right thing to do. The woman wanted to thank her; she could be gracious and accept those thanks. In all honesty, she knew she wanted to meet Daina Buchanan, anyway. The memory of that grin, and her reaction to it kept gnawing at her. She had nothing to lose by agreeing to meet with her.

Feeling much more at ease, she stood, stretched luxuriously and headed for the door to go for her run.

CHAPTER FOUR

Awakened in the early hours by the flurry of activity attending a cardiac arrest at the other end of the ICU, Daina lay quietly, watching without fully comprehending the tableau playing out across from her. She felt thick and stupid from the aftereffects of the morphine, and annoyed that her sleep had been disturbed. She struggled to make her brain work, but it was only when the crash cart was rushed over that she was able to make sense of the scene.

Overcome with a feeling of horror, she decided right then and there that she wanted to be out of the ICU as soon as possible. She turned her head away and closed her eyes, but she could not shut out the sounds as the team worked. She squeezed her eyes tighter. The quiet, urgent voices of the team overrode her attempts to block them out. A moment later, she felt a touch on her shoulder, and at the same time a gentle voice asked, "Daina, are you okay?"

Her eyes flew open to take in a slender figure wearing scrubs. She looked up into the compassionate face of her night nurse. Attempting to affect a casual air, she tried to say, "Oh, sure", but what came out was hardly recognizable as anything other than a strangulated croak. Gagging suddenly as her throat constricted, she effectively distracted herself from the scenario beyond her, but was now in her own little panic. Immediately, her nurse was uttering soothing words, cutting through her fear and focusing her, as she quickly raised the motorized bed up to a forty-five degree angle. Hit with a wave of nausea, Daina paled and clutched at the blankets. The nurse offered her water, which she managed to sip through a straw. Her stomach spasmed and the nurse reached for a kidney-shaped basin. Almost immediately, the ill feeling passed and Daina waved the proffered basin away.

"Good Lord," she muttered wearily.

"Sorry about that," the nurse commiserated.

Daina sipped at the water, eyes closed, while the nurse puttered around her bed. Remembering the scene she had woken to, she cracked her eyes open. She was grateful to see the curtains across the way were now drawn.

The nurse noticed the look and said, "Not a pleasant thing to wake up to, I know. How are you feeling, any pain?"

Daina took stock of herself, discovering the pain to be tolerable, but still bothered by the disturbing image of the recent activity she'd witnessed.

"The pain's not bad," she said slowly. With a slight frown, she asked, "What time is it?"

The nurse checked her watch. "Almost three thirty in the morning. Do you think you can get back to sleep or would you like a sedative?"

"If it's not too much trouble—" Daina began, knowing she would never get back to sleep on her own.

"No problem at all," her nurse said, giving Daina's leg a gentle pat. "I'll be right back."

When she next woke up, it was to the ordinary bustle of the unit's morning activities. Blearily blinking her eyes, she shifted ever so carefully, feeling stiff and sore. She had been cautioned against moving too vigorously, due to the still-attached leads from the monitors, but she thought it an unnecessary warning. Moving vigorously was hardly in her repertoire at the moment.

With her new sitting position, though, she found her view much improved. She saw right off that the bed which had been occupied across the room, and which had been the site of last night's activity, was empty. Feeling as if a lead ball had just dropped in her stomach, she swallowed hard and looked away. She saw a nurse coming toward her, the day nurse this time, and she locked onto her, willing the memory of last night's crisis from her mind.

"Good morning, Daina. How are you feeling this morning?"

Clearing her throat, Daina ventured carefully, "Not too bad." She was pleased to find her voice in better working order. "A bit stiff and sore," she added, "but pretty good, otherwise."

"Excellent!" The nurse, Shelley Montgomery according to her name tag, beamed. She was tall and somewhat large, dark haired, and beautiful in an unadorned way. Her smile lit up her entire face. "That's what we like to hear." Looking over the monitors, she asked, "Are you feeling up to something more substantial than Jell-O for breakfast? You can probably tolerate it, considering how well you're doing. I think we could probably even get you out of that bed today for a while, get the ball rolling, so to speak."

"Sure, I guess." Daina smiled tentatively, not quite sure what was meant by "get the ball rolling."

"We'll take some more blood this morning and do another workup," Shelley continued conversationally. "Plus, we'll get you off that catheter, make sure everything is working the way it should." She gave Daina a warm smile. "If everything is fine, I think today we might get you transferred from here to another ward."

"Oh. Wow." Daina tried not to sound too surprised. "Great."

"Not until this afternoon, sometime," the nurse said, with a quick glance at her. "We don't want to rush anything, but you're doing very well."

Daina was pleased. After last night, she had begun to feel vulnerable and almost depressed, feelings which were alien to her. She'd always thought she was a strong-minded, forward-looking individual; she found her current situation not terribly conducive to happy thoughts. The thought of the transfer relieved her greatly. She had been less than five days in the hospital, but already she was beginning to feel restless and edgy. The sooner her circumstances improved, the better.

It was going on nine A.M. by the time the tasks that needed to be done were complete. She now had the option of self-administering her medication with a patient-controlled analgesic, through her own IV drip. By the time her parents showed up, she was feeling stronger and much more herself.

She had been moved to a chair beside the bed, but it was far from an ideal setup. With the IV in her right hand, her left arm in a sling, and her entire left side feeling hot and itchy from the surgery and sutures, she hugged her parents awkwardly.

"You're up!" her mother exclaimed happily.

"Yeah, Ma," she said with a rueful grin. "It's all part of their plan to get me out of here."

"And then *we* get to deal with you," her father said with a wink. He was a tall man, just over six feet, but his shoulders were slightly stooped, as if he'd never adjusted to his height. He had a shock of wavy blond hair, wide-set brown eyes that radiated a strong warmth, and an easy, disarming smile.

"Isn't it still a bit early, dear?" Marlene Buchanan's concern was obvious.

"Well, Ma, I don't know." Daina tried not to sound exasperated. "I assume they know what they're doing. Try not to worry, okay? Hey, how did it go with those phone calls you were going to make? Did you happen to get hold of Kendra? That's something *I'm* worried about."

"And you *should* be worried," her mother said sternly. "I wasn't able to get hold of her, but I left a message on her voice mail to return my call, for all the good *that* will do." With a frown, Marlene asked, "She's not going to run off with your money or anything, is she?"

Daina had to chuckle. "Ma, I haven't got any money for her to run off *with*, or anything else of any use to her. So whatever else is going on, I sort of doubt it's that."

"Do you know what might be going on, Daina?" Steve Buchanan asked quietly.

"No, Dad, I don't," she replied tiredly. Sitting up was already beginning to wear on her. "I'd like to think it isn't anything too serious, but regardless, I'll deal with it, okay?" She gave her mother a pointed look. "Don't worry so much, Ma."

"Oh, Daina," her mother sighed, her exasperation clear.

Daina shifted her position slightly and winced. "Oh, hey, were you able to get in touch with that police officer?"

"Oh, my God, yes!" Marlene brightened. "We didn't talk long, but she sounded so nice. And she was very happy you were recovering and that you weren't in a coma anymore. She said she could come by today at three, so I've cleared it with the nurses and—"

"Oh, Ma, *today?*" Daina groaned. "Why today? I said there was no rush—"

"Oh, hush," her mother admonished her. "It may as well happen today, you wouldn't be happy with *any* day I chose. Besides, she's on her days off, from what I understand, and right now she has some time."

"But I look like hell," Daina grumbled.

"You don't look like hell, and even if you did, I doubt it would matter to her in the least."

Daina held onto her poor form for a few moments longer, before finally acquiescing with a heavy sigh. "All right, all right, we'll do it your way." In a tone that held a definite hint of long-suffering, she added, "Not that I have any say in it, anyway."

"Finally figured that out, have you?" Steve Buchanan sounded amused.

"Steven!" Her mother gave her father a light slap on the

shoulder, which her father made a show of trying to avoid while cowering in mock fear.

Daina burst out laughing, her first real laugh in days, but one which she instantly regretted, as the pain it caused was so blinding, her vision actually swam and then grayed. She felt herself flush hot, and then, sickeningly, broke out in a cold sweat. She uttered a single moan, certain she was going to lose her breakfast. A second or two later, she felt strong hands steadying her in her chair, and heard gentle, soothing words in her ear.

"Easy, just breathe, nice deep breaths, you're fine…"

She did as instructed, and after a while was able to open her eyes and focus once more on her surroundings. At her side, Shelley Montgomery reached over and applied a cool, damp cloth to her brow. Daina swallowed, and tried to look at her.

"Don't. Just stay still for now." The nurse's tone brooked no argument.

"Is she all right?" Her mother's voice, extremely concerned.

Daina couldn't turn to look for her. She opened her mouth to speak, but nothing came out. She didn't know if she was all right or not.

"She'll be fine," Shelley said, with gentle reassurance. "She just has her limits, that's all. Mr. Buchanan, if you'll give me a hand, let's get her back up into bed."

Daina was so completely taxed, she was barely any help at all. But she did manage to help them get her into her bed, and Shelley administered a dose of painkiller through the dial on her IV. Daina saw the concerned faces of her parents, and tried to give them a reassuring smile and wave. She had no idea if she succeeded or not. The drug acted swiftly. She was out of commission in no time.

She awoke with a start to the sound of her name being called. Shelley, standing at her bedside, smiled warmly as she opened her eyes, and greeted her with a soft, "Hi there."

Daina blinked a few times as she focused, and then she yawned. "Hi."

"How are you feeling?"

Daina frowned, considered, then replied, "Fine, I guess." She grinned crookedly. "I hope you didn't wake me up just to ask me that."

"No, but I will next time, just for that." The nurse's warm smile held, as she added, "I woke you for a couple of reasons. First, we've received the preliminary results of your blood work and everything looks fine. We'd like to transfer you to a general surgical ward this afternoon. Are you comfortable with that?"

Again, Daina considered. She gave a very slight shrug. "I suppose. Are the nurses there as nice as you?"

"No, they're terrible," Shelley replied dryly. "I've spoiled you, I'm sorry. It's a failing of mine."

Daina's grin was met with a wink from the nurse, who said, "The other reason I woke you is because you have a visitor in the waiting area that no one has cleared with us."

"Oh. Who is it?"

"She says her name is Kendra Morrow. Apparently she's your partner...*and* your manager?"

Daina felt no surprise, only a vague sort of annoyance. She shook her head. Of course Kendra would feel it necessary to clearly state both positions.

"You mean she isn't?"

"Oh, yes, she is," Daina hastily stated, realizing her headshake had been misinterpreted. "No one cleared her with you, though, because no one thought she'd show up."

"Oh. Well, she did. And she's a bit PO'd we wouldn't let her in."

"Yeah. She would be." Daina sighed.

"So..." Shelley paused. "Did you want to see her?"

No, truthfully, I really do not, was Daina's first thought. Quickly followed by, *But, of course, I have to.* She sagged. "Yeah, I guess I have to."

"If you like," her nurse broached carefully, "I can keep an eye on you while she's here."

"Oh. No." Daina managed a half-smile. "Thank you, but I'm sure it'll be fine."

When Kendra showed up, it was obvious to Daina, noting the careful tread and wary expression, that Kendra was unsure of her reception. She silently watched her approach the foot of the bed, where she stopped, resting one hand on the metal frame, her briefcase in the other. She wore white slacks, a light blue button-down shirt, and a navy blazer. She appeared a bit pale and haggard, and more than a little tense. She bent to place the briefcase on the floor, then straightened.

"Daina," she said guardedly, nodding slightly in greeting.

"Kendra," Daina returned, with almost no inflection. "Fancy seeing you here." She paused a beat, then added, "Figured out pretty quickly why my mother was calling, did you?"

Kendra lifted her chin, coloring slightly. "Look, don't start with me," she said tightly, with hardly a trace of her Southern accent. "I realize I have some explaining to do, and I realize you're probably not too happy with me right now. But there are things we need to talk about."

"Well, at least we're agreed on *that*." Daina's mild tone was edged with contempt.

Kendra set her jaw. "If all you're going to do is try to score points off me—"

"Oh, *please*," Daina interrupted in the same mildly contemptuous voice. "After your sterling behavior, anything I could come up with as a repartee would hardly compare."

The comment seemed to bring Kendra up short. Her color deepened, and she glanced sharply away. Then she looked back at her, seemingly collected once more. "You look good, by the way," she stated, a bit lamely, into the silence.

"No, I don't," Daina countered. "I look like hell and I feel like shit." She paused, then added rather snidely, "But thanks, anyway."

"Oh, for *God's* sake," Kendra finally snapped. "If this is how you're going to be—"

"Get to the point, Kendra," Daina interrupted wearily. "You forfeited your right to respectful behavior a little while back, remember? Hurting your feelings is the least of my concerns at the moment."

Kendra blinked, stared at Daina, then bluntly stated, "The tour has been canceled."

It was Daina's turn to stare. "*What?*"

"You heard me. It's been canceled, all of it, all of the North American dates, canceled."

Daina felt something lurch inside her. "Why? I don't understand, we weren't set to tour again until next month. Why cancel, why not postpone?"

Kendra frowned. "Daina," she said slowly, her Southern twang deepening, "next month is only two weeks away. It's the middle of July. You're in a hospital bed, in an intensive care unit, fresh out of a coma. I don't mean to rain on your parade, darlin', but you ain't going *nowhere* for a while, let alone on the road."

Realizing for the first time the truth behind those words, Daina fought off a feeling of despair and held tightly to her anger. "Answer my question, why cancel, why not postpone?"

"Postpone until *when*, exactly?" Kendra's frown deepened. "You were comatose, for Christ's sake. There were no little LED readouts to tell us when you were going to come out of it. We were lucky as it was to give those venues two weeks notice. If we had waited, who knows—?"

"If you had *waited*," Daina practically snarled, "you could have included me in your little discussion."

"You think this is just about *you*?" Kendra narrowed her eyes and her expression hardened. "Daina, there are a hell of a lot more bodies involved here than just yours, alone. Bodies that I became responsible for when—"

"*Wrong*, Kendra," Daina shot back. "Every single one of those contracts was approved by me, which means every single one of those *bodies*, as you put it, is my responsibility. Not yours to assume. *Your* responsibilities are determined by *me*, remember?"

"Someone had to speak for you," Kendra countered tightly, flushed, but obviously determined to gain the contested ground.

"Well, that someone is not and *will* not be you," was Daina's rapid-fire response, "because *you* are fired."

Kendra's expression of shocked disbelief was almost comical, but Daina didn't laugh. If at all possible, she was doubly surprised at her words. But once uttered, she knew she had spoken rightly. Anything else would have been a concession, and the time for making concessions was well over.

"You can't *fire* me," Kendra said hoarsely, her color very high.

"I can and I *have*," Daina stated flatly. "I have watched you over the months trying to wheedle your way into areas where I don't want you. And you still keep trying. I've had enough, Kendra. I'm ending it, all of it, right now."

Kendra's look sharpened. "What do you mean *all of it?*"

And again, before she had even formulated the thought, the words were out of Daina's mouth. "You, me, all of it, the whole thing, it's over," she said shortly. Her head was starting to pound and she was beginning to tire, but she continued doggedly on. "You and I both know there've been problems between us for a while now."

"So *this* is how you deal with it? You just *end* it? What the hell kind of a solution is that?"

Daina chose to view the question as rhetorical, and so didn't answer.

"Daina, don't you think we should talk about this?" Kendra's voice was strained. "How can you—?"

"After the little fiasco you just pulled," Daina cut in, a dangerous edge to her voice, "I really don't think we have anything to talk about."

"You were in a *coma*, for God's sake. What in the hell was I supposed to do?"

"Anything would have been better than what you did." Daina's contempt resounded in the enclosed space, all the more so because her voice was so soft. "I may have been in coma, but I wasn't dead."

Kendra stiffened. Her face became expressionless, as she seemed to realize that whatever entreaties she attempted would be a waste of time. She stared at Daina for a protracted moment, her eyes keen, before saying, "I hope you realize what you're doing."

And Daina, as softly as before, said, "Kendra, I just hope *you* realize what I'm doing."

Kendra's green eyes flashed. Daina returned the look unflinchingly. Even so, she was thankful when her now ex-partner and ex-manager gathered up her briefcase without a further word, turned, and left, curtains billowing in her wake. Only then did she sag back into her pillow, feeling decidedly ill.

And when Shelley Montgomery came in, a look of concern on her face, Daina gave her a wan smile.

"Guess I told her," she muttered thinly.

Twenty seconds later, she suffered a grand mal seizure.

CHAPTER FIVE

"So, you're actually going to get to meet her?"

Perry's tone was casual, but there was a definite hint of curiosity that caused Emma to look at her partner with a slight frown.

They were descending the stairs to the basement of the Public Safety Building, to get in some practice at the shooting range. Emma had suggested the idea to Perry when he'd called her this morning to find out how she was doing. She had casually mentioned the call she'd received from Marlene Buchanan.

"Yes," she replied cautiously, "I actually am."

"So, when is this supposed to take place?"

"Later this afternoon. Around three."

"Well, I hope it goes well," he said.

"Why wouldn't it?" she asked, more to draw him out than because she actually felt like participating in the conversation.

"Will it just be the two of you?" He spoke gently, as if she were a child, or incredibly dense. Or both.

"Well, yes, as far as I know," she said shortly, taking exception to his tone.

"I think you should take advantage of the opportunity," he said with a slight shrug.

"Oh? And what opportunity would that be? Opportunity for what?" She eyed him behind narrowed lids.

"Oh, come on, Kirby, aren't you even a *little* interested? She's cute, she's gay—"

"*Interested?*" Emma could not suppress her incredulous laugh. "Just because she's cute and she's a dyke? What, is that supposed to mean we're perfect for each other?" She shook her head in disbelief. "My God, Perry, grab a brain," she muttered, throwing a look of complete disgust at him, and continued on her way down the hall.

"Well," he said, following after her, his tone reasonable, "I just think you've been alone too long."

"Oh, is that right?" she replied, slowing and turning to face him. "So now you're my dating consultant?"

Another shrug. "Couldn't hurt," he said simply. "You might not like my taste in women, though."

"Yeah, well," she replied, with an eloquent shrug of her own and a tight, humorless smile, "you don't like mine, so we'd be even."

"*You* must not like yours, either," was his quiet rejoinder, "or you'd stick with them longer than one night."

Emma's gut clenched unpleasantly and her spine stiffened; she exhaled sharply. "Perry," she said with extreme care, "if you have something to say, then say it. Don't play with me."

"I'm not," he told her with a serious expression. "I just think it's time you gave someone a chance."

She got a sudden inkling of where this might be going. Her expression hardened. "Don't try to psychoanalyze me, Perry," she said coldly.

"Look, Emma, I just think it's time you realized—"

"Mind your own goddamn business, Perry, do you hear me?" She kept her voice low, which only served to underscore her implicit threat. "If you have a problem with how I conduct my sexual affairs, that is *your* problem. I don't want to hear about it. Understand?"

"Kirby," he said heatedly, "just because your parents dumped you doesn't mean everyone will. Give it a chance, why don't you?"

For one or two brief seconds she was stunned into utter speechlessness. His audacity astounded her, even as his words stung her like a slap in the face.

"*Fuck* you, Perry," she snapped,   teeth meeting and lip curling in a snarl.

And then she moved past him, heading for the exit door which led out into the underground parkade. She hit the door at full stride, slamming it open and flinging it wide. Her lean body was rigid, her mind a thunderous cloud shot through with incoherent rage. He had never before pushed her like this. He had never crossed her boundaries. What had possessed him now to do so, she could not guess. And couldn't be bothered to. She reached her Pathfinder, threw her gun case onto the seat, and leaped in after it.

She left the parkade with a squeal of tires.

Fifteen minutes later, just outside the city limits, she had the presence of mind to realize that she had absolutely no idea where she was going.

"Jesus Christ," she muttered, whipping off her sunglasses and tossing them onto the dash.

She pulled over to the shoulder, then into a little-used drive that led onto a farmer's field. Facing a sea of waving greenery she assumed to be flax, judging by the multitude of tiny blue florets, she switched off the ignition.

She fingered her key chain briefly, eyes moving across the soothing expanse of blue before her. Behind her, traffic zipped past, hell-bent for leather. A shudder ran through her. She sagged back into her seat.

"Good God," she sighed heavily.

Head thrown back, eyes closed, breathing deeply and evenly

as she attempted to restore her equilibrium, she heard birdsong and traffic noise through the open windows as well as the irregular ticking of the Pathfinder's engine as it cooled. Over all of that, the sound of the wind as it blew through the crop and the grass and cattails in the ditches on either side of her, calmed her in a way her mindless driving couldn't.

"Shit," she whispered. *That was a bad scene, Kirby. Very bad.*

And yet, what was she supposed to do? How was she supposed to react? In complete trust and confidence she had discussed with him certain personal details and family matters. She had never wanted any advice. She had told him because he was her partner and her friend and she had felt she could share such things with him. Never once had she thought he would throw her confidences back in her face. She felt angry and betrayed and hurt. And tired. So very tired.

Yet she knew he had confronted her out of concern. Perry cared about her. She knew that. There was no misplaced sympathy, no attempt to counsel in matters he could never understand. He genuinely cared for her and about her. He had only been trying to get her to realize how potentially damaging her behavior was to herself and to those around her, close or otherwise. And on some level, she herself was aware of what she was denying herself and others by allowing no one any closer than what she considered safe.

Just because your parents dumped you, doesn't mean everyone will. Perry's words echoed through her mind, bringing life to a whole host of memories, thoughts and feelings she had tried to put to rest years ago.

"Goddamn you, Perry," she whispered, but there was no heat behind the words.

Leaning forward to rest her elbows on the steering wheel, she put her hands to her face, digging the heels into her eyes, fingers buried in her hair. Unbidden images flashed behind her eyelids, long-unheard voices from the past filled her mind. Unlike so many times in the past, though, this time she allowed them free rein. She threw open the door she had slammed shut and locked so long ago, and allowed herself the first real look she had taken in years.

Growing up in the smaller city of Brandon, she had always known she was different in some way. In a very crucial way. Her own private agony for many years had been viewing what passed for normal all around her, and knowing she did not fit in. She sought confirmation of her own questionable identity, but had no idea where to look. Romantic notions of the past and present confused her. And yet, struggling as she was, and as troubled as she felt, she kept her feelings to herself, preferring to find her own answers rather than seek assistance from individuals whose understanding could not be guaranteed.

In high school, she managed to keep up appearances by accepting a few dates with guys. Maybe what she was feeling was wrong, she just had to find the right guy and everything would be fine. But she knew there was never going to be the right guy. Her dates never coalesced into anything solid. And while these intermittent outings convinced her friends and family that she was no different from them, *she* became more convinced that she was.

One area of her life where she *was* successful was academics. She was awarded a scholarship to the University of Winnipeg, and she left home to attend full-time, residing on campus. It was there that she discovered gay and lesbian collections in the libraries, and finally, coffeehouses and gay bars. She hooked up with a few other women and proceeded to cultivate her sense of self. She met a woman named Crystal, who was slightly older. Intimidated at first, and completely unsure of herself, she awkwardly stumbled through a world that was as new and foreign as it was welcome. She was blindly thrilled when their relationship quickly became intimate.

Armed with a newfound strength and confidence, she finally came out to herself, and felt a huge weight being lifted from her shoulders. Accepted by her peers outside of her home turf, she saw no reason why she should not share her personal happiness. Courage and conviction in hand, she had approached her family, to include them in the rightness of her self-discovery.

She chose to gather her two sisters and her parents together one Saturday night after dinner. So much easier, she thought. She looked at their expectant faces and, after a few false starts, and a couple of hesitant, half-finished referrals to her past, had finally told them, with care and concern, that she was a lesbian.

With her heart pounding in her chest, she awaited their reactions, not sure exactly what to expect.

Her sisters, Debra and Alison, seemed puzzled but not overly affected. Her mother just blinked, becoming rather pale, her mouth forming a soundless *Oh*, before she immediately closed it and glanced at her husband. It was Emma's father who broke the silence. Emma's father, after years of unquestioning and unconditional love and support, the one person she had ever really idolized, and the only person whose approval she had ever sought, slowly got to his feet. His expression was as hard as steel and his voice colder than a January wind. He rose before her and said, plainly and without inflection, "Get out of my house."

Shocked into complete immobility, she stood rooted to the spot, mind frozen, eyes staring. "Wha-what?" she finally managed to stammer out.

In the same flat, cold tone he said, "Whatever the hell they're teaching you at that university, it doesn't belong here. And you don't either. Now get out. I don't want to see you in this house again, unless you lose these sick ideas of yours."

She had flinched at that, flushing hotly. Unbelieving, her eyes had darted between her mother and her sisters, but saw no help or support there. Her eyes flew back to her father as he said, "Get out. Now."

Her mind whirling, her actions completely automatic, she threw her stuff into her single suitcase. Within minutes, she was out the front door, not bothering to even look back at a family that, for all she knew, was still grouped together in the living room in a silent cluster, reeling from her announcement.

It was only on the bus ride back to Winnipeg that night that she had finally begun to realize, with something very akin to horror, that she had, in effect, just been disowned. As the full meaning of her father's words registered, she suffered a horrible moment where she felt she might just simply throw up. She struggled to get herself under some sort of control, reining in her emotions so she wouldn't break down completely on a Greyhound bus at eleven o'clock at night.

Over the days and then weeks that followed, her emotions vacillated wildly between anger, betrayal, fear and sorrow. She railed at the injustice and unfairness of her situation and found herself filled with an overwhelming sense of self-loathing. And one night, full of rage and self-denial, she ditched her girlfriend, Crystal, found some guy at a local bar, got drunk with him, and in a very short while, lost her integrity. Some time later, she turned up on Crystal's doorstep, sobbing, diminished, and lost. Crystal, upon hearing the turn of events, did not turn her away. Being older and a little wiser, she voiced her understanding of Emma's torment though she could not support her indiscretion, regardless of the reasons behind it. What she did the next day was arrange an appointment with a therapist she knew, in the hopes that Emma might find some peace from the demons that tormented her.

And over time, with the help of the therapist and her own resilient nature, Emma was able to come to some sort of terms with herself and the rejection by her family. But she'd lost her naïveté and her faith in people. She would never again take anyone or anything for granted, and her trust would be very difficult to gain. There was a new wariness, a certain watchfulness that threw some people off, even as it attracted others. She became cool and aloof, reserved and cautious. And any relationships she embarked upon were on her terms, and her terms were that they never lasted more than one night.

Since that night twelve years ago, she'd had no contact with her family and they had not contacted her. She had no intention of setting herself up for any further pain. Her conscious choice had been to put it all away, considering it over and dealt with. When, of course, it hadn't been. The time had come to feel it once more and turn it over in her mind.

"Goddamn you, Perry," she muttered again, but this time with a rueful grin and a shake of her head. For the better part of an hour she pored over her memories and feelings, searching for a peace that would, most likely, continue to elude her for some time yet. But when she again decided to lay it to rest once more, she did so with the knowledge that she was much further ahead than she had ever been. Reliving her past did not destroy her, and the pain she felt was the merest shadow of what she once had.

Mentally giving herself a shake, she glanced at her watch. With a start, she saw that it was almost one forty-five P.M.

"Shit!"

She still had to drive clear across town to get to her apartment, shower and get ready, and then drive all the way to the other side of town to get to Winnipeg Memorial.

"Shit, shit, shit," she repeated, reaching for her sunglasses and keys.

"God*damn* you, Perry," she cursed her partner yet again, as she threw the truck into reverse and waited for a break in traffic. "If I'm late, I'll kill you."

CHAPTER SIX

Grabbing the small bouquet of flowers she'd picked up along the way, Emma hopped out of the Pathfinder and headed across the parking lot to the hospital. At the information desk she was given directions to the ICU and told she would have to report to the nurse's station.

Never one to fuss overmuch about her appearance, she nonetheless took a few moments to step inside a public washroom and check herself over. She had deliberately dressed down, in jeans, boots and a clean-fronted, button-down, short-sleeved white shirt, an embroidered knotwork motif adorning half the length of the front. The design lent her appearance a casual stylishness that pleased her. She cocked her head slightly, and then reached up decisively to undo the top two buttons. *No point in looking uptight.*

Flowers in hand, she headed for the elevators. Without knowing exactly why, she realized she was feeling somewhat nervous. Since the night she had saved Daina Buchanan, she had felt different somehow, affected in a way she could not put her finger on. The short elevator ride gave her a chance to collect herself. Exiting, she straightened ever so slightly, resisting the urge to smooth the front of her shirt. A tall, attractive nurse rose from her seat at the nurse's station and came around to meet her.

"Constable Kirby," she said softly, her hand outstretched, "it's so good to meet you. I'm Shelley Montgomery, Daina's nurse." She smiled warmly.

Emma, very much aware of the solemn atmosphere of the unit, pitched her voice to match the nurse's as she replied, with an answering smile, "Hi, thank you." She shook the woman's hand and added, "Please, just call me Emma."

"Daina's resting right now, but she is expecting you. She suffered a bit of a seizure earlier, so we had to give her a mild sedative to relax her."

"Oh!" Emma's smile faltered. "Is she all right?"

"She's fine, now," Shelley immediately reassured her. "It was something we were able to rectify right away, a low sodium level, quite low, actually. She gave us quite a scare, I can tell you."

Emma wondered if her being there at that time was a good idea. Her hesitation must have shown, for Shelley Montgomery took a light grip on her elbow and brought her forward.

"The sedative we administered was a mild one. It happened a couple of hours ago, so it might even be wearing off by now." They were moving toward a row of four beds, separated by curtains. "A seizure can be very exhausting and disorienting to a patient, not to mention upsetting. We administer the sedative just to calm them afterward."

Emma nodded her understanding, but her attention was on the beds and their occupants. She guessed which one was Daina, second from the right, by the spiky blonde hair. She seemed to be sleeping.

"I'm glad you didn't wear a uniform," the nurse was saying, bringing Emma's attention back to her. "It can be upsetting to the patients to have a uniformed officer in the room."

"Well, I'm off-duty and wasn't told otherwise."

"Not a problem, you did fine. I like that shirt, by the way."

"Oh, thank you." Emma was pleased.

"I'll let you go ahead and introduce yourself."

Emma realized that was her cue to get on with it. Her boot heels sounded loud in the relative quiet of the unit. She wondered at the seeming impropriety of just waking the woman up. A moment later, Daina opened her eyes a bit sleepily. She blinked a couple of times, her forehead creased in a frown, but then she smiled, a puzzled, tentative smile. "Hi," she said.

Daina's face was badly bruised and puffy beneath the bandages, and both eyes sported fading circles of exhaustion. She was pale and drawn, and her resemblance to the vibrant performer Emma recalled on stage was vague, at best. But when she smiled, Emma's heart did that same confusing little leap in her chest. "Hi," she said, and offered a smile of her own.

"Let me guess." Daina's frown disappeared as her smile widened. "Constable Kirby, right?"

Emma was a little surprised by the strained harshness of Daina's voice, but merely inclined her head slightly in acknowledgment. "That's right, but call me Emma, please, Ms. Buchanan."

"I can do that, if you'll call me Daina." The singer sounded amused.

Emma nodded, with another small smile. "I can do that."

"Well, then, it's a pleasure to meet you, Emma." Daina reached to shake Emma's hand. She gasped sharply.

"Oh, hey, can I—?" Emma extended her right hand and Daina, with surprising strength, grabbed it with her own.

Features contorted, Daina breathed, "It's okay, I'm just—" She took a deep breath, held it a couple of moments, and then exhaled forcefully, "—sore." She released Emma's hand, and added with a strained smile, "Just give me a sec here."

Emma watched as Daina fiddled with the IV line.

"My memory seems to have been affected," Daina muttered. She looked up with a rueful grin. "I keep forgetting I'm an invalid." She bent to her task once more.

Smiling, Emma spoke with gentle candor. "Well, if it makes you feel any better, you look a lot better than the last time I saw you."

For some reason the statement seemed to strike a nerve with Daina. As she patted the IV line back into its original place at her side, she said waspishly, without raising her eyes, "Well, that pretty much goes without saying, now doesn't it?" Color immediately flooded her face, but she kept her eyes downcast.

The remark brought Emma up short. She realized that she was not the only one feeling awkward. She brought forward the bouquet of flowers, and said in an easy, conversational tone of voice, devoid of any sarcasm, "These are for you, by the way, in case you were wondering."

For an instant, she thought Daina wasn't going to look up. When she reached for the flowers, she stared at them for a few moments. Finally, she looked up again. "I'm, uh, sorry for that." She paused, her color rising, and cleared her throat. "That was rude, I'm sorry. I, uh, have a bad habit of speaking without thinking."

"Well," Emma said gently, casually putting her hands halfway into her pockets, "I have a bad habit of thinking without speaking." With a slight shrug of her shoulders, she added, "Makes us even, I guess."

Daina fixed her with an appraising look, and then her mouth quirked in a small, sardonic grin. "Well, I don't know about *that*." She held up the flowers. "Thank you."

"You're welcome."

Daina swallowed, and seemed to think her next words over carefully. Voice and expression earnest, she said, "I really am sorry for that remark. I realize I owe you a great deal—"

"Oh, whoa, wait a minute," Emma interrupted. "You don't owe me anything, okay? I didn't come here expecting some big production and I'm not here holding my hand out, looking for some sort of payoff." She took a breath. "Believe me, I would rather have met you under different circumstances, but I just happened to be in the right place at the right time." She added, "To tell you the truth, I've never been in this position before."

Daina gave a fleeting smile, and then her expression sobered. With extreme care and dignity, she said, "Thank you, Emma, for...not giving up...when everyone else had."

Emma's breath caught in her throat and her heart staggered in her chest. She managed to respond, with equal dignity, "You're very welcome."

It occurred to Emma that the meeting was effectively over, and she found herself with nothing more to say. She could also see that Daina was tiring and she was loath to overstay her welcome. She tried to come up with an appropriate exit line, and had only begun to formulate the words when Daina spoke up.

"Okay, that was hard work. Could you pass me that glass of water, please?" Her voice was noticeably weaker, as if the emotion of the last few minutes had drained her. She managed a faint smile. "I'm feeling a bit parched here."

Emma watched as Daina took a couple of sips. When Daina cleared her throat, Emma looked at her with concern. "Are you okay?"

Daina swallowed and gave another tired smile. "Yeah," she said, sounding disappointed, "guess I'm just fading. I'm sorry."

"I should be going anyway," Emma said quickly.

"I'm really glad you came by." Daina's voice was little more than a harsh whisper.

"So am I," Emma replied.

"I was wondering..." Daina said nothing more, as if she were still wondering. And then she sighed, and came out abruptly with, "I was wondering if you might like to get together, you know, after I'm out of here." She was obviously exhausted, and blinked rapidly a few times. "When I can actually walk and talk."

Emma felt herself go very still inside.

"You know, just for coffee or something. Or a beer, I don't know." She smiled, as if to make the invitation light-hearted.

It occurred to Emma that smiling in return was what was called for here, but the muscles required for that seemed to have frozen along with the rest of her. It took her a few moments to finally say, "Uh, sure."

Daina narrowed her eyes. "Really? Are you sure? Because—"

"No, yes, really." Frustrated, Emma waded through her confusion, struggling to find a clarity which had been eluding her for too long. "I'd like that, really," she added more firmly, "that would be nice."

"Okay, well, you know where to find me for the next little while, I guess. After that..."

Without giving herself time to think, Emma pulled her wallet out of her back pocket and extracted one of her little-used business cards. "Tell you what," she said, reaching for the pen on the table by the bed, "when you're ready, call me. I'll give you my home number." She quickly scribbled on the back of the card and handed it to Daina, who looked at it with interest.

"Thank you, I appreciate that."

"You're welcome. It's been a pleasure."

"My mother would be thrilled to hear that," Daina said dryly.

"You can tell her I said so." Emma took a step back, raising a hand slightly in farewell as she said, "Take care."

And she turned and left, the sound of her boot heels loud in her ears, but not as loud as the voice in her head demanding to know what the hell she was doing. As she stepped out into the brilliance of the afternoon sunshine, the only thing she knew for certain was she was definitely attracted to Daina Buchanan. Maybe not enough to matter. And maybe it didn't matter. But the attraction was there. And that did not please her in the least.

CHAPTER SEVEN

Wednesday found Daina in high spirits. She had just been transferred to the general surgical ward and the move granted her more freedom and was indicative of her impending release. It also meant that she was now allowed visitors other than immediate family. Her parents had informed her there were quite a few people clamoring to visit her, to wish her well. Her first two visitors were the two detectives she now faced, and they might very well be her last, if she were to seriously entertain the possibility they were presenting her with.

Detectives James and Cameron were as different as two men could possibly be. James was tall and spare and rather nattily dressed in a charcoal suit jacket and pants, pale grey shirt, and a shiny pewter colored tie. The jacket, however, was not a perfect fit. It appeared to hang from his frame rather than be tailored to it, and the smart-looking tie cinched his shirt collar tightly below his prominent Adam's apple. Whenever he swallowed, it looked almost painful. His hazel eyes were intense, his gaze sharp, his thinning hair was tousled, and his mouth narrow and tight.

Detective Cameron was a good foot shorter than his partner, possibly only an inch or two taller than Daina. His suit was a plain brown, his tie a shade lighter, laid over a shirt of nondescript beige. His eyes were large and brown and warm; in his round face they tended to make him appear placidly bovine. He wasn't exactly obese, was likely strongly stout; next to James, the point was moot.

Initially, they asked after her health, and explained that the doctors had denied them access while she was in the ICU. Otherwise, they would have made an appearance sooner to take her statement. As it was, the delay had proved beneficial, as there had been developments in the investigation that warranted serious consideration.

"What do you mean, 'developments'?" she asked with a frown.

"Well, not necessarily developments," Detective James replied. He seemed to be the speaker for the two of them. Detective Cameron, other than introducing himself, did nothing but write things down on his notepad. "More just lines of thought."

Daina raised her eyebrows dubiously. "'Lines of thought?'"

"Ms. Buchanan, please understand this is an ongoing investigation. One which really isn't going *anywhere* currently. We know what kind of bomb it was, we know it had a rather complex timing device; we've taken statements from over a hundred people. In our minds, there could be any number of reasons why someone would do something like this. We have to consider everything, including anti-gay groups, current or ex-lovers, overzealous or misguided fans, it could be anyone from anywhere. But no one has claimed responsibility for it. Which is unusual, considering it was a fairly high-profile night. So we have no motive, no suspects, no leads."

"Just *lines of thought*." Daina's expression was mild, but her tone was laced with contempt. "You have no idea the confidence that inspires."

Detective James blinked a couple of times. "Please, ma'am," he said, maintaining his professional, calm tone, "if we could, we have a few questions for you."

Detective Cameron waited with pen poised.

She shrugged. "Fire away."

She proceeded to answer their questions, but she hadn't the slightest notion who could have done this or why, and could provide little in the way of insight into their investigation.

"Ms. Buchanan, we have other questions, but we'd first like to assure you that your safety is of paramount importance to us. And we ask that you keep an open mind, since we are, in effect, theorizing here."

Daina nodded and smiled, trying to look politely interested. But she had a suspicion regarding their "theorizing" and sincerely hoped they would disappoint her.

"One line of thought we're seriously considering is that whoever planted the bomb had a specific target. We can't know for sure who that target was, but considering the circumstances, you come up as the number one choice." A split-second pause, then, "So, as a safety precaution, we would like to place a twenty-four hour police guard outside your room, for the duration of your hospital stay."

Her smile thinned and tightened. She could handle the fact that her career was on hold indefinitely; she could handle the fact that her personal life was pretty much in a shambles; she could even handle, just barely, the fact that her future rested entirely on the success of her recovery. *This* scenario, on top of everything else, she could not handle. This and the implication that any hope of returning to her normal everyday life had just been blown completely out of the water, was too much. Her initial impulse was to deal with it in her typical fashion, to just push it aside and refuse to deal with it.

Detective James was one step ahead of her. "I realize it sounds a bit over the top, but it's a possibility we have to consider. To not do so would be negligent, and your safety would be compromised. That's not a chance we're willing to take. The police guard would lessen that risk. And just so you know," he added, "anyone else who performed that night has been advised to take extra safety precautions, as well. We're not just focusing on you, but you are our main concern."

"Just because I happened to be on stage alone when this whole thing happened?" she asked him.

"Are you comfortable with viewing that as a coincidence and nothing more?"

The question was put forth mildly. She stared at him a moment or two before the wind went out of her sails completely. "Okay, no, I guess I'm not."

"Neither are we. The investigative team is working hard at this but with nothing much to go on, we've got nowhere to go. So, a few more questions?"

"This is where you ask me if I have any enemies, right? Do I know of anyone who might've done this? The answer is no, I don't." Her irritation was rising and she couldn't help it. "I don't have any enemies; I have never received any hate mail. I've never gotten any death threats, and right now the only person I can think of who's likely to be seriously pissed off at me is my partner, my manager, because I just fired her yesterday."

Detective Cameron consulted his notes and spoke up for the first time. "Your manager is—uh, *was*, Kendra Morrow, is that right?"

"Yes." She eyed him carefully.

"And the two of you were also…um—" He floundered, coloring slightly, obviously at a loss for words.

"Lovers?" Daina provided helpfully.

Detective Cameron blushed crimson and glanced at his partner once, quickly, before returning his attention to her. "Yes. So, um, where would she be…right now? Can we contact her? If we needed to question her?"

"You could certainly try." Daina recalled her mother's difficulty in that area. "I would imagine she's back in Nashville, but don't quote me on that. I haven't spoken to her in the last twenty-four hours. She could be in Timbuktu, for all I know."

Both detectives were obviously confused, judging by their respective frowning countenances.

"But, I thought…" Detective Cameron began, his color rising once more.

"We *were* lovers," Daina explained. "We're not anymore. I'm sure I don't need to expand on that."

Neither of them said anything.

"Do you need to know anything else?" Daina asked abruptly.

Detective James looked at Cameron, who shook his head quickly. "No, just the address and phone number in Nashville."

She provided both, then asked a question of her own. "How long am I going to be under police guard, did you say?"

"At least until you're released from the hospital," answered Detective James. "Definitely that long while we consider whether the threat against you is real or not. Or someone claims responsibility. We are treating this very seriously."

Daina softened a bit at that. "This is going to freak out my mom," she stated quietly. "Am I still allowed visitors, by the way?"

"Yes, but they'll have to check at the nurse's station and with the officer on duty and provide identification. And absolutely no media."

"Oh, I don't care about that." She waved the concern away.

"Unless you have a preference," James went on, "we'll split the watches between male and female officers." He looked at her carefully. "*Do* you have a preference?"

"I, uh…I don't know." Daina frowned, wondering at the look. Perhaps he thought she would prefer a female officer rather than a male. Which actually had not occurred to her. Could she request Emma Kirby? She realized there was a certain level of comfort there, perhaps even a sense of safety. It wasn't attraction. It was definitely interest, but on exactly what level, she wasn't sure. Certainly the woman was attractive, and certainly she was enigmatic and intriguing, but she was also almost certainly straight, and straight or not, she was almost certainly not single.

"Ms. Buchanan?" Detective James asked, interrupting her reverie. "Can we go ahead, then?"

"Sorry. Yes, definitely," she replied, and as soon as the words left her mouth, she realized her moment of opportunity was lost, and she didn't know how to feel about that. She blinked away her confusion. "Thank you. I mean that. Really."

The two detectives graciously accepted her thanks. There was already an officer on deck for the first shift, a beefy, younger fellow, and he was introduced to her as Constable Yukowski. Daina acknowledged his presence with a nod. And once the detectives had left, James leaving his card and asking her to call if she thought of anything else, Daina had to laugh. Her life was in turmoil, her career up in the air, but she could take the time to think about some woman who fit in absolutely nowhere. She shook her head and pushed Emma Kirby to the back of her mind, bringing to the forefront instead her mother. Making sure her mother didn't have a cow when she found out her only daughter was now considered to be the target of a mad bomber was what she should be focusing on.

She reached for the phone.

CHAPTER EIGHT

"So, have you heard the latest?" Perry's tone was conspiratorial, drawing a sharp glance from Emma.

"I just got here, Perry," she told him. "I do have a life, you know. And since when have you become a gossipmonger?"

The two of them had just left the briefing room and were on their way to the sixth-floor parking level to get their cruiser. It was five twenty-five P.M. and they had just started their evening shift, a four-day stretch which ended at three in the morning. Not her most favorite shift, but today she found herself looking forward to it.

"This isn't gossip," he said seriously. "I just heard that your little country singer friend has been placed under twenty-four-hour police guard."

Emma shot him a dark look. "She's not my *little country singer friend*, Perry." She shook off her irrational irritation. "Why is she under guard? What happened?"

"Well, they think *she* was the bomber's target." He shrugged. "Which, you have to admit, is pretty much the way it looks. So they're taking precautions."

Emma felt at a loss for words. Distracted, pulling her keys from her pocket, she headed for her door.

"See?" Perry said.

She looked up, over the roof, in time to see him wink at her with an obvious smirk.

"I knew you'd be interested." His smirk grew.

"Okay, you know what?" Emma slammed her door shut and walked to the front of the patrol car. "Let me tell you something." She leaned forward, placing her hands flat on the hood. "I think we've gone about as far with this as we're going to, okay?"

Perry blinked, managing to look both contrite and amused at the same time.

Emma took a breath, reining in her displeasure. "I appreciate your concern, I do," she went on, more patiently. "I even appreciate your interest, twisted as it is at times. But quit with this Daina Buchanan thing. I'm not interested in your little matchmaking ideas. I'm not going there. I'm not even considering it. So give it a rest." She gave him a meaningful look. "Are we clear on this?"

He gave her a tiny frown, a tiny pout, but his eyes twinkled with amusement. "You're no fun."

"Oh, please, I'm tons of fun," she returned dryly. "Now get in the car." She straightened, then added, "Wait, one other thing."

He looked at her with interest, good humor intact.

"About the other day," she went on.

In an instant, his humor disappeared, to be replaced by sober attentiveness.

She hooked her thumbs in her gun belt and smiled gently, "I

want to apologize for…flying off the handle the way I did. Like I said, I do recognize and appreciate your concern. And just so you know, you weren't too far off the mark. But we need to be clear on one thing: if I tell you something personal, it's because I trust you." She paused a moment, letting her words sink in, then added, "I don't want to have to think twice before telling you something, Perry."

He nodded, looking sheepish. "Sorry," he said quietly.

She inclined her head, grateful for his understanding and acceptance. "Thank you." She tossed the keys in the air, caught them, and threw him a wink. "Now let's get out of here before we get arrested for loitering."

The next couple of days flew by; she was almost surprised when Friday night rolled around. She welcomed the routine familiarity. She had not received any phone calls, had heard nothing more about Daina Buchanan's situation, and had not inquired into it. Perry had remained silent on the subject, whether he knew any more or not. She admitted to herself that she was interested, curious, perhaps concerned, but whether there was something going on or not, she wasn't about to involve herself.

Before Friday night's shift ended, a couple of cruisers were called to the Palliser, a downtown bar where a fight had spilled out onto the street. By the time Perry and Emma pulled up, the scene was chaos, the street and sidewalks full of people, as if everyone had decided to throw a huge block party. Emma was hard pressed not to stare openmouthed at the people who sat in groups or staggered about with their drinks in hand. Her ears were assaulted by music blasting from the windows and doors of vehicles parked on the street. At either end of the street, a couple of cruisers sat with lights flashing, as if their sole purpose was to provide a light show.

She took in this weird tableau as they came to a stop. She glanced at Perry, who looked back and shrugged.

"It's downtown Winnipeg on a Friday night. Are you surprised?"

By the time they found the officers who'd first arrived on the scene, everything seemed under control. Gathering in the lobby of the Palliser, they looked on as an inebriated, scruffy fellow was led out in handcuffs, protesting angrily, "None of this is my fault! I just got in the way! Where's my knife, dammit? Why don't you arrest the bastard who stole it!"

A chorus of yells and the sound of breaking glass came from the street.

Emma and Perry bolted out the doors, to a mob scene unexpected and unprecedented. The boisterous, mostly good-natured crowd, which had seemed to be diminishing, appeared to have swelled. Two groups were trying to flip two cruisers, one of which happened to be theirs. Both Emma and Perry's first reaction was to jump into the mêlée and rescue their cruiser. And then they both checked themselves.

"Call for backup," Emma said, shaking her head. "We are *not* going into that without backup."

Perry didn't argue. He got on the radio, but obviously a call had already been placed. Three more cruisers pulled up at either end of the street, lights flashing, sirens wailing, trailed by two fire engines and three rescue units.

Emma raised her eyebrows at Perry. "Wow. You're good."

Perry choked back his laughter and Emma grinned. Together, they ran down the steps to meet the other officers just stepping out of their cruisers. The crowd had decided that it had gotten a little too busy for their taste and were abandoning the party. The police let them go, and converged instead on the two groups manhandling the cruisers.

Emma was mildly alarmed to see that their cruiser was very close to being overturned. But as the police rushed the group, many of them bolted and the few that remained were pulled to the ground and cuffed. The cruisers dropped back to the pavement on all four tires.

By the time the excitement was over and they had returned to the station, it was close to three forty-five A.M. By four-thirty that Saturday morning, their reports had been filed and they were free to leave the station.

As Emma drove home, the very first vestiges of dawn were showing. Exhausted as she was, she felt that thrill she always did when she caught a sunrise. With the windows wide open and the morning summer air rushing past her, the promise and beauty of the day presented before her took her breath away. She reveled in the drive, reluctant to end it, but sleep beckoned to her.

As she entered the lobby, her attention was caught by a white envelope stuck in the frame of the building's mailbox. The print on the envelope, bold and black, caught her eye. She frowned and took a step closer. It was addressed to her. She removed the envelope from the frame and headed for the stairs, tearing open the envelope as she went.

The sheet of paper within contained a half-dozen typewritten lines.

What is it with you fucking dykes?
Do all of you stick together
and look out for each other?
You saved her ass once
Don't try it again
I have no problem taking out two of you

"What the hell?" she muttered tightly. She whipped her head up to take a quick look around. There was no one around and nowhere anyone could hide. She read it through again and the full impact of its meaning slammed home. The threat to Daina Buchanan was obvious. The threat to herself shocked her. Whoever had written the letter obviously *knew* her. Knew who she was, knew what she did for a living, knew where she lived. As that realization ripped through her, Emma jerked her head up again.

Her first reaction was to climb the remaining stairs and get to her second-floor apartment. Her training made her realize that it was probably not wise to retreat to the questionable safety of her apartment. Whoever had delivered the envelope had entered her building. The small hairs on the back of her neck stood up. Her apartment might not be the haven she wanted it to be. She stepped back onto the landing, carefully refolded the letter, and slid it back into the envelope.

Cautiously, she headed back down the stairs to the lobby. It was four fifty-five A.M. She could get to the station in less than fifteen minutes. She had to let the detectives in charge of the Buchanan case know that the threat to the singer was very real and obviously not past. As an added bonus, she would also get the opportunity to lay her own private life out in the open for all to see.

Wonderful. Could this get any better?

CHAPTER NINE

During the drive to the station, Emma prepared herself for the inevitable. She'd never been outed before, and she certainly had never gone about openly declaring her sexuality. But now, one innocuous-looking piece of paper was going to do both for her, neatly, succinctly, and without preamble.

She reminded herself that the letter wasn't about her. This was all about Daina. The irony was not lost on her that the more she tried to distance herself from the singer, the closer, it seemed, the two of them were being drawn together. She knew events would happen as they did, and she couldn't control those events, but she would not let herself be controlled by them, either. She hoped that once she presented the letter to the sergeant on duty, her involvement in the situation would progress no further.

Sergeant Michaels looked up from his desk as she appeared at his door. He was perhaps ten years her senior, an unremarkable looking man, with pale gray eyes and a tanned, well-lined face that was open and often reflective of exactly what he was feeling. Her eyes were constantly drawn to his fashionably short-cropped hair, which was entirely, almost shockingly, white. He didn't lack confidence, seemed to have it in excess, in fact, and this, coupled with his solid build, made him seem larger than his average height. He was professional and, to her knowledge, competent and friendly enough, yet she had never warmed to him. He was her superior and she respected him as such and that was the extent of their relationship.

"Emma, what can I do for you?" He seemed surprised to see her, which she could understand. She'd only just said goodbye to him.

She held up the envelope. "I found this, this morning," she said, "stuck next to my apartment mailbox. It's addressed to me, but it has to do with the Daina Buchanan case."

He stood, frowning. "What is it?"

"It's a letter—well, it's a threat, actually, against Ms. Buchanan." She paused, then added, "And myself, in a way. You'll want to read it."

"Are you the only one who's touched it?"

"As far as I know. It was sealed when I opened it. I had no idea what it was about."

"Let's get it in a protective casing, then I'll have a look at it." He pulled a clear plastic casing out of a drawer.

Opening the envelope once more, she withdrew the letter carefully, making sure to handle it now only by its edges, and slid it into the casing. She then slid the envelope in beside it and sealed the casing. She handed the plastic sleeve over to the sergeant. And while he read the letter, she watched his face carefully, keeping her own face expressionless.

When he looked up, his eyes were keen. He locked his gaze on hers. "What's your take on this, Emma?"

The question was ambiguous. She wondered if that was his

intent. "Considering the circumstances," she replied carefully, "I think we should take it very seriously."

He nodded decisively. "We'll need to get some copies of it, then I'll send this one to the lab." He held up the original. "I'll make some phone calls, see how many of the investigative team I can get together. You're okay to hang around for a while?"

"Of course," she said quietly. She knew she didn't have a choice, but she appreciated his asking. The investigative team would need to question her regarding her involvement, not only in the finding of the letter but also how and why she was involved.

She took a seat in one of the chairs across from his desk, waiting while he busied himself with the tasks at hand. When he was done, and a clerk had come to retrieve the original to take it to forensics, he looked at her with some concern.

"Are you okay with being dragged into it like this?"

She cocked her head ever so slightly. "Does it matter?" she asked, keeping her tone and expression impassive.

"No, I guess not." He paused, then added, "You'll have to answer a lot of questions, personal questions, you realize that, don't you?"

"I'm aware of that, yes."

"You'll be treated with respect and consideration, I promise you that. We'll be as discreet as possible."

She gave a single nod. "Thank you. I appreciate your saying that."

He nodded, seemed about to say something more, then dropped his gaze to the copies of the letter on his desk. When he looked back at her, he asked, "Any thought on who might be behind this?"

At any other time, such a question might have been laughable. But Emma had to give him credit; they were obviously thinking along the same lines.

"No," she replied, in the same careful vein. "But it would… appear to be someone who knows me. The fact that they know where I live, they know I'm a cop, they…know my personal life, it would pretty much have to be someone who knows me. To some extent, anyway."

He nodded and held her eyes. "But not necessarily someone you know."

It sounded more like a statement than a question, and a rather odd one at that. It brought her up short. She was unsure if he actually expected a response. There was already a good piece of herself out on the table. She felt more than a little reluctant to offer up anything more. And so she kept her expression neutral and said nothing.

"Could it be someone *she* knows?" he went on, without missing a beat. "Someone who knows *her?*"

Emma blinked, caught off guard. "Who? Daina Buchanan?"

"Yes. Do you think that the person who wrote this," he indicated the letter with a gesture, "who's responsible for all this, knows *her?*" He was looking at her intently.

She returned his look unflinchingly. "I have no idea. I suppose. Why are you asking me?"

"Well, at this point, you're really the only one who can provide some insight." His tone was sympathetic. "I'm not trying to put you on the spot; you're already there, unfortunately. I just want your opinion."

Emma's discomfort was growing with each passing minute. But she knew it would likely only get worse. She clamped down on her feelings, as she said, "My *opinion*, then, is that it's possible." She allowed herself a small frown. "Anything is possible. You know that."

"Yes, but is it *probable?*"

"Probable?" Her frown deepened. "Honestly, I have no idea." She paused, then asked, "What if it is?"

He looked down at the letter. Then he said quietly, "Because if it is," and he looked up, meeting her eyes once more, "then it's someone who knows her *and* you."

Emma went very still. She returned his look steadily, but as his words sunk in, the implications startled and confused her. He'd gotten ahead of her, which she hadn't expected, and broached a line of thought she'd come nowhere near considering.

"It may be a perfectly harmless connection," the sergeant went on. "It may be...the garbage man, who knows? But it may not be. If there is a connection between the two of you, and it certainly seems there may be, we have to find it. Which means both of you will have to be questioned. About some very personal things. Do you understand?"

Emma gave a very small nod. "I'm starting to." And the more she came to understand, the more unhappy she became.

"I can appreciate that we may be walking into a delicate situation here, and I'm sorry it had to come out this way." Sergeant Michaels indicated the letter; whether he realized the pun or not, she didn't know.

"Thank you," she said quietly.

"And, of course, I *am* just speculating here, that's all we can do at this point."

Emma pressed her lips together, but said nothing. There was nothing to say.

"Why don't you go get a coffee, Emma?" the sergeant suggested to her gently. "It's already been a long night and morning and it isn't over yet. And I have some more calls to make before anyone else arrives. I want you to carry your weapon twenty-four/seven, I'll get the authorization. And I want you on admin leave, effective immediately, for five days."

She nodded and got to her feet.

"I'll have a unit sent to your apartment, so it'll be there once you leave here. We'll want to make sure everything is secure there."

She nodded again. "Thank you."

She turned and left his office, heading for the stairs to the basement. She badly wanted coffee, but getting her handgun and holster took precedence. As she descended the stairs, she was aware of the tension in her shoulders and back, and made a futile effort to shake it off. But neither the tension nor the questions and concerns tripping over themselves in her mind could be banished so easily. She was troubled that Sergeant Michaels' line of reasoning hadn't occurred to her. Because it made perfect sense. It would have to be someone who knew both of them. There really was no other explanation.

"Jesus, you're slippin', Kirby," she muttered to herself in the abandoned stairwell.

As much as she felt scattered personally, professionally she was completely focused. As much as she disliked the idea of having her private life exposed and dissected, she knew she would cooperate fully, without hesitation. Someone's life was at stake. And the cinderblock that had taken up residence in her gut would, she knew, eventually disappear.

She reached her locker and removed her gun and two holsters, an ankle holster and a belt holster. The belt holster was more of a clip really, designed to be worn at her back on the inside of her pants. Both allowed her to carry her weapon out of sight. She fixed the belt holster in place, strapped on the ankle holster, and slipped her gun in. She checked to ensure her ID badge was in her pocket where she always carried it, then slammed her locker shut.

Time for that coffee. She was more than a little tired, but figured that between the coffee and the tension thrumming through her nerves, she'd be able to hold out awhile longer yet.

By the time she got back, coffee in hand, there were already a couple of members of the investigative team present. Emma went and sat once more in Sergeant Michaels' office. Some fifteen minutes later, Michaels came to get her. She was shown into one of the smaller debriefing rooms where there were three other individuals seated, none of whom were familiar to her. All eyes were on her as she entered.

Two were in uniform, both constables, fresh faced and serious looking younger men who looked far too alert for the early hour. Just looking at them made Emma feel even more tired. The other wore a charcoal gray suit jacket which looked a size too big for him, and a light gray shirt open at the throat. His pewter colored tie was very loosely knotted, hanging down almost to his breastbone. The sight bothered her; she looked away from his prominent Adam's apple.

As Emma chose the empty seat at one end of the eight-foot table, facing the sergeant, she filled a glass from the pitcher of ice water before her. She could see that each of them had a notepad and a copy of the letter before them. She was introduced to the three of them, including Detective James, who was in the process of readjusting his tie. She nodded in return, and then settled herself into the chair, placed her hands in her lap with fingers interlocked, and proceeded to answer their questions.

Nothing could prepare a person for laying their private life out in the open, before what basically amounted to a bunch of strangers. And yet she felt she was handling herself well. She bridled, however, when Detective James said, "Please describe your relationship with Daina Buchanan."

"My *relationship?*" She raised her eyebrows and then shook her head. "I have no relationship with Ms. Buchanan." Her flat tone did not invite further discussion.

But James looked down at his notepad and quickly leafed through it. He stopped halfway through and read what was before him, saying, "I understand that you visited her at the hospital." He looked up, met her eyes, and politely inquired, "Is that correct?"

Emma had no idea how he'd come by that information, since the request for her visit had not gone through the usual channels. But she returned his look levelly. "I didn't initiate the visit, Ms. Buchanan did. She wanted to thank me. Is there a problem with that?"

"It's just unusual that no one knew about the visit, that's all."

Emma kept her tone and expression unchanged as she said, "Obviously someone knew about it, if you're bringing it up. The woman wanted to thank me, there's nothing more to it than that."

Still the detective pressed. "How did she know how to get in touch with you?"

Emma thinned her lips, bringing the edges of her teeth together. "I'm in the phonebook, Detective."

"But how did she know it was you?" he asked patiently. "How did she get your name?"

Emma finally saw where he was going. "My name was somehow leaked to the press. I'm sure you know it was in the papers the next day. I don't know how, but I *can* tell you there were individuals that I know who were at that concert."

He nodded. "Okay, well, we'll need the names of those individuals, as well as any others you deem relevant to this investigation, say within…the last four years?"

Emma nodded.

"Obviously, we're looking for someone the two of you have in common," the detective continued. "That *may* extend to… romantic partners, past or present." His voice and expression were both keen and kind. "Are you okay with that?"

She looked him steadily in the eye as she considered how best to respond. She had known something of this sort would be necessary. She hadn't had the time to even think of how to answer it. Now, with a sinking sensation in her gut, she chose her words carefully.

"It's not that I'm not okay with it, it's that there may be some…difficulty in that area."

The detective and the sergeant frowned, and Emma was aware of a subtle shifting of the room's two other occupants. She ignored them and said, with utmost care, "I don't date. And I don't associate with my…romantic partners, as you put it, for longer than one night." She paused, then added, almost coolly, "And I don't usually get last names."

Nobody said anything. Detective James, frown still in place, glanced down at the table, obviously thinking, then looked back up at her. His expression had softened. He cleared his throat and said gently, "Okay, well, forgive me for asking this, but what kind of numbers are we looking at here?"

Emma narrowed her eyes. "In the last four years?" She looked away and cast her mind back, making a quick calculation. She looked back at the detective and shrugged. "Off the top of my head, twelve, thirteen, somewhere in there."

"Women?" he asked.

She shot him a tight, dark look but said nothing.

The detective had the decency to blush. "I'm sorry," he said quietly. "I meant no offense. Do the best you can, whatever you can remember about them, whoever you think is relevant, in whatever capacity. It'll take some time, I'm sure, to compile but get it together as quick as you can and get it to the sergeant here. We'll ask the same of Ms. Buchanan. Speaking of which," he added, after a quick glance at his notes, "considering the nature of this letter, are you comfortable with her knowing its contents? Because we don't have to tell her, verbatim, what it says. Nor do we need to give out your name in reference to it."

Again, though the idea had not completely formed in her mind, something of the sort had already occurred to Emma. She responded, "If it will further the investigation, you have my permission to tell her whatever you need to. Otherwise, I'd prefer not to be brought into it."

"Okay." He nodded once, sharply. "Good enough. You've been a great help, Constable, thank you. And my...apologies for any discomfort this may have caused."

Emma merely nodded and got to her feet. She glanced at Sergeant Michaels and inclined her head slightly toward him, a gesture he returned.

And as she drove home for the second time that morning, it suddenly occurred to her that she had forgotten to mention that she had given Daina her phone number. She wondered if it was relevant, and then immediately dismissed it. It no more meant there was a relationship between them than anything else had. *And besides, it's not likely she'll call anyway, considering the way things are going.*

CHAPTER TEN

Saturday morning found Daina awake early and chafing at the agonizingly slow passage of time. She was to be released at eleven, but it was now only seven thirty. The breakfast rounds had begun and while she'd never been very big on breakfast, in the hospital she'd made a habit of consuming as much of the meal as she could. Her recovery and, indeed, her release depended on a continual gain of strength. The nurses were adamant that she be eating, and keeping down, what she was given. She did her best to comply.

She was healing quickly, and while still suffering from a great deal of pain and stiffness, she'd made the decision to cut herself off her pain medication. She even refused the usual T3s generally prescribed at her stage of recovery. She didn't want to become dependent on anything, and she didn't like the foggy feeling from taking the medication. She learned to accept and tolerate the pain, and even welcomed it, as a reminder of her limitations. She had never really paid much attention to the "lessons learned" school of thought, but she did know that what had happened to her had affected her, changed her. She just wasn't exactly sure how. And she'd been too busy with business affairs to give it the consideration it probably deserved.

Over the last couple of days, she'd called her lawyer, her banker, her road manager and the record company. She had received faxed copies and signed and sent off other copies of pertinent documents which effectively removed Kendra from any and all decisions and obligations regarding Daina's career. She was pleased with the progress she had made; her mother had been an enormous help, going so far as to release an innocuous statement to the press on Daina's behalf.

What she hadn't been able to accomplish was to get in touch with Kendra. And that troubled her. Not because she was particularly heartbroken over the demise of their relationship. She'd initiated it and she felt right about it. But Daina disliked loose ends, and Kendra and whatever business still lay between them was starting to resemble just that. She had called her once, on Wednesday, and left a voice mail. There was no point in calling again. Kendra would either get the message and return the call, or not. That she hadn't annoyed Daina to no end. And she hated feeling annoyed. On top of that, she felt powerless, and edgy and restless as a result. Sleep had become more of an acquaintance of hers than a real friend.

Finished with her breakfast, she swallowed the last of her apple juice and pushed the tray aside. She'd been sitting on the edge of the bed and now gingerly lowered her feet to the floor. She'd begun physical therapy on Wednesday and had made progress since then, but her movements were still cautious and restricted. She made her careful way to the bathroom, stopping to pick up the change of clothes her mother had brought her. She was tired of hospital gowns and robes. Today, she would clean herself up on her own, wash her hair, and dress in something other than hospital garb. Today, she was going home.

Fifteen minutes later, she opened the door to leave the bathroom. Her mind once again overrun with her concerns, she didn't even see the person standing right outside the door until she practically walked into him. Every muscle in her body contracted and a wall of pain slammed into her. The agony was so intense she almost dropped where she stood. She fell back against the doorjamb. Her vision grayed, her heart pounded, and whatever she'd managed to eat of her breakfast headed back up the way it had gone down. *Oh no, you will not throw up.* She swallowed hard, and then swallowed again. She felt hands on her arm, on her shoulder, but for the next few seconds could only wait until both the pain and the nausea subsided.

She heard someone say, "Is she okay? What happened?" And then another voice, this one vaguely familiar, asked, "Ms. Buchanan, are you okay?"

She cracked open an eye and saw the concerned face of Detective James. Through clenched teeth, waves of pain still crashing through her and a sickening heat washing over her, she practically spat out at him, "Yeah, I'm fine, just—dandy."

She managed to straighten, using the doorframe for support. She irritably knocked James' hands away, then fixed him with a venomous look. "Jesus Christ, don't you people knock?" she asked testily.

"Actually, we did," he said, his expression filled with concern. "I guess you didn't hear us," he added, just as Daina flicked off the switch to the bathroom light and fan; obviously the latter had been just loud enough to drown out their entry.

"So knock louder," she threw back at him.

With extreme care, she moved away from the doorjamb, her entire left side on fire and her belly churning unhappily. Her surgical site felt as if someone had ripped it open, dropped a red-hot brick in it, and then closed it back up again. *That just can't be good.* But she was still on her feet, still conscious and still moving.

She made her slow and painful trek back to her bedside. James again made as if to help her, but she stopped him with a baleful look.

"Don't," was all she said.

She didn't even bother trying to get up onto the bed. That, she knew, was currently beyond her. Ever so carefully she lowered herself into the chair beside the bed. She let her muscles relax, and a new wave of agony coursed through her. For a moment she seriously reconsidered her stand against pain medication, but eventually the pain subsided to a dull ache. She was able to look up at the detective, who stood where she'd stopped him. She swallowed, cleared her throat, and smiled thinly. "So, Detective, to what do I owe the… *pleasure* of this visit?"

James blinked, then took two steps forward. "There's been another threat against you," he said, his tone and expression caught somewhere between concern and professional courtesy. "We received it this morning. It came in the form of a letter."

Daina could only look at him blankly. And then, as his words registered, she closed her eyes and slowly shook her head. "Wonderful," she muttered.

"The letter was delivered to us by a third party," he went on, and Daina looked up at him once more. "The threat against you is obvious and, we believe, legitimate. You weren't named, but the content and the context left no doubt that you're the target."

Still, Daina just looked at him. Her mind and body felt thick and slow. "So where is this letter? Can I see it?"

James shook his head after the briefest of hesitations. "Unfortunately, no. We need to protect the privacy of the third party. I can't divulge the contents of the letter and I can't show it to you. I'm sorry. I *can* tell you that there's no question that the threat *is* directly against you. But there's no indication of how that threat will or could be carried out. Just that the intent is there."

Daina felt certain that what he'd just told her should have made some kind of sense.

"So…" she began, choosing her words carefully, "a letter

was delivered to *you*, which contains a threat against *me*, but you won't tell me what it says or let me read it, because you need to protect someone *else?*" She narrowed her eyes. "Is that what you're saying? Because if that's what you're saying, what the hell am I supposed to do with that?"

"I'm sorry, it's…complicated, I know." And he did look and sound apologetic. "But the individual who…delivered it asked that their privacy be upheld. We have to respect that."

Daina still didn't get it. "So why can't I see it? Is this person named in the letter? Why can't I read it?"

The detective hesitated once more, as if considering, then abruptly shook his head. "I'm sorry, I can't. No one was named, but I can't discuss it any further. It's complicated."

"That's not *complicated*, Detective," Daina snapped at him. "That's *bullshit.*"

Detective James put his hands out in a placating gesture. "Ms. Buchanan, if you knew the situation, you'd understand. But I can't even explain it to you because, well…I can't."

"Okay, fine," she said tightly. "So why are you here then?"

"Because we need to ensure *your* safety."

"And how do you intend on doing that? I'm in here in the first place because somebody didn't do their job. And now you're fudging things. So what exactly do you have in mind?"

"Well, actually, that's largely up to you." He briefly eyed her T-shirt and her nylon black and white track pants. "When are you getting released?"

"Today. This morning, at eleven." Daina was actually no longer as excited about that as she had been. She had a feeling her life was about to get rather complicated itself. She wasn't happy about that at all.

Detective James was nodding. "Okay, I figured as much. We'll have to get the ball rolling quicker than I expected, but first, I need to know where you're going, and if you'd be comfortable being under guard there. You're not leaving town, are you?"

"No. Why?"

"Well, if you leave our jurisdiction, there's nothing we can do for you."

"Really." Daina sighed. "Okay, well, I'm here for a couple more weeks, to recuperate. The doctors have advised me not to fly yet."

"Well, that does make it easier. Where will you be staying?"

"With my parents." As soon as the words left her mouth, the full reality of the situation hit home. And what she hadn't considered, hadn't wanted to consider, now stared her full in the face. "Wait a minute, Jesus, is that even an option?"

"Actually, yes it is, and it's probably your best one," he told her. "You shouldn't be alone, and if you choose to be placed under guard, that protection would extend to your family, as well."

"If I choose?" Daina frowned. "What do you mean *if I choose?*"

"As I said, anything we plan to undertake is largely dependent on what you're comfortable with. We're not going to surround your house with a SWAT team, that's not realistic, but depending on the layout, we'd probably assign two cruisers, one at the front, one at the back, to watch twenty-four/seven. Or," and he shrugged, "if you so choose, you could tell us to get lost, that you don't want any protection."

Daina contemplated him for a moment, then said dryly, "Well, that would just be stupid, now wouldn't it?" Her comprehension of the seriousness of her predicament was growing steadily. There might have been a time when she would have refused such measures, but that time was past. She didn't know what she required, but she was willing to accept that she required *some* kind of protection.

"We're not trying to force anything on you, Ms. Buchanan," James went on. "It's your life, it's your choice. We're here to help and to advise you. If you want protection, you can have it. If not..." He shrugged.

"My life is in my own hands," she finished for him. "Yeah, I think we've covered this ground already." She took a couple of moments to collect her thoughts, then asked, "How long would I be under guard?"

"Until you or we determine it's no longer necessary."

She gave him a look of narrow-eyed annoyance. "That's not a very definitive answer, Detective, but I get your meaning: either nothing happens, or something happens, right?"

"Simply put, yes."

This time, Daina took several seconds to ponder his words. It seemed that every time she thought she could take a step forward she was sent two steps back. What he was saying, what he was suggesting, was beyond disturbing. It was practically beyond comprehension. But whatever logic existed in this crazy, upside down world of hers strongly dictated that she take his words and her situation seriously. And so she said firmly, "Okay, then let's do this."

He nodded. "Good. I'll see that the arrangements are made." He added, "There is something else I need from you, though."

Of course there is. She cocked her head and feigned polite interest. "And what's that?"

"We've been over this before, I know, and I know you've said you don't have any enemies, but we need you to compile a list of names of anyone you can think of who, for *any* reason, would want to harm you. Anyone in the last four years."

"Four *years*?" Daina gaped at him. "How the hell do I remember everyone I've met over the last four years?"

"Not everyone," he said gently. "Just those who might have a reason to want to harm you. Anyone. Like, for instance, your ex—uh, manager." He stumbled a bit, as if he was still unsure of how to refer to Kendra. "Who, by the way," he quickly added, "we have questioned and who does have an alibi."

Daina was startled, more at the realization that they had spoken to Kendra when she hadn't, than by the information provided. "Well, I didn't seriously think it was *her*—"

"Well, *we* have to seriously consider everyone. Whoever you put on this list we will question, if we can find them. But your list should consist only of those individuals who have reason to hold a grudge against you; a bad date, a bad relationship, a bad business deal, anyone who might want to get back at you for a real or imagined wrong against them."

Daina frowned as she listened to him, as she considered the task he'd set before her. "When do you want this by?"

"As soon as you can. The faster we get it, the faster we can get to work on it."

"And you're saying my ex is cleared?" She wondered why she felt the need to clarify the matter.

"Well, we haven't taken her off our list completely. Even though she has an alibi and it checks out, she'll remain under consideration, simply because of your relationship."

His words caused Daina to feel a sudden and distinct discomfort, but she said nothing. And then another thought occurred. "What about this third party you mentioned? How did they get this letter? How do they fit in? Or do they?"

The detective shifted slightly. "We're not...entirely clear on that. We're looking into it."

She eyed him keenly for a couple of moments. She badly wanted to ask more questions in the same vein, but knew she would just get shut down. That he did refuse to talk about it told her there was more to it than someone simply finding a letter, delivering it, and wanting to remain anonymous. She was no dummy. This individual's privacy was being protected for a reason. But she could no more guess the reason than she could their identity. And so she let it drop. "Okay, well, is there anything else?"

He shook his head. "Once the arrangements have been made, I'll get back to you with the details. It'll take about an hour."

"Okay, fine, whatever. I'll be here." She knew she sounded dismissive, but she didn't care. Her head felt like it was going to explode. She needed to get her thoughts and feelings in order. It felt as if her life was spinning out of control, and she wanted him gone so she could deal with it in private.

He must have sensed her need, because his expression softened. "I know it's a lot to deal with. I'm sorry."

And that was all it took. As Daina gave him a cursory nod and he turned to go, her throat constricted and her sinuses burned. And as he left the room and the door closed after him, she could hold it in no longer. She started to cry.

CHAPTER ELEVEN

By the time Emma got home, there was already a team assembling to investigate the grounds, the building and her own apartment. She parked on the street behind the cruisers and approached on foot a group of four officers who'd obviously been awaiting her arrival. Once introductions were made, she proceeded up the front walk to give them access to the building. She showed them where she'd found the letter, answered a few questions regarding the layout of the building and its tenants, and then took them up to her own apartment. There, she unlocked her door and stepped aside. The officers entered, sidearms drawn, joined by Detective James' partner, Detective Cameron, while she waited in the hall, her own weapon in hand.

A few minutes later she was assured her apartment was empty and secure. She thanked them, and confirmed that nothing had been moved or removed, that everything was as it should be. She set about making a pot of coffee. The team would dust for fingerprints in the lobby wherever they deemed relevant, and would question as many people in the building as they could. She could not possibly sleep before that was complete. She could, however, take a shower and enjoy a cup of coffee, and she set about doing just that.

Fifteen minutes later, clean and refreshed, in khakis and a black tank top, she sat at her dining room table reading the newspaper and drinking her coffee. She felt neither tense nor troubled. She let the team do their job, secure in the knowledge that she, at least, was not in any danger provided she not involve herself further in anything to do with Daina Buchanan.

By the time eight o'clock rolled around, the team was wrapping up. The building and grounds were secure, and no one in the building had seen anyone suspicious hanging around. When Detective Cameron asked if she wanted a car left behind for surveillance, she declined, citing the obvious fact that whoever had gained entry could probably do so again with little trouble. She told him she had no intention of further involving herself in any aspect of the Buchanan case. Also, she was currently armed and could take care of herself should the need arise. Cameron departed, taking the rest of the team with him.

With a semblance of peace restored to her home and her psyche, Emma, now starting to feel the weight of exhaustion dragging her down, drained off the last of her coffee. She reached for her gun on the dining table, removing the weapon from its holster and hefting its familiar weight. She doubted she'd have any real need of it, but still she was comforted by its presence. She removed the magazine to ensure it was full, snapped it back in place with a neat little *snick*.

The phone rang, and in the silence of the apartment it startled her.

She glanced at the clock on the microwave. It read 8:15. *Who the hell is calling me at quarter after eight in the morning?*

She crossed the room and glanced at the caller ID; it only read Unknown Name, Unknown Number. She considered briefly not answering, then remembered how Daina's mother had called out of the blue the other day. She picked up the receiver.

"You just couldn't keep your goddamned nose out of it, could you?" demanded a harsh, unfamiliar male voice.

Emma's immediate reaction was cold shock. Her mouth dropped open, her heart slammed in her chest, and she almost lost her grip on the phone. She gripped it convulsively, and clamped her jaw shut with an audible click.

"You just had to go to the cops, didn't you?" continued the caller. "Well, guess what? Now you're both dead. I warned you, you didn't listen. The minute she's out of that hospital, she's done. And so are you. Count on it."

The line went dead before she could even think of a response. "Shit!" she snapped, as she stared at the handset, and then gave in to her frustration by slamming it back into its charger.

"He's watching me," she muttered, with a certain amount of incredulity. "The son of a bitch is *watching* me."

She didn't even bother going to the patio doors to look out. She hadn't seen him earlier. She sure as hell wouldn't see him now. She looked down at the gun in her hand, mind racing as she went over his words, then made a decision. She grabbed up the phone and punched in the sergeant's number.

He picked up on the first ring.

"Sarge, it's Emma. He just called me. The guy who's doing this, the one who's after her, he just called me."

"*What?*"

"Yeah. He knew I was home, he knew when it was safe to call, and he knew I brought the letter in to you. He's watching me, Sarge."

"What did he say? Tell me." Michaels was all business, crisp and sharp.

Emma quickly repeated what she'd been told, finishing with, "He ended by saying 'Count on it.'"

After a pause, Michaels asked, "Are you okay, Emma?"

She took a couple of moments to take stock of herself. "Yes,

I'm okay," she replied, and she was. A little wired, perhaps, but otherwise okay. She realized that in her agitation she was tapping her gun against her outer thigh. She carefully placed the weapon on the coffee table, then straightened and sighed with frustration.

"I'm sending a car over," the sergeant began, "we can at least—"

"No," Emma interrupted, "I am *not*—"

"Emma—"

"*No*, Sarge," she cut him off again, more emphatically this time. "It won't make any difference. There was a whole team here and he just waited until they were gone. He'll just watch, like he has been, and wait for an opportunity."

"Did he say anything about what he plans to do?"

"What, you mean other than kill the two of us?"

"Okay, I know, I'm sorry," Michaels responded immediately. "I just don't like the thought of one of my best officers being the target of a madman."

"Well, I don't like it, either. But I refuse to run or hide like a scared rabbit."

"Okay, I hear that. So what do you want to do?"

Emma considered carefully and then, with a shake of her head, said, "Honestly, what I think needs to be done—and you might not like this, I'm not even sure I like it—but I think I should meet with Daina Buchanan. I think we need to compare some notes."

There was silence on the other end, and then, "Are you sure that's wise?"

"Doesn't it make sense to you?"

"Well, sure, I suppose—"

"Look, I'm speaking more in terms of expediency here," she explained. "I don't know what she knows, I don't know what she's been told, I don't know if she's been told *anything*. But she's not the only one involved in this now. She needs to know *that*, if anything."

"And you think you should be the one to tell her?"

"Well, if not that, then I should at least be there. But yes, my preference is to speak with her alone. In terms of comfort levels, hers *and* mine, I think it might work best that way." What she was proposing might not be a good idea at all, but it *felt* right, and she would rather trust that, than the protocol that would suggest her idea was too unorthodox to implement.

Again there was silence from the sergeant's end, and she waited patiently for his response.

"Okay," he said finally. "I'll allow it. *But*," he added quickly, "you don't go *anywhere* until I've sent a couple of units to check out your immediate area. Is that clear? You don't step foot outside your apartment until they give you the all clear. Now, when did you have in mind to go and see her?"

"Uh," Emma blinked and raised her eyebrows. "As soon as I get the all clear?"

Michaels made a sound that could have been a chuckle. "Right. Well, shouldn't you get some sleep?"

"I honestly don't think I *can* sleep, Sarge."

"Okay, I get that." Then he said, "I think you might want to consider one more thing, Emma."

"What's that?"

"Relocating. At least for a while. You're a sitting duck there. We both know it. And I don't like it."

"And where would I go?" she asked, with a certain level of tension.

"Well, my suggestion would be one of our safe houses. You'd be under constant surveillance, nobody could sneak up on you, but you'd still have freedom to move around and not feel like a prisoner. What do you think?"

Emma was only vaguely familiar with the concept of the safe houses. She knew they existed, but that was all she knew.

"No one's ever gained access to a safe house," Michaels went on. "*I'd* feel better knowing you were there. And I think you would, too."

Emma pressed her lips together momentarily, and then said, "You've got a good point. Let me think about it."

"Well, don't take too long. If you go, I want you there by the end of the day. Now let me get those units on their way to you. Hang tight, okay?"

"Not going anywhere, Sarge. I promise."

Emma was again left holding a dead phone to her ear. She dropped it unceremoniously back into its charger, picked up her gun once more and strode across the living room to the patio doors. Being on the second floor, she rarely closed her blinds. But her apartment faced east and when she worked a night shift she usually closed the blinds before she left so she wouldn't have to deal with the bright early morning sun after a long night's work. She sidled up to the far left side of the doors, and with the muzzle of her gun, eased aside the blinds a fraction.

There was her Pathfinder, just where she'd left it. There were no other vehicles in evidence that she could see from her narrow field of vision. She shifted slightly to get a better view of the rest of the tree-lined street, but from what she could see, it was deserted. Which wasn't unusual. Emma had specifically chosen the neighborhood because it was so quiet. Her apartment faced a park, which took up the whole block. On her side was her building and one other with a swimming pool and playground between the two. On each side were three houses. Behind the buildings were the parking lots and past them, a ten-foot wide strip of lawn which ended at a sound wall bordering Carmichael Drive, a main thoroughfare.

She glanced left and right again, leaning forward, and bumped her forehead against the glass door. She jerked back and made a sound of annoyance in her throat. "Oh, fuck it," she muttered.

She pushed the blinds aside to unlock the glass doors. Sliding them open, followed by the screen door, she carefully stepped out onto her balcony. Above her was another balcony and below, a patio, but nothing on either side. She had a clear view and there was nothing and no one to be seen. She realized she was making herself a perfect target by standing out on her balcony, but the alternative was to cower in her apartment, and she wasn't about to do that. Besides, there really wasn't anywhere anyone could hide. From where she stood, she could see clearly in three directions and there was nothing out of the ordinary.

She was nowhere near tired now, and had no intention of going back into her apartment. She glanced back to where she kept lawn chairs stacked against the wall. She grabbed one, unfolded it and sat down. Gun resting in her lap, she stared out through the wrought- iron railing enclosing her balcony and waited for whomever it was the sergeant had sent.

Twenty-five minutes later, she stood in the lobby of her building, speaking to Michaels and the officers who'd just performed a sweep of the area.

Emma had been surprised to see Michaels, but somewhat relieved. Much as she resented what was happening, and much as she might not want to admit it, she was very troubled by what was going on. And she was grateful for any show of support. Michaels had explained to her that he wanted to ensure she was okay and the current situation stable before heading over to the hospital to see that Daina Buchanan was made aware of the latest development. He'd already doubled security there. And he'd gotten in touch with Detective James and the rest of the investigative team to update them.

Now, he met her eyes as he said, "I'm leaving a unit behind, whether you want it or not. There's no way I'm leaving you unprotected. Just humor me, okay?"

She eyed him thoughtfully. An idea was formulating, and she dropped her chin slightly as her eyes skated off to the right, unseeing. The idea took root and bloomed in the space of a couple of seconds, and she brought her gaze up to his once more. "I'll humor you, if you'll humor me."

"Tell me."

"I want to go with you, now, to the hospital. I want to talk to her."

"Why?"

"You know why," she told him bluntly. "It has to happen sooner or later." She shrugged. "I just think sooner is better."

Michaels glanced around the lobby, obviously giving her request the consideration it deserved. He sighed heavily. "Okay. Okay, you're probably right. If you're comfortable with it, it's your call."

Emma didn't think they could afford to waste very much more time because of a delicate situation. If she wasn't comfortable with it now, she'd just have to become so. She couldn't see any other options.

"You follow me in your car," he said. He then instructed two of the officers to follow in one cruiser behind Emma on the drive to the hospital. The other two officers he stationed at either entrance of the apartment until Emma returned. He looked at her and raised his eyebrows. "Let's go."

CHAPTER TWELVE

Daina's crying jag didn't last long. It hurt too much. As soon as she started to sob, her body protested of its own accord, reminding her that such exertions were not currently factory recommended. She'd been about to bring her hands up to cover her face, but instead slammed them down to grip the arms of the chair.

"Jesus *Christ*," she moaned, squeezing her eyes shut as the pain ripped through her for the second time in less than an hour.

Her knuckles whitened and she could feel the edges of the metal armrests digging into her palms. Her muscles spasmed as she fought against the emotional tide that threatened to swamp her, creating even more pain. Eventually she was able to control the sobs, but she couldn't stop the flow of scalding tears. She cried out of a sense of confusion, she cried out of fear and anger, she cried out of a combination of despair and denial. She cried out of frustration and she cried from the pain of her injuries. But mainly, she cried because she hadn't yet. And she was overdue. She hung her head and the tears fell like rain into her lap, but the only sound that escaped her was that of her own ragged breath, hissing in and out of her open mouth.

The emotional storm passed; her pulse thudded dully in her ears as she blearily stared ahead at nothing. She sniffed a couple of times and brought the heels of her hands up to rub her eyes. She wiped the tears from her face with quick, almost angry swipes, sniffed again, and then carefully got to her feet. Grabbing the untouched coffee from her breakfast tray, she limped her way over to the window.

The view from the window was of the parking lot and the busy street beyond. It was mindless and soothing in a way, and for a short while all she did was stare at it and sip at her tepid coffee. She felt drained and hollow, but as the minutes passed, she felt a calm steal over her and infuse her. Expelling one last shaky breath, she tossed aside the blinders she'd knowingly or unknowingly kept in place for so many years, and took a long, hard look at her life as it now was.

Her career was on hold, she had come to accept that. She needed to heal and that would take as long as it took. The doctors had estimated an almost complete recovery by mid-September. It was now only mid-July. If breaking down and throwing a temper tantrum at this point would accomplish anything, she probably would have done so. But there was nothing she could do. She wasn't happy about it, but she accepted it. She could still sing and play guitar, of that she was sure. So her career might be on hold for a while, but it wasn't dead in the water.

The thought of playing caused a sudden sharp pang deep inside of her. Her guitar was like an extension of herself. She missed the feel of the wooden body against her own, missed its curves, and missed the strong, smooth feel of its neck, the steel strings beneath her fingertips. She missed the sound of its voice, which called to her even now, a voice that was for her and her alone. And she knew, right then, that she'd have to buy another guitar, today, if at all possible. She'd lost two the night of the concert, and the two she had at the house in Nashville she doubted she'd be seeing anytime soon. There were some things she was willing to do without in her life. A guitar was not one of them.

A manager, on the other hand, she was certain she could do without, at least for a while. It was the least of her concerns. She hadn't really given much consideration to the fact that Kendra was out of the picture. The woman's absence, either professionally or personally, wasn't going to affect her all that much. Kendra was not irreplaceable. She would do the footwork herself. She had in the past. She could do so again.

She wondered at the ease with which she'd let Kendra go. All it had taken was one show of disloyalty for her to cut Kendra loose. It occurred to her that Kendra, herself, could not have been too deeply invested in the relationship either, or she wouldn't have, couldn't have left while Daina had been in a coma. The thought that the two of them had been merely going through the motions for who knew how long was not a pleasant one. Nor was the realization that neither of them had ever bothered to acknowledge that there was even a problem with their relationship.

Okay, so we both suck. That was pretty much all the solicitude she could summon up. It was done, it was over, she couldn't fix it and she didn't want to even if she could. What she wanted to do was learn from her mistakes, and widen her pencil-thin beam of focus to take in every aspect of her life. She could no longer continue concentrating on her career to the exclusion of all else. She needed to be realistic and open-minded, and face the new challenges that had been set before her.

She leaned against the window frame and crossed her arms. She felt better, stronger, now that she'd cried. Finding out on the day of her release that she was still in danger, that things were seemingly going to get worse instead of better, had been just a little too much for her. She had crumbled, but who wouldn't have? Now she felt steady and clear-headed, able to actually look at the predicament she was in and ask point-blank, *Who in the hell is trying to kill me?*

She knew she had to consider what Detective James had said, that they not rule anyone out. She knew that haters existed, and that over the years a smattering of gay-bashings had occurred in Winnipeg, yet she had lived her entire life here. She had come out at the age of nineteen, and been out and visible ever since. She had never experienced any negative attention, unless you considered someone not liking her music. The city was mostly gay-friendly; the prevailing attitude was one of acceptance, not intolerance. Granted she'd been away for a good portion of the last three years, but during that time nothing much had changed.

The *why* of it really didn't matter to her. People had their own reasons for doing things. And sometimes those reasons were baseless or just plain off-kilter. So who mattered more to her than why. And now the detective wanted a list? She really had to laugh at that. She couldn't even think of who might want to do such a thing, let alone compile a list. And she had given it some thought. But each and every time, she drew a blank. There was no one in her past or present that she could think of who would do such a thing. And so she had to think it was someone she didn't know, some crazy person who had a hate on for her for their own reasons.

And what the hell am I supposed to do with that? she wondered, not for the first time. Because this person had gone to great lengths to try and take her life. Surely there were easier ways to kill someone. Why a bomb on the night of a well-publicized event? Had it been for recognition? Maybe, except that the attempt had pretty much failed. Which could explain why no one had claimed responsibility.

Her mind kept returning to the night of the bombing. She couldn't recall much of it, but it wasn't that which troubled her. It was the fact that, not only had *she* been injured, but dozens of other people had been as well. No one had been killed (that honor was to have been mine alone, she thought grimly), but that wasn't the point. Whoever had done it, whoever was after her, had no qualms whatsoever about anyone else who might get in the way. What did it mean? Why an attempt so spectacular, yet so singular in its purpose?

For the first time in days, she found herself craving a cigarette; she'd smoked for the better part of ten years. But her doctors had forbidden it. No smoking now or, quite possibly, ever. And while there was no obvious damage to her heart, she had suffered cardiac arrest. So, no smoking.

Ah, well, the head rush from the first drag would probably drop me to the floor, anyway.

Feeling more clear-headed than she had in days, she hoped she would feel less like a prisoner at home under police guard than she did in the hospital. Having the door closed at all times, while certainly conducive to her safety, had left her feeling claustrophobic. Complaining about it would accomplish nothing, and so she had kept silent on the matter.

Shaking herself out of her reverie, she glanced around the room, not really seeing anything, until her gaze skipped past the bedside table. Her attention was caught by a small flash of white peeking out from beneath a *Time* magazine. She lifted the magazine to reveal Emma Kirby's business card, back facing up, with Emma's number and the word HOME in neat black handwriting.

"Oh, wow," she said softly, raising her eyebrows.

I almost left that behind. She stared at it, rereading the word and numbers, aware once more of that feeling of security and comfort, of a sense of calm whenever she thought of the officer. She didn't know if she would ever see Emma Kirby again. *And that would be a shame.* She still felt that she would like to get to know her, beyond the original circumstances which had brought them together. If *only* to get beyond that, which was a fair enough reason in her mind.

There was a knock on the door. She slipped the business card into her pocket.

"Yeah," she called out.

The door opened and Detective James walked in, followed by a serious-looking older uniformed officer.

"Daina, sorry to barge in like this," James said, "but we need to talk to you."

It was the first time he'd used her first name. And it should have gotten her attention. But it didn't. Her attention had been caught, and was now held, by the entrance of Constable Emma Kirby, who came in right behind them.

CHAPTER THIRTEEN

Emma was aware of Daina's eyes on her the second she walked into the room. She was also aware that she was in a state of low-grade anxiety. But she gave Daina a small smile and a single nod in greeting while trying to ignore the slow tumble her belly took at the sight of her.

Looking more than a little perplexed, Daina gave a small nod in return, and then cast her eyes back to the detective and the sergeant. "What the hell is going on?" she asked, a definite edge to her voice.

Emma came to a stop just to the left of Sergeant Michaels and assumed a relaxed but alert *at ease* position. She noted the edge in Daina's voice, but it sounded more annoyed than alarmed. She hoped that what was about to be presented to the singer would go over well.

When they'd arrived at the hospital, Michaels had touched her arm and asked, "What exactly are you thinking of telling her?"

She'd shaken her head, shrugged. "Honestly? I really don't know. I just know that *she* should know what's going on, that it's not just her anymore. Then maybe we can find a connection that much quicker."

"Will whatever you tell her make her think or feel differently toward you?"

"Possibly." She hesitated, then added, "Okay, yes, most likely."

"Do you *know* how she thinks or feels toward you?" His eyes bored into hers.

"I have a *sense*," she answered carefully.

"Does she know you're gay?" he asked bluntly.

"I don't believe so," was Emma's immediate reply. She shook her head. "Honestly, that's not the impression that I get."

As they stepped out of the elevator, Michaels took her by the elbow, turning her in the direction of the hallway. "I know you trust your instincts, Emma," he said. "And I trust your instincts as well. But I had an idea on the way over here and I want to present it to both you and Detective James, before we go any further. If she loses her objectivity, this idea won't work."

"Okay, I'm willing to listen."

Just ahead was the nurse's station where Detective James stood. He started walking toward them. Beyond him, farther down the hall, two uniformed officers were standing outside what she assumed was Daina's room. She turned her attention back to the detective who was just coming abreast of them.

He said, without preamble, "I just found out she's being released in a couple of hours."

"Okay then, let me tell you both what I have in mind." Michaels looked at Emma. "Remember I mentioned the safe house to you?"

She nodded.

"Well, it occurred to me that Daina will need to be relocated as well. We have to get her *and* you somewhere he can't find either of you."

He looked at James, then back at her. "So I was thinking, it makes sense to have you both in one place, house the two of you together."

Emma's immediate response was complete rebellion. "Oh, no, now *wait* just a minute—" she began heatedly.

"Just hear me out, Emma," Michaels said, putting his hands out to forestall her protests. "I'm thinking of a more professional setup, as opposed to two women targeted by a madman stuck in a house together."

"Okay, go on," she said, a bit tightly. She was still willing to listen, but her tension level had just increased tenfold.

Detective James chose that moment to jump in. "Are you thinking more along the lines of, say, a bodyguard approach?"

"Yes, exactly." Michaels looked back at Emma, whose mouth had thinned to a straight line. "The idea is that she shouldn't be alone, and neither should you. So we assign one of our officers to stay with her, kind of like a bodyguard. That would be you, obviously. This way, neither of you is alone. And it's easier for us to keep an eye on the two of you, if you're not spread out."

Michaels and James looked at her, and she looked back and forth between the two of them, arms crossed, completely unhappy and not at all convinced.

"Look," Michaels went on, his tone somewhat more mollifying, "this makes sense and it saves time, energy and manpower. I understand you're not completely comfortable with it, and maybe I even understand why, to an extent. But she doesn't have to know why you're really there. I need the two of you comfortable with each other. Which is why you can't just waltz right in and tell her whatever you're thinking of telling her. I know I can count on your professionalism. I need to be able to count on her objectivity." He paused, and then added quietly, "And I need to know that I can keep the two of you safe. That *is* my job."

Emma again looked back and forth between the two of them. She could not ignore her misgivings about the idea, but she couldn't discount the logic of it, either.

"Just keep in mind," Michaels added, "that this is for *your* protection, as well. I need to keep you safe as well, because he will kill you to get to her."

"He'll kill *anyone* to get to her," was her grim response. "And I'm already on his list, remember?" She gave a heavy sigh and shook her head tiredly. "Okay, fine, if *she* goes for it, I will. But if she—"

"I know, I know," he said, hands raised in a calming gesture. "Let's just see how it goes, okay?"

Emma had grudgingly quieted then, and the three of them headed down the hall to Daina's room.

Now, in response to Daina's question, Detective James answered, "There's been a change in plans, a drastic change."

Daina looked at him with an expression that was either disgust or exasperation, or a combination of both. "Are you *ever* going to bring me good news?" she asked him.

Emma quickly repressed a grin. Michaels' voice, when he responded, was tinged with a lightness that could have been amusement as he answered, "Well, that *is* my goal."

"Well, that's good to hear." Daina's eyes then darted between the three of them, as she asked, "So, what is this 'drastic change'?"

Michaels took a couple of steps forward. "Ms. Buchanan, I'm Sergeant Michaels. I'm in charge of this—your case and the investigation."

Daina glanced down at the bed that separated them, then leaned slightly forward, her right hand extended. "Nice to meet you," she said with a curt nod as they shook hands.

"You know Constable Emma Kirby?" he asked, looking over his shoulder to nod in Emma's direction.

Daina's eyes flashed to Emma's and then, somewhat disconcertingly, did a quick up and down, before locking eyes with her once more. "Yeah, we've met," was all she said.

The once-over caused Emma to stiffen minutely. No one seemed to notice, least of all Daina, and for that she was grateful.

"We've come to let you know," Michaels continued, "that the individual who's threatening you is becoming more…direct in his threats. He's now indicated—"

"Wait a second," Daina interrupted him. "'He'?"

"Yes," Michaels said. "We've discovered that it is a male, that's all we know. And we just found that out."

"Okay," Daina said levelly, "go on."

"He's indicated that the minute you leave this hospital, he… *intends* to take your life."

Daina's eyes once more jumped between the three of them, her eyebrows raised. "So…what, you mean I have to stay here?"

"No, no, not at all." Michaels shook his head. "It just means the original idea of you staying with your parents is no longer feasible. That, and when we *do* move you, it has to be done in complete secrecy."

Daina just stared at him, frowning, as if he'd spoken in a foreign language. Emma noticed how tired she looked, that her eyes appeared red and puffy as if she'd been crying recently.

Jesus, this can't be easy on her. It said a lot about Daina's character that she still had fight and fire in her.

"What we're proposing is setting you up in one of our safe houses. We have a few of them in various parts of the city. They're not fancy, but they are inconspicuous and comfort is key. Since you might be there awhile, you'll understand why we stress that. Everything is provided, except whatever clothing you need or have. Obviously, the main feature is security. These houses are highly secure, with alarm systems and cameras, all monitored twenty-four/seven by an independent security company."

Michaels continued in a slower, more cautious manner. "Even with those security features in place, we still believe you shouldn't be alone. So what we'll do is…*assign* one of our officers to you, so you aren't alone—"

"What, you mean like a bodyguard?" the singer broke in.

"If you care to look at it like that," Michaels allowed.

Daina gave him a look of near-disgust. "How else should I look at it? We're not talking pajama parties here."

Once more, Emma had to repress her grin.

From across the bed, Daina suddenly pinned her with an intense look, and for the first time Emma noticed that Daina's eyes were a clear, almost impossibly brilliant shade of blue.

Nailed in place by the intensity of the look, her amusement evaporated. A moment later, Daina shifted her gaze to Michaels.

"Okay, fine," she said, decisively crossing her arms. Shooting another quick glance and a nod at Emma, she looked back at Michaels and said, "I want her."

Emma blinked and stiffened at the blunt, unexpected statement. Still somewhat transfixed by those eyes, she had been right in the middle of thinking *How did I miss that?* She made an effort to gather her thoughts.

Michaels, sounding surprised himself, said, "Excuse me?"

Daina inclined her head in Detective James' direction, speaking calmly but firmly. "The detective here gave me a choice once before, which I didn't take. If you're giving me a choice now, that is my choice." Again the glance and nod at Emma. "Constable Kirby."

Michaels said, almost casually, "Um, okay." He shrugged and nodded. "Sure. Of course you have a choice." He turned to look at Emma. "How do you feel about that, Constable?"

Emma returned his look with a dark and thoughtful one of her own. She knew she was not the only one to catch the irony of what had just transpired, nor was the implication lost on her that she no longer had a case to argue. Daina had neatly swept aside the one issue that might have kept Emma out of the situation entirely. *How convenient.*

"Oh, shit," Daina suddenly uttered. Emma quickly looked back at her.

"I'm sorry," the singer said, her eyes on Emma, looking and sounding puzzled, "I thought—isn't that why you're here? I hope I wasn't out of line with that request."

Emma made a supreme effort to quell her emotions and hide her discontent. "No, not at all," she responded, with a coolness she did not feel. "It's fine, not a problem."

"Are you sure?" Daina pressed, her expression now troubled. "I don't want—"

"Yes, really, I'm sure." Emma adopted a kinder tone and expression of her own. "It's fine."

Daina stared at her as if she expected her to say more. But

words eluded Emma, and so she kept her silence, all the while meeting those ocean-blue eyes steadily with her own.

Daina finally blinked. "Okay," she said simply, and looked at Michaels. "Okay," she said again, more firmly this time. "Because it's *her*," and she inclined her head toward Emma, "I'll go along with it. But only because it's her. *And*, I want my parents to know what's going on. I want them to know everything."

"Well," James said, "we can't tell them *everything*—"

"Fine, fine," Daina interrupted with obvious annoyance and impatience, "the whole secrecy thing, yeah, I get that. But you have to allow me to call them and tell them what's going on. Before I disappear off the face of the earth, for God only knows how long. Okay? Can I do that?"

"Yes, of course," Michaels reassured her. "They can come here, you can talk to them. But we have to get on that right away. We have a lot of arrangements to make if we're going to get you set up in the house today."

"Well, they were planning on being here at eleven anyway, so I'll call them now."

"Make sure you arrange to have your clothes and whatever personal items you need or want brought here. You'll be leaving right from here."

"What about food, groceries?" Emma suddenly thought to ask, forcing herself into the moment and trying to think practically.

"The house is stocked with the basics," Michaels said. "Anything else you need or want, you make a phone call, it gets delivered. We pick up the expense."

Emma nodded. "Sounds good." She glanced across at Daina.

Daina looked her way at the same time. Their eyes met and Daina raised her eyebrows and nodded as well.

"Okay," Michaels said briskly. "All right then, any more questions?" He looked at Emma, who shook her head.

They both looked at Daina, who nodded.

"Uh, yeah…is there a pool?" she asked, completely serious.

Emma's earlier amusement returned. This time she didn't even bother trying to hide her smile.

"What?" Daina asked. "I was thinking in terms of

hydrotherapy. I get my stitches out in a few days. It's a good question, isn't it?"

She assumed an almost injured air, and the smile that Emma was trying to get under control broadened instead.

"Actually, it is a good question," Michaels responded. "And yes, there is a pool. Anything else?"

"Yeah, actually, there is." Daina looked from the sergeant to Emma and asked of her, "Can you…stay a bit longer? I'd like to talk to you, if I could."

A bit thrown by the request, Emma collected herself quickly enough to answer smoothly, "Yes, of course." Her reply sounded cool and professional, and not in the least enthusiastic. She turned to Michaels, her back to Daina briefly, and Michaels met her look with a subtle questioning one of his own. And she recalled his earlier words of caution, and knew what he was thinking and what he wanted to say. And even though she was annoyed with him, she understood that he was concerned. But she couldn't respond to that concern, not here, not now. And so she just smiled and said, "I'll be right out." Michaels nodded and he and the detective left the room. And Emma, her mind churning and her body fatigued, turned once more to face Daina.

CHAPTER FOURTEEN

Daina actually hadn't intended to ask Emma to stay behind. At least not consciously. But she did have a couple of questions. And she'd caught Emma's amusement and thought it boded well for the development of a good rapport. Considering the way things were going, a good rapport was going to be necessary in the days ahead, she knew that much.

As Emma made the half turn back to face her, her expression, for one brief moment, was completely unguarded. And what Daina saw in Emma's eyes, in her face, was utter exhaustion. In the next moment the usual wall of cool professionalism was thrown up and she wondered if what she had seen had actually even been there.

"Are you okay?" she asked, moving to the right to reach the foot of the bed, all the while watching Emma closely.

Emma's expression didn't change as she answered, "Yes, I'm fine." She shoved her hands halfway into the pockets of her khakis. Coupled with the black tank top and running shoes, she looked so casual and so attractive, Daina had a hard time remembering the woman was a police officer. But if her attire belied her profession, her stance and attitude, even her build, was a subtle reminder of it. Her arms and shoulders were well-defined without being muscle-bound, which complemented her lean frame. She carried herself with a smoothness and grace underlined by a certain tension, like a dancer balanced on a knife edge. And while her expression was invariably mild, her eyes were keen and watchful, and Daina doubted they missed much. She didn't know how anyone could be so relaxed and so alert at the same time.

"And you're sure you're okay with all this?" she asked carefully, watching Emma's eyes. "Because I really didn't mean to—"

"Yes, I'm sure," Emma broke in, calmly but firmly. And then with the slightest of frowns she asked, "Are *you* okay with it?"

"Oh, yeah, I'm fine with it," Daina hastened to reassure her. "I mean, sure, it takes some getting used to, but I'm adapting." She paused, then added, "It's just…I don't know, these are unusual circumstances, you didn't seem to give it much thought. Don't you have a…husband, or a boyfriend or—"

"It's not a consideration," Emma interrupted her flatly.

Daina blinked, effectively shut down. "Okay, then," she said into the silence, feeling a bit foolish.

At that, Emma's look softened. "I'm sorry. I don't mean to be harsh. But it's really not a consideration." She hesitated, then asked, "What about you?"

"No," Daina replied, then added hastily, "I mean, no boyfriend or husband, obviously, and, well, no girlfriend, either, because…" She shrugged. "I fired her."

Emma said, completely straight-faced, "Wow. I didn't realize you could do that."

Daina started to smile, her smile broadened into a grin, and finally she laughed outright. "That was good," she said, with an appreciative nod. "Very funny."

Emma merely smiled.

"She was my manager, as well. I *did* fire her, and then broke up with her, almost in the same breath. Not that you need to know that, but…" Daina shrugged again, "that's what happened."

"I see."

Daina said, "So, I do have another question."

"Sure, shoot."

She blinked. "Make that two questions." She considered a moment, before asking, "Are you…going to be in uniform?"

Emma gave her a blank look. "Excuse me?"

Daina didn't know how else to ask the question. "Are you going to be in uniform?" she repeated, then added helpfully, "During your bodyguard stint."

"Oh!" Emma said with a start. "Right. No, no, just…street clothes, what you see here. No uniform."

"Okay, good." Daina gave a relieved laugh. "'Cause that might've felt a bit weird." A smart-ass comment popped into her head, having to do with women in uniform. She quelled it. "Second question is, will you be armed?"

"Yes," Emma replied immediately. "Are you okay with that?"

"Oh, yeah, definitely," was Daina's quick reply. "I mean, otherwise, it's like…having a watchdog but keeping it chained to the doghouse." She shrugged. "What's the point?"

"Good analogy," Emma said, with a nod and a smile.

Daina smiled in return, and then cleared her throat. "I'd like to say something," she began carefully, her eyes on Emma's, "and I'm not quite sure how to say it, but…"

Emma's expression was mildly curious while she waited, and Daina was bolstered by it. She swallowed, and continued, saying, "I *chose* you because…I feel…safe with you. And I don't mean that in some kind of…creepy way, because you saved my life. I don't. It's just, I can't—" She broke off, jerking her eyes from Emma's and raising them to the ceiling briefly before, with an inarticulate sound of frustration, she looked back. "I can't find the words to explain that any better. But that's what

I meant, when I said 'because it's you.' *Because* it's you, I'll go along with this; *because* I feel safe with you." She paused, then added, quietly, "And I wanted you to know that."

Only about five feet separated the two of them, so Daina was close enough to see Emma's expression change into something almost resembling surprise. She opened her mouth as if to speak, but nothing came out. And then, to Daina's absolute alarm, Emma's eyes brimmed with tears.

"Oh, my God, what—?" Daina spoke quickly, fearfully, her hands out in a gesture of appeasement. "What did I do? I'm sorry."

Emma blinked and shook her head, and the tears fell from her eyes to slide down her cheeks. "No," she said, and sniffed. "No, it's not you. Please, I'm sorry." She put one hand out toward Daina, as if to calm her, while she wiped away the tears with the other. "It's not you," she repeated, and sniffed again.

Daina just gaped at her.

Emma turned ever so slightly away, wiped her eyes with both hands, took a deep breath and once more faced Daina. She said, almost sheepishly, "You, uh, caught me off guard there." She gave a weak smile and a small shake of her head. "And I'm sleep-deprived and I, uh…really think I need to regroup." She sniffed one last time, and then added, "So, if you'll excuse me?"

Daina looked at her a bit dumbly and said, "Yeah. Sure. Go."

With what was obviously a grateful smile, Emma said, "Thank you. I'll, uh, catch up with you later."

Daina could only nod. "Great," she muttered, as the door closed behind Emma. "I just made my bodyguard cry."

She stood there a few moments longer, trying to make sense of Emma's reaction, but in the end, gave up. The woman must be extremely tired or extremely sensitive. Or both. She sincerely hoped she hadn't misjudged the woman's competency, or how safe she might actually be with her.

She had to call her parents. *That* was her priority. And if Emma had a problem with what had just happened, well, they could talk about it over dinner tonight, she supposed. The thought struck her as so patently absurd that she actually laughed out loud, a single, harsh sound that had an edge to it she didn't like. She instantly squelched it and limped over to the bedside table.

Priorities, she thought, as she picked up the phone. *Remember your priorities.*

Emma wasted no time heading down the hall to the elevators. She needed to get out of the area to somewhere private so she could deal with what had just happened.

"Emma!" Michaels called out behind her, halting her in her tracks.

She took a deep, steadying breath before turning to face him.

As he got closer, he frowned. "Are you okay? What happened?"

"Nothing," she replied coolly. "I'm fine."

"You're fine? You don't *look* fine."

She had no idea what she looked like; she only knew how she felt. If that was reflected in her face, she'd have to make a conscious effort to cover it up, or else explain her countenance to Michaels. She didn't feel she had enough energy for either. With a heavy sigh, she said, "Really, Sarge, I'm fine. I'm just tired."

He seemed to buy her explanation; his expression became sympathetic, as he said, "Oh, yeah, of course."

And suddenly, on top of the myriad other emotions she was feeling, Emma realized she was once more annoyed. She was annoyed that he stood in front of her, wanting to know what, if anything, was wrong, and annoyed that whatever was wrong, she couldn't possibly tell him, because she wasn't quite sure herself. And even if she was sure, she still couldn't tell him. She was annoyed that she couldn't tell him she was annoyed, and the piéce de rèsistance, she was annoyed that she had just walked out on Daina, likely leaving her standing there thinking she had done something wrong.

Michaels was still looking at her closely. "Did everything go okay in there?" he asked.

"Yes, it went fine." She assumed a casual air. "It's all good."

"She didn't bring anything else up? She seems okay with everything?"

"Actually, yes, she seems more comfortable with it than I expected." *Which is more than I can say for myself.*

"Largely due to you, apparently."

"Well," Emma said, with a slight, dismissive laugh and tilt of her head, "so she says."

"That was quite the little twist of fate there, her asking for you," Michaels commented. "Worked out for the best, I think. You're okay with it?"

Emma sighed inwardly. "Honestly, Sarge, I'm as okay with it right now as I can possibly be. If she wants me there, then I'm it. I mean, she won't go for it otherwise, so it's a moot point. I think I just need some time to adjust, get used to the whole 'being a victim' thing. That and some sleep and I should be just fine."

Michaels' intense look eased. "Well, you're going to have to go without sleep for a bit longer, I'm afraid, if you think you can handle it."

Another inward sigh. "Sure, I'm good for a while yet," she told him, not surprised in the least by the delay.

He motioned her toward the elevators and fell into step beside her. "We'll get you to your apartment so you can get your things together, but I want you in and out. I want you back here."

That surprised her. "I have to come back here?"

"I'd like to keep the two of you together. It makes sense to move you both at the same time."

Emma supposed he was right. "How are you moving us?"

"We're still working on that."

He said no more on the subject, insisting instead that he accompany her to her apartment, which she agreed to.

It was only after he'd left and she was alone and certain of complete privacy that she allowed herself to look closely at what had happened at the hospital. She felt reluctant to do so, not because she didn't know what was going on. She wasn't naïve. In fact, she almost couldn't believe what was happening and therefore didn't feel she could trust it, couldn't trust her feelings or her perception.

The truth of the matter was, Daina touched her in ways she had never experienced before. Certainly she was abrupt and brutally candid, almost to the point of annoyance, but she also exhibited a genuine honesty and guilelessness that could not possibly be feigned. The woman was so sincere and so open, it was disarming.

Emma knew that she was interested in Daina, attracted to her, drawn to her. She could deny it to anyone else, but she couldn't deny it to herself, not anymore. She'd never met anyone who was so alive, so captivating, so free of restraint. And yet, nothing really had changed. She was still a cop in Daina's eyes. She would have to maintain her professional objective distance. There was no way she would jeopardize the integrity of the investigation or Daina's safety. Regardless of the fact that she'd shed a few tears earlier in front of the woman.

She felt a sudden irritation with herself and abruptly got to her feet. She headed down the hall to get her things together, and to push Daina Buchanan from her mind.

CHAPTER FIFTEEN

Daina's parents took the news of the sudden change in plans better than Daina had expected. She'd explained nothing over the phone, merely told them that the original arrangements had been scotched, that she was being relocated, and would explain as best she could once they were at the hospital. She'd asked them to get together whatever belongings she'd brought with her from Nashville, knowing it wasn't all that much since she'd only been planning on staying a couple of days, and she recited a quick list of things she thought she might need or want in addition.

When they arrived they brought with them her suitcase and her shoulder bag; she'd always been a light traveler and she guessed that the few extras she'd requested had already been transferred to her luggage. Her father, however, carried something else, and when Daina saw it, she was elated.

"Thought you might be wanting this," he said, as he placed the hard shell guitar case on the bed. "All things considered."

"Oh, my God," Daina breathed, placing her hands on the case. "I'd forgotten it was at your house."

She undid the clasps and lifted the cover. Nestled inside was one of her favorite guitars, a blond Seagull six-string acoustic. Its flat finish seemed to absorb the light rather than reflect it. She'd bought the guitar when she was nineteen and it was still in excellent condition. When she'd moved out of her parents' house she had decided to leave it there, so there would always be a guitar available.

She hugged her father as best she could with her one good arm. "Thanks, Dad, for remembering."

"That's what I'm here for," he said, returning the hug and kissing the top of her head. He then stepped back, holding her at arm's length, and looked at her gravely. "Now tell us what's going on, honey."

Keeping in mind the restrictions put in place by Sergeant Michaels, Daina shared with them only the most prudent details regarding the recent threats and her relocation. She stressed the safety factor, and the fact that she wouldn't be alone; she didn't mention Emma Kirby's name, just the fact that a police officer had been assigned to guard her. She was unsure what more she could share, but felt she couldn't possibly say much less.

Her parents took it all calmly and asked few questions. She explained that their safety was also a concern, so she was limited in what she could share. They accepted that without argument. Shortly afterward, there was a knock on the door.

"Oh, you're here already," Sergeant Michaels said to Daina's parents as he entered.

After he'd shaken both her father's and mother's hand, he looked back at her and asked, "What have you told them?"

"Only what we need to know, obviously," her father

spoke up. He then proceeded to reiterate her words and their questions, and finished with, "My daughter has a good head on her shoulders, Sergeant."

"Well, yes, I'm sure she does," Michaels said gravely, "but this is a dangerous situation—"

"I could have said more," Daina interrupted him softly, eyeing him steadily. "I opted for less. I'm aware of the situation, Sergeant. I'm not going to endanger my parents."

At that, Michaels' expression softened. "I didn't mean any offense," he said with a slight smile. "You did fine." He looked then at her parents. "Do the two of you have any more questions?"

"I do," her mother spoke up. "Will we be able to have any contact with Daina? Will we be kept informed?"

"Those are details we'll have to work out," Michaels replied, addressing all three of them. "Yes, you will be kept informed, and it's entirely possible you can maintain *some* level of contact, but we'll have to work out something agreeable to everyone, that doesn't compromise security. Let's deal with one thing at a time, shall we?"

He shook hands with them once more, saying, "We'll take good care of her. It was nice meeting both of you." And with that, he turned and left.

Marlene Buchanan finally broke down and turned into her husband's arms. As he embraced her, Daina went to both of them and attempted her own measure of comfort, even as she sought to be comforted in turn.

Emma was back at the hospital by ten o'clock, sitting in the cafeteria having yet another cup of coffee and a passable grilled cheese sandwich. It was only ten in the morning, but she'd been awake for too many hours to be in a breakfast frame of mind. And besides, grilled cheese sandwiches had always been a comfort food for her, and she was in need of a bit of comfort at the moment.

She had packed quickly, neatly and efficiently. She'd even

remembered her swimsuit. She had been just about to reach for the doorknob, when the phone rang.

Her heart slammed in her chest. For a moment, she was frozen, completely incapable of moving. It rang again. She hadn't even considered that the guy who'd called earlier might call again. She quickly checked the caller ID, and saw with complete and utter relief that it was Perry.

"Emma, hey, what're you doing up?" Perry said in surprise when she answered. "I expected to get your machine."

Usually after a late night shift, Emma was asleep by eight A.M. She always turned her phone's ringer off, letting her answering machine pick up any calls. She was suddenly unsure if she should tell Perry what was going on, and then decided that the fewer people who knew, the better. "I just had some things to do," she answered him casually. "What are you doing up?"

"Oh, the girl just left. I was bored."

Emma grinned at that. "The girl" was Deirdre, Perry's girlfriend, but for some reason he couldn't pronounce her name to save his life, and he refused to call her Dee because according to him, that was just a letter and not a proper name. Emma had no idea what he called her when there was an actual need for it. *Honey*, she supposed, and suppressed a laugh.

"You were bored so you called me? Even though you thought I might be sleeping?"

"That's how bored I am," he sighed. "Reduced to talking to your answering machine. It's one step above talking to myself, so I'm safe."

"Yeah," she said with an easy laugh, "you just keep telling yourself that."

"Actually, I did want to ask you something, that's why I was hoping you might be up. But now I'm thinking I'll just save it for tonight when I see you."

"Oh, uh…" *Shit*, Emma thought. She quickly gathered her thoughts together. "I actually, um, won't be coming in tonight, Perry. I'm taking some time off, starting today."

"Oh. Are you okay?"

"Yeah, yes, I'm fine, I just…have to get away for a while." That sounded lame even to her ears.

"Well, where are you going? And for how long?" He sounded confused.

And she suddenly ached to tell him, to have someone else on her side, to have someone else's support. But she couldn't. She knew that. "Perry, I can't tell you. It's personal."

There was silence on the other end, and then Perry asked, "You're not still sore at me for the other day, are you?"

"What?" Emma was surprised. "No, my God, Perry, no, that's—no, that's over, that's past."

"You still trust me, don't you?"

Taken even further aback, she hastily reassured him. "Perry, yes, I still trust you, okay? This has nothing to do with any of that."

"Okay, good, I'm glad to hear that." He paused briefly, then asked casually, "So, are you going to ask that girl out?"

"*What?*" The abrupt change of topic completely threw her.

"Well, if you've got time off," he said reasonably, "why not ask her out?"

"'Ask her out'?" Emma was flabbergasted. "Perry, she's in the *hospital*. What am I going to do, pack a picnic lunch?"

"Well, she's not going to be in there forever."

His tone of voice bordered on condescending and she was immediately irritated.

"Well, I wouldn't know about that, Perry," she said shortly. "And I'm not having this conversation with you. Do you *not* have better things to do?"

"Well, actually, if I'm not going to see you tonight, I wanted to ask you something."

"Fine, ask me," she tersely invited him, glancing quickly at her watch. "But make it fast, because I do have to go."

"Okay, well…" A pause, and then he continued. "I wanted to ask my girl to marry me, and I wanted to know what you thought of that."

Maybe the stress of the morning had finally caught up with her, or maybe she'd just had enough of him. She lost her patience. "You want to know what I think of that? What do I *think?* Perry, you can't even pronounce her fucking *name*, and you're going to ask her to marry you? You might want to work on getting her name right first, since it's only her last name that'll likely be changing if you *do* get married. There, are you happy? That's what I think."

"Whoa, Emma—"

"And you know what else?" she broke in heatedly. "I don't have time for this shit. I have to go. Take care of yourself."

And she hung up on him. And grabbed her keys from the coffee table, picked up her bags, and left her apartment.

Now, sitting in the cafeteria, tearing apart her grilled cheese sandwich and eating it in small bites, she lamented losing her temper. It wasn't Perry's fault. She was on edge, terribly on edge, and he had annoyed her in his usual fashion, which normally she could tolerate. But not this time, not today. She knew she should apologize, and she would. In a while. Right now she just wanted to calm herself and eat her sandwich. The magazine she'd picked up at the counter should be enough distraction until she had to go back upstairs.

She was supposed to be ready to leave in an hour; apparently their accommodations were being readied. Beyond that, Emma knew nothing. *Which is just as well.* She already had her reservations. The less she knew at this point, the better.

She sincerely hoped that this plan would work and not blow up in their faces. She still felt as if there were some form of deceit going on, but was that really her concern? If the end result was that the two of them remained safe while they tried to catch this guy, wasn't that what mattered? Which was likely what Michaels was telling himself, and trying to convince her of. She smiled to herself. *Good luck with that,* was all she could think.

She turned the page of the magazine and the article on the next page actually caught her attention; it dealt with women in law enforcement. Interested, she leaned back in her chair, rocking it slightly on its back legs, pulled the magazine closer, and began reading. Very shortly, she was engrossed. She didn't know there was someone behind her until a male voice spoke softly almost right into her ear.

"You're lucky you're being saved 'til last," he said.

She never even had time to react. His voice, his words, had barely registered when her chair was yanked brutally backward. She caught a blurred image of a retreating lab coat before she crashed down, striking her head a solid blow against the floor.

CHAPTER SIXTEEN

Emma's head hit the floor so hard she actually saw stars. A part of her marveled at that, in a detached kind of way, even as she gamely struggled to gain her feet. A sound disturbingly similar to that of the ocean roaring in her ears, she rolled over onto her hands and knees. The view of the tile floor swam nauseatingly before her eyes, its irregular black diamond pattern first doubling, then tripling. With a singular effort, she forced herself to look away. She was aware of the close proximity of other chairs and tables; with her right hand she reached up to grab the back of one of the chairs, managing to haul herself halfway up. With her left hand reaching back to the table behind her, she pushed herself up the rest of the way, lurching drunkenly to a standing position. Suddenly there were hands at her arms and shoulders, helping her to stay upright.

"Easy, Emma, take it easy." She recognized Michaels' voice on her left.

"Have you got her?" a female voice asked on her right.

"Yeah, I've got her."

The woman was either a nurse or a doctor, she couldn't tell which, clad in scrubs and a lab coat. She had Asian features with beautiful and expressive dark eyes, her black hair pulled rather severely back and up in a bun. She was looking at Emma with concern even as Michaels was easing her back into one of the chairs.

"Sarge, no," Emma said, struggling against his efforts. "It was him, that guy, he's here."

Michaels swore softly. He kept one hand on Emma's shoulder as if to restrain her, and grabbed for his radio with the other. He spoke quietly, urgently into it.

Emma decided to sit still for the moment. Her head ached beyond anything she'd ever known, and moving only exacerbated it. She was going to have to move, she knew that, but for now she brought both hands up to the back of her head, interlocking her fingers and cradling her head with her forearms. She just wanted to stop her head from feeling like it was going to split apart.

"Emma?" Michaels crouched in front of her. "What did he look like?"

She leaned back in the chair, keeping her hands in place. "I don't know. All I saw was a lab coat, which he could have ditched."

Michaels shook his head, rose to his feet. "Did *anyone* see this guy?" he asked the room at large.

Emma heard a couple of voices raised in assent, and Michaels stepped away from her. He was immediately replaced by the woman in scrubs and lab coat, who crouched before her.

"Hi, I'm Dr. Lang. You took quite a hard fall there, how're you doing?" The woman's voice was soft, concerned.

Emma dropped her arms. "I'm okay, I think." She placed her left hand gingerly to the back of her head and winced. "It hurts like a son of a bitch, but I think I'm okay. I'm not bleeding, am I?" Her hand was free of any blood.

"Any dizziness, double vision?"

Emma shook her head and regretted doing so immediately. "No," she said. "Initially, but not now."

"Well, that's good." The doctor brought out a penlight. "It could come back, though. You fell pretty hard. Look straight ahead." Lang flashed the light in her eyes, nodded, and repocketed the light.

Emma smiled. "You make house calls, Doc?"

Lang smiled in return. "Does anybody? No, I was on my break, I heard you fall. Pay attention, follow my finger."

Finally, the doctor nodded. As she rose from her crouch in front of her, Emma felt a hand on her shoulder.

"We need to go," Michaels said. "Are you okay?"

"Yeah," she said, and shot a look at the doctor. "Aren't I?"

"Pay attention to your reflexes and your vision," she was told. "Any dizziness, nausea, vomiting, get checked out right away. But just monitor yourself for now."

As Emma moved away, Dr. Lang called after her, "Try to stay awake for a couple of hours yet. If you have a concussion, falling asleep right away could be a bad thing."

Emma looked back with a wry grin. "No worries there, Doc. Sleep isn't on my agenda this morning." She continued after Michaels.

"What've you got?" she asked him as they hastened to the elevators.

"Blue jeans, dark hair, a lab coat," he told her. "Nobody really saw him. He was quick. Went out the side exit."

"He could still be in the building," she stated, unnecessarily.

"Not much we can do about that," Michaels told her. "I need to get you upstairs. Our two guys up there are on alert. That's where I want you." At the elevators, he looked across at her. "What exactly happened, by the way? He blindside you?"

She puffed her breath out in disgust. "Nothing that spectacular. He came up behind me and pulled my chair out from under me. I whacked my head on the floor. End of story."

"He say anything to you?"

"Yeah, that's how I knew it was him. He said I was lucky I was being saved 'til last."

"Lucky you, then, huh?" Michaels said dryly.

Emma could have cheerfully told him to piss off. She shook her head, and then squeezed her eyes shut against the accompanying ache. *Jesus, I have to stop doing that.* "So, now what?"

Michaels waited until the elevator doors had closed before saying, "Now, we get you two out of here, ASAP. I've called for backup, for all the good it'll do, and the chopper is on its way."

She looked at him sharply. "Chopper? You're moving us by helicopter?"

"It's the quickest and the safest," he replied with a nod. "This hospital has a helipad on the roof. All I have to worry about is getting you safely to the roof and out of here. Especially now. This guy could be anywhere. I don't have the people to cordon off the floor or to conduct a room-to-room search. So, I get you to the roof, then to the military base and from there to the safe house. There's no way he can follow. It's a good plan."

"No shit," Emma murmured, impressed.

"You going to be okay?" he asked, his concern obvious.

"Yeah, sure, I'll be all right," she reassured him. "I've just got a whopper of a headache, that's all."

He continued to look at her while reaching for his radio and speaking into it, asking for an all clear as they got closer to their destination. They exited the elevator cautiously but quickly, and then Michaels' radio came to life once more. He listened, coming to a stop.

Emma slowed, but he shook his head.

"Daina's room. Go," he told her.

She went, her long strides carrying her quickly down the hall. At Daina's room she was brought up short by the identical looks of consternation on the faces of both constables stationed there.

"What?"

"She's...getting her stitches out," the taller of the two replied with obvious reluctance. "I was...told to wait out here."

"What are you, *stupid?*" Emma uttered in complete disbelief.

She reached for her gun as she knocked on the door. "Is it locked?" she asked the officer.

He shook his head.

Emma withdrew her gun, smoothly racked the slide. "Daina? I'm coming in," she called. She motioned the other officers to flank either side of the door. Gun at her side, she grasped the handle and eased the door open, stepping partially into the room, exposing only her left side.

Daina lay on the bed on her back, covered with a blanket which she held against her chest. There were two nurses present, one with a pair of scissors and tweezers in hand at Daina's left side, the other, basin in one hand, caught in the process of pulling a curtain around the bed. They wore twin expressions of surprise. Daina's expression, however, was amused.

"Well, at least you knocked," she said.

Emma fluidly reholstered her gun at her back, holding the door open with her foot. She leaned back to nod at the two constables, then stepped into the room, releasing the door so that it closed behind her.

"I'm sorry, but you can't be alone," she told Daina.

Daina looked first at one nurse and then the other, before looking back at Emma.

"Right," was all she said.

"I mean, without protection," Emma amended.

Daina never lost her amused expression. "Oh, well, I thought that's what the two goons outside my door were for." She then indicated the chair at the side of the bed with a slight inclination of her head. "We're almost done here, if you want to have a seat."

Emma glanced at the chair. "Uh, no thanks, I'll pass."

"Suit yourself."

And with that, the nurse pulled the curtain the rest of the way around the bed. Emma contented herself with stepping back and leaning against the wall next to the door. She heard murmured voices from behind the curtain and the occasional *ouch!* or sharp intake of breath. At a knock on the door, she straightened abruptly.

"Grand-fuckin-Central Station," she heard Daina mutter.

Then Michaels said, "Emma, it's me."

She opened the door, losing both her grin and her good humor.

"Everything okay?" he asked.

"Yes," she said, in a tight, low voice, "no thanks to Milli and Vanilli there. What kind of idiots do you have on duty here?"

"I know, I know," he said, one hand out in a placating gesture. "They assumed that since I told them to be on the lookout for a male, two women in scrubs weren't a threat. You did the right thing, and I've already torn a strip off them."

"Well good, saves me the effort."

"I just wanted to tell you, ETA for the chopper is fifteen minutes. Will she be ready then?"

"Hang on, I'll check." Emma deliberately closed the door, then craned her head around. "Daina, can you be ready to leave in fifteen minutes or so?"

"Yeah, no problem," Daina said. "We're done here."

Emma turned back to the door, opened it a crack. "She said yes," she told Michaels.

"Great. I'll need her stuff and yours."

"My things are at the nurse's station. Hang on another sec." Emma spied the suitcase, shoulder bag and guitar case by the closet and handed them through the door.

She closed the door just as the two nurses stepped out from behind the curtain with a tray of instruments, swabs and disinfectant.

"She's all yours," one of them said. "She's just getting dressed."

Emma nodded and held the door for them as they left. She then turned to face the curtained-off area and listened to Daina dressing. She felt distinctly uncomfortable. She was supposed to be in the room for her own protection, so she couldn't leave. She glanced around the room, trying to find something to occupy her attention.

"You okay out there?" Daina asked from behind the curtain.

Emma brought her gaze down from the ceiling, back to the curtain. "Yes, I'm fine."

"Okay, I won't be much longer." A few moments later, the curtain was pulled back. Daina peered around the edge of it. "You sure you're okay?"

It suddenly occurred to Emma to wonder if Daina might be obliquely referring to her earlier abrupt departure. She had absolutely no intention of discussing that event. She quickly said, "Yes, I'm sure. You look well. No more bandages?" The dressing on the left side of Daina's head was absent.

"No more bandages and no more sling. I still have to be careful though, and I'll need to continue with the physical therapy for a while yet, but otherwise it's all good." She sounded immensely pleased. "Oh, and the staples in my belly, they come out next week."

"That sounds…painful," Emma observed. "Why the staples?"

"Well, apparently I ruptured my spleen and almost bled to death, which is why I arrested. They had to remove it. They used staples to hold me together."

"Oh, wow, I didn't know that, any of that."

Daina shrugged. "Not many people do, I'm guessing." She reached up to gingerly touch the wounded area at her left temple. It looked angry and tender.

"Does it hurt?" Emma asked.

"A little." Daina's brow furrowed. "How does it look?"

Emma, meeting her eyes, saw the worry there. She smiled gently. "You look fine," she said, with complete sincerity.

Daina colored slightly, but her look of relief was unmistakable. She gave a small smile. "Thank you."

"Are you sure you're ready? Because the chopper will be here in about ten minutes."

"Chopper?" Daina's eyebrows rose in surprise. "Do you mean as in helicopter?"

She nodded. "I couldn't say anything while the nurses were present. But it's the quickest and safest way to get you out of here." She decided that was all she would say on the subject. She was barely clear on what was going on herself. And besides, her head still hurt abominably. She really didn't feel, either mentally or physically, up to answering any questions.

Daina looked at her thoughtfully. "You take your job very seriously."

"There's a life at stake," Emma returned quietly.

Daina nodded, her face expressionless. They were both startled by three sharp raps on the door. Emma moved first, heading for the door.

"Yes," she called out.

"It's Michaels."

She cracked open the door.

"We're going up now. Everything's in place, chopper's almost here. Ready?"

Emma saw that the hall was crowded with uniformed police officers. Their escort, no doubt. She nodded at Michaels, then looked back at Daina and smiled at her. "Let's go," she said easily and, holding the door open, allowed Daina to exit first, then quickly followed after.

CHAPTER SEVENTEEN

Daina had never been in a helicopter and she wasn't quite sure if she was nervous or excited at the prospect. Her adrenaline was up and her heart was pounding, but she didn't let on about her current state. She carefully stilled her expression to neutrality before leaving the room. As she stepped into the hall, she was startled to see so many police officers and that those officers wore Kevlar vests.

"What the hell is going on?" she asked, some of her surprise creeping into her voice. "Why so many cops?"

"Don't let it bother you, just keep moving," was all Emma said.

Daina felt Emma's hand at her back, gently urging her

forward in the direction of the elevators. She saw Michaels a little way down the hall, also wearing a vest. Everyone was looking at them, and as they came upon the nurse's station, the staff on duty murmured well-wishes and goodbyes. It all began to feel somewhat surreal; she almost felt as if she were going to her doom instead of her supposed salvation.

Daina was aware of police officers falling in behind them and as she and Emma entered the elevator, she ended up in one corner. Michaels stood directly across from her, Emma beside her, and two other officers blocked the doors.

Daina shook her head. "When did this become a SWAT exercise?"

"We've decided this is necessary," Michaels answered.

"Why, did something happen?"

His eyes flicked briefly in Emma's direction, before he looked back at Daina. "I really can't say anything, either way."

"Okay, you know what? *Fuck* you," Daina snapped at him. "I've had enough of your cryptic little remarks and your bullshit secrets." Everyone in the elevator had tensed, but she didn't care. "When are you going to get it through your head that this is *my* life we're talking about here, and I deserve to know what the hell is going on?"

"Daina, hey—" Emma started to say, her voice pitched low as she reached out to touch Daina's arm.

"No, *piss* off!" Daina snapped, rounding on her as well. She knocked Emma's hand away. "And don't fucking touch me. Any of you. Just *piss* off."

Emma's face briefly registered hurt surprise, and a part of Daina was instantly sorry for her actions, her words, even while another part snidely congratulated her on being the poster child for overreacting. A moment later Emma's expression had closed down, reverting once more to that cool inscrutability Daina had become familiar with. And she was just fine with that, content to hold onto her anger and brandish it again if need be. She couldn't believe their arrogance or their ignorance, and she was fed up with all the secrecy. She crossed her arms and stared straight ahead.

The remainder of the elevator ride was completed in tense silence. They filed out singly, into a large, enclosed concrete and glass area, to be met by another Kevlar-clad officer.

"All clear," he said to the sergeant. "Chopper's ETA is one minute."

Daina took a couple of steps off to the side, putting some distance between herself and the rest of the group.

Emma glanced over and then dropped back to stand beside Daina, seemingly undaunted by her earlier behavior. "Are you all right?" she asked, voice lowered.

Daina didn't look at her, just gave a single stiff nod in answer.

Michaels looked back. "Have you ever flown in a helicopter before, Daina?"

She shook her head once.

He eyed her briefly, then asked, "Are you okay with flying?"

She looked him dead in the eye. "Bring it on," she said quietly.

Surprisingly, he grinned. "Damn, you're a tough one," he said, with a shake of his head.

Daina said nothing. A moment later, the thumping sound of helicopter blades announced the arrival of the police helicopter. When it came into view, she watched as it hovered over the pad momentarily before touching down.

"Blake?" Michaels said to one of the other officers present. "You're with Daina, get her in safe and strapped in."

Michaels addressed Daina. "Keep your head lowered and stay away from the rear of the helicopter. That rear propeller can be hard to see and it'll chop you to bits."

Nice, Daina thought. She shook her head and made ready to follow Blake, when she felt a light touch on her left arm. She looked across at Emma.

"Are you afraid of heights?" Emma asked her, keeping her hand in place. She spoke in that same low tone that Daina, almost in spite of herself, was quickly coming to find quite riveting.

She frowned. "No."

"I didn't think so." Emma almost seemed to smile, without actually doing so. "I just want to tell you something then: Planes and helicopters are two totally different birds. They fly completely different. You'll see what I mean. I think you'll be fine."

Daina blinked, a little nonplussed. "Okay. Thank you."

A few minutes later, everyone was on board. She tensed as the helicopter powered up and then lifted off, but within seconds she relaxed. The ride was smooth and the view incredible and she gave herself up to the pleasure of the moment. Certainly they were high in the air, but everything that lay below was identifiable and on scale. Just being able to see traffic was immensely comforting. She had been stuck inside the hospital for a week; the sense of freedom was indescribable. So she was surprised and disappointed when the pilot's voice came over her headset, informing them that they would be landing in a few minutes.

Once they had touched down and disembarked, she glanced back at the chopper, filled with a vague sense of yearning. But then, with a soft, derisive laugh at herself, she shook her head and turned away, only to come eye to eye with Emma. She must have paused, even as Daina had, but not likely for the same reason.

With a slight nod of acknowledgment Daina said, "You were right. It was great." She glanced over her shoulder once more at the chopper, then again met Emma's eyes. "I'm going to have to get me one of those."

She stepped past Emma to follow in the direction of Michaels. Beyond him, parked on the tarmac, were a plain white sedan, and a black SUV with darkly tinted windows. Both were flanked by two men in plainclothes; more police officers, she guessed. Michaels came to a stop at the vehicles and spoke briefly with the two men. Daina did her best to ignore them, concentrating instead on the warmth of the summer sun beating down on her, the breeze brushing past her, and the wide open space surrounding her, all of which uplifted her spirits and calmed her fractious state of mind.

Michaels turned to face the two of them, as the plainclothes officers strode off to the white sedan.

"Okay, the two of you will ride with me," he said, jerking a thumb at the SUV. "They'll tail us and then we'll leave the

Explorer with you. This way, if you need a vehicle you'll have one. We sent your personal belongings ahead, they're already at the house." He turned to open the back door on the passenger side. "Now then, shall we?"

The drive was silent and for that Daina was grateful. She wasn't in the mood for conversation of any sort, and thankfully, neither Michaels nor Emma seemed inclined to make any small talk. She contented herself with staring out the window, trying not to give any thought to the multitude of issues that were clamoring for her attention.

Fifteen minutes later, the vehicles slowed near the outskirts of the city. "Here we are," Michaels announced, and he turned into a paved circular drive which led up to a moderately sized ranch-style house.

The house and neatly landscaped property were encircled with what Daina guessed to be a seven foot high wrought-iron fence, an impressive and rather daunting counterpoint to the comfortable façade of the house itself. There were two other vehicles in the driveway, parked in the loop. Michaels pulled the SUV up to the gate, beyond which sat a two car garage. He pulled his visor down to reveal what appeared to be two-garage door openers.

"Okay," he said, "you're going to want to park behind the fence, obviously, not that I foresee you going anywhere, because realistically you shouldn't. Anyone else who comes, like cleaning staff—they're here once a week—will park on this side of the fence. They will buzz you on the intercom here." He pointed at the box attached to the fence, which also housed a keypad. He then reached up to press the button on the smaller of the two black remotes. The gate proceeded to retract.

"Only you, the security company, and select members of the police force have access to the code. Anyone other than you wishing to gain entry must be cleared first by the security company. You receive confirmation and then you let them in. There is no deviation from that procedure. It's foolproof, so no mistakes are made. And the cameras are constantly on, monitoring twenty-four/seven."

Michaels drove the SUV ahead about fifty feet and stopped before the garage. Daina looked back to see that the gate had already closed behind them.

"This remote," Michaels went on, drawing her attention back to the larger of the two, "is for the garage, obviously." He pressed the button; the garage door opened and he drove inside. The garage door trundled down behind them.

The three of them left the garage and Michaels led the way to the house, taking them around to the back to show them the grounds and the large inground pool. They entered the house through the back patio doors and Michaels gave them a quick tour of the interior.

The house was roomy, boasting four bedrooms and two bathrooms, one of which was attached to the master bedroom. One of the bedrooms had been converted into an exercise room of sorts with a treadmill, Stairmaster, and a rack of free weights against one wall. The overall floor plan of the house was open and airy, with both a tasteful décor and comfortable-looking furnishings. There was a finished basement complete with a pool table and an entertainment area with sofa, armchairs, TV and stereo.

Daina was impressed and pleased. Stealing a glance at Emma, she could see that she obviously was, as well. Their forced confinement and seclusion would not be too hard to endure, at least from the perspective of material comforts. Their personal belongings they found in the living room.

Michaels instructed them in how to go about ordering anything they might need and, finally, went over the security features and codes. "This house is a little more...lavish than what we might normally have set you up in. But we thought it a good choice, since we have no idea how long you'll be here." He then clasped his hands together. "My job here is done."

He looked at Daina. "Anything you need, whatever you need, let us know and we'll see that you get it."

"Thank you."

He turned his attention to Emma. "Can I speak to you privately for a moment?"

Taking her cue, Daina decided to go sit by the pool. Making her careful way outside to one of the patio chairs, situated a few feet from poolside, she eased herself down. With a sigh of contentment, she leaned back and closed her eyes.

A short time later, she heard the patio doors open, and the approach of murmured voices. Emma and the sergeant came into view. Michaels stepped close.

"So, what do you think?" he asked her.

Daina shaded her eyes against the late morning sun. "I'm trying not to," she replied with a half smile.

"I can understand that," he acknowledged with an answering smile.

Never once taking her eyes off him, she said, "I do still have questions, and I deserve answers to those questions. In case you'd thought I'd forgotten."

"I didn't think that."

"Good. Then we understand each other." She straightened in her chair, and then carefully rose to her feet. They shook hands. "Thank you, again."

"Take care of yourself. I'll be in touch."

Hands thrust into her pockets, Daina watched him go until he disappeared around the corner of the house. Finally, after almost a full minute of silence, she spoke up. "Do you realize that this is the first time I've been outside in a week?" She turned then, and smiled as she met Emma's eyes. "It's heaven."

Emma merely dipped her head slightly, a smile touching her eyes and the corners of her mouth.

Daina looked away, her gaze roaming over the beautifully landscaped yard. "I certainly didn't expect a setup like this," she said, admiration creeping into her voice.

"It *is* very nice," Emma agreed. After a brief pause, she added, "I thought that all things considered, you would be better off in the master bedroom."

Daina glanced around, a little surprised. "Thank you. That's very thoughtful."

"It just makes sense," Emma replied with a shrug.

The contemplative look that Daina fixed upon Emma was

returned steadily. Daina finally blinked and looked away, to squint in the direction of the pool.

"Are you okay?" Emma asked into the silence.

"Yeah," she replied without looking back. "I think…I'd like to stay out here for a while. Just enjoy the sunshine."

"All right. Sure."

She heard Emma walk away but remained where she was, blinking against the brilliance of the sun reflecting off the surface of the pool.

CHAPTER EIGHTEEN

Entering the house through the patio doors, Emma looked out at Daina's unmoving figure. Doubtless the woman needed some time to herself. Things had happened so fast for both of them, they both needed to regroup. But the sight of Daina, standing alone by the pool, hands in her pockets, her back straight and her head slightly raised, struck a poignant chord. She stood there for quite a few moments, just looking at her, with no clear or cohesive thoughts. Finally, with a shake of her head, she turned away.

She gathered up Daina's things and made the trip down the hall to deposit them in the master bedroom. She then got her own things and went to her own room. Someone had had the foresight to convert what had most likely been a den or office into a bedroom. It was situated at the other end of the house and allowed for a measure of distance and privacy. It too was comfortably furnished and tastefully decorated.

She put her things off to the side, to be unpacked later, and sat on the edge of the bed. She felt a certain longing to just lay back, close her eyes and go to sleep. But now, when she actually *could* sleep, she wasn't supposed to. Her head no longer felt all that bad. Still, she supposed it was in her best interests to stay awake for a while yet. She was more thirsty and hungry than tired.

With a sigh, she pushed off the mattress and headed for the kitchen. She quickly searched the cupboards and the fridge, but other than the staples and some canned Sprite, there was nothing to eat. She grabbed one of the Sprites, picked up a pad of paper and pen by the phone and the order list for the groceries, and sat down at the dining room table. From where she sat she could see right through the patio doors out to the pool. Daina was now seated on the ground at the pool's edge, shoes and socks off, pants rolled up, her feet dangling in the water.

Emma smiled and bent to her list. Fifteen minutes later she grabbed another Sprite from the refrigerator and headed outside.

As she approached, Daina craned her head around. Her eyes dropped down to take in the items Emma carried, then rose once more. Emma stopped beside her.

"Sprite?" she asked, holding out the can.

Daina smiled that crooked little smile. "Sure."

Crouching down beside her, Emma passed the drink over.

Popping the tab, Daina took a sip. "What've you got there?"

"Grocery list." She handed over the papers and pen. "Your turn."

Daina grinned. "Are we a little short on supplies?"

"You could say that," Emma replied with an answering grin.

"All right then, let's see what we've got here." Daina gave the papers a shake and looked over Emma's list. And then, with a little snort, she glanced over at her. "Pop-Tarts?" she asked, eyebrows raised.

"I—" Emma began.

"I'm just bugging you," Daina said, her amusement obvious. She looked back at the lists. "Okay, well," she said finally, "looks good so far." She looked up, assuming a serious expression. "I approve of your choices."

"Except for the Pop-Tarts."

"Well, yeah, I have issues with that, but, you know, don't let that bother you." Daina reached for her Sprite, took a sip.

Emma grinned and ducked her head, looking out over the sparkling surface of the pool. After a silence of a few moments, she said, "So." And then, with a sidelong glance, asked, "Are you okay?"

"Yeah, I was just thinking…you know what would make me happy?"

"What?"

"If I could move my bed out here, poolside, like right over there." Daina pointed to the far side of the pool. "I could be out here twenty-four/seven. And in the morning, when I woke up, I'd just have to roll over and fall into the pool." She sneaked a glance at Emma and said, "It's heated, you know."

Emma laughed.

Daina grinned and then looked back at the papers she held. "I'll get on this right away," she said. "And yes," she continued, raising her eyes, "I'm okay. I apologize for being so short with you, you didn't deserve that. I was a little pissed off. But you're very patient and very thoughtful, and I appreciate that."

Emma nodded in acknowledgment, but kept silent.

Daina looked out over the pool. "I still think this is fucked up, though. I mean, keeping me in the dark when I'm the bloody victim, but what do I know?"

Her words caused a twinge in Emma's gut, but still she said nothing.

"This," Daina went on, making an inclusive gesture to indicate her surroundings, "has helped enormously. I could

almost let all of that bullshit slide. Almost. But I'm offended and
annoyed and I have too many questions to just let it go."

"I understand," Emma said quietly.

Daina looked at her. "Thank you." Her expression became
thoughtful. "You're a cop; do you...know anything more than I
do? To answer my questions, I mean."

"Oh, I...might." Emma tried desperately not to flounder as
she replied. "But...Michaels is really the one you should talk to.
Look, I still have some things to do." She jerked her thumb over
her shoulder at the house. "If you'll excuse me?"

"Of course, sure. I'll get to work on this list so we can get
some food in the house." Daina paused, then finished with a
completely straight face, "Even if it's only Pop-Tarts."

Emma's grin felt a little wooden as she rose and left. In the
living room, she dropped onto the sofa, put her elbows on her
knees and covered her face with her hands. *I don't think I can do
this.* She had to laugh at her pathetic excuse. What the hell had
that been? *I still have some things to do.* Like what? Rearrange
the furniture? As much as she had been thinking she *would*
answer Daina's questions if she asked, now that she *had* asked,
she suddenly didn't feel as if she could. The thing was, Michaels
in his infinite wisdom had given her something in case this
scenario should present itself.

She reached into her back pocket and withdrew a folded
piece of paper. It was a copy of the now infamous letter.
Michaels had passed it to her when they had been alone,
saying, *Just in case.* Emma had no idea what that meant. Just
in case what? She needed proof? The whole situation was so
patently ludicrous no amount of proof was going to make it
any less so.

She continued to hold the piece of paper. She could only
imagine what Daina's questions were, and she couldn't think
of a single thing she might say in response. With a sigh, she
refolded the letter and shoved it back into her pocket. *Cross
that bridge when you come to it,* she told herself.

Feeling suddenly very tired, not to mention uncomfortable
with the gun at her back, she got to her feet and went to her room.
She removed the gun with the belt clip, and slid the weapon in

between some clothes in her duffel bag. She stretched out on the bed. Her head no longer ached, but she almost wouldn't have cared it if did. She closed her eyes, comfortable in the silence of the house.

She was startled awake by the sound of the phone ringing. She was on her feet and heading for the door, when she heard Daina's voice.

She entered the kitchen just as Daina disconnected. She looked up almost guiltily at Emma's sudden appearance, then held the cordless phone out like the culprit it was. "I had *no* idea they were going to call back. I'm sorry."

"Who was it?" Emma ran her fingers through her hair, feeling disheveled and out of sorts.

"The grocery store, to confirm the address. I didn't know they were going to do that. It scared the shit out of me."

"It's all right, don't worry about it." Emma shook her head, blinked rapidly a few times. "They didn't...ask your name or anything...did they?"

"No, and I wouldn't have given it anyway," Daina assured her.

Emma was instantly contrite. "I'm sorry, I meant no offense. I don't mean to imply—"

"It's okay, I'm not offended. And you implied nothing." Daina flashed that patented crooked little grin of hers. "I may be a little hot-tempered but I can be sensible once in a while."

Emma dropped her eyes and looked away. That grin had the effect of loosening Emma's moorings each and every time. Sliding her hands halfway into her pockets, she looked up and delivered a brief, almost perfunctory smile of her own. "I think I'd like to take a shower, wake myself up a bit. My sleep pattern is a little messed up. I'm still feeling a bit foggy."

The irony of the situation suddenly struck her. She grinned

and puffed her breath out in somewhat shamefaced amusement. "Some bodyguard, huh?"

"Hey," Daina said, her tone and expression open and sincere, "I have no complaints."

"Well, maybe not yet," Emma returned quietly, cocking her head and retaining the tiniest smile. "Just wait until you expect me to share my Pop-Tarts. Then we'll see."

She saw the look of...what? Surprise? Amusement? And perhaps something else, forming on Daina's face. But with an innocent look and smile, she turned and headed back to her room, content to leave on a lighthearted note when in truth she was feeling anything but.

CHAPTER NINETEEN

For as long as she could remember, Daina had always turned to music as a means of solace. Whatever was troubling her, whatever negative emotions she was feeling, whatever poisons they filled her with, music was her antidote. As a child, she would listen every chance she got to the radio or to her parents' tape and LP collection. When she was twelve, they bought her her first guitar and she learned to create her own music. And that music became a tool which she used to dismantle the machines of self-destruction that often threatened to undermine her foundation and bring her to her knees. In music, she found strength and courage. And through music, she learned humility and grace.

As Emma departed from the kitchen, Daina stared after her doubtfully, her look of amusement fading. Unless she was mistaken, she was almost certain the woman had been flirting with her, albeit very subtly. Was that possible? The situation which had brought them together and the circumstances that required they stay together provided a huge enough argument against any kind of personal involvement or attachment on Daina's part. She was completely unprepared to even consider Emma's motivations if she *was* flirting with her.

"No," she suddenly said firmly, as if refusing a party crasher entry to a private function. She abruptly turned on her heel and headed for her own room, all the while muttering, "No, no, no, no."

She grabbed her guitar case from against the wall and made her way back outside, where she noticed a little side table that would double quite nicely as a stool. Removing the instrument from its case, she plunked herself down and just sat there quietly for a few moments, cradling the wooden body against her own. And then she carefully tuned it by ear and began to play.

She played tentatively at first, refamiliarizing herself with the guitar as if it were a lover's body from which she'd been separated for too long. Her fingers picked out the simplest notes, the simplest melodies; she felt and she listened. And as she became more comfortable, and the instrument responded to her touch in the way she remembered, she let go of her inhibitions and allowed her passion free rein.

She had no concept of the passage of time; she just played. Occasionally, she sang. She experimented with some combinations and riffs and fiddled around with some ideas that had been in her head for some time. She heard the phone ring distantly, but paid no attention to it.

Some time later, she became aware of a feeling of being watched. She glanced back over her left shoulder. Emma stood behind the screen of the patio doors; with Daina's attention on her, she slid open the screen door and came out to where she sat. She'd changed clothes; she now wore a pair of khaki shorts and a dark green tank top. And sandals.

Nice legs, Daina thought. "Hey," she said, by way of greeting.

"Hey, yourself," Emma returned with a small smile.

Her hair was still slightly damp, Daina noted. The scent of shampoo, of clean, wafted to her. She breathed it in.

"You play and sing beautifully. I could listen to you for hours."

Hours. The sentiment, coming from Emma, struck deep, and she was startled to feel herself blushing. She dropped her eyes. "Thank you," she said, strummed an A, and looked up once more. "You realize, of course, I don't believe you, since you *did* just interrupt me."

Emma smiled again, and sent her gaze off in the direction of the pool.

And Daina thought that one of the singular, most rewarding things she was able to do at this particular point in time was to make Emma Kirby smile.

"The groceries are on their way," Emma said. "That's why I interrupted you. I think I'd like you to remain unseen when they arrive."

"Oh. Do you think that's necessary?"

"I have no idea," Emma admitted. "I just know it's what I'm comfortable with."

"Oh. Well." Daina gave her a doubtful look. "You're not going to...send me to my room or anything...are you?"

She was rewarded with a soft laugh from Emma. "No. I'll save that for a more appropriate occasion." A grin teased the corners of her mouth.

"Okay, well, no problem," Daina said, "I'll head down to the basement, play a game of pool. I need the practice anyway."

"I'm sorry."

Daina looked up from putting her guitar in its case, surprised. "For what? For looking out for me?" She snapped the case closed. "I'm a little embarrassed *I* didn't think of it."

"It's not an easy frame of mind to get into," Emma said gently. "And it's not an easy frame of mind to get out of." She shrugged. "I'm just programmed to think that way, I guess."

Daina cocked her head at that and frowned, feeling an odd

mix of curiosity and sympathy. The only sound she made was a polite, "Hmm."

She headed into the house. She reflected, as she returned her guitar to her room, that Emma Kirby was not an easy person to read. And in spite of her obvious reserve, she had a playful side that had shown itself on a few occasions already. Daina now thought it was entirely possible that she was confusing this less than overt playfulness with flirtatiousness. She knew how dangerous that could be.

And then she had to laugh at herself. She had overlooked one crucial fact in her considerations, one very important detail: she had no clue as to whether Emma was gay or straight. The realization stopped her in her tracks.

Oh, Christ, I am such an idiot.

And then another thought occurred to her: she could ask. The boldness required for that had never been a problem in the past. With Emma, though, such audacity was daunting. Her relationship with Emma was tenuous at best. She wasn't about to cause any friction. No, she couldn't ask. And she wouldn't.

With that decided she went to the basement. She flicked on the lights, mostly track lighting, which accented the tastefully finished area nicely. The space, dominated by the pool table, was wide open and roomy like the rest of the house. There was a triangular seating arrangement off to one side, a sofa and a couple of chairs facing a TV, a DVD player, and a compact stereo system in an entertainment unit against one wall. She noted the mirrors and light wood paneling on the walls, the nondescript but tasteful framed prints, the soft lighting that bounced unglaringly off the light-hued walls. This room, like the rest of the house, had been designed to evoke comfort, and it accomplished that nicely.

A girl could get used to a place like this. And then added, a tad cynically, *There's no place like home.* Even if that home, temporary though it might be, was what basically amounted to a prison decorated with attractive accoutrements.

She tuned the stereo to a local FM station, then made her way to the pool table. She turned on the overhead light to illuminate the table, surveyed the domain that was for the time being hers alone, and proceeded to rack the balls. She retrieved a pool cue from the rack on a nearby wall, chalked it up and eyed the table. *This should prove interesting.* She wasn't even sure she was flexible enough to play a game of pool. Things felt a little tight as she leaned forward to break, but even so she managed to scatter the balls nicely.

"Oh hell, I can do this," she muttered confidently.

She was a little out of practice and she'd never been a shark to begin with, but she'd always been able to hold her own. It took her about ten minutes to clear the table. During that time, she heard noises from upstairs and the sound of muted voices, but paid no heed and just continued with her game.

Halfway into her second game, she was interrupted by Emma asking, "Is this a private party or can anyone join in?"

She looked around, to see Emma at the foot of the stairs. With a smile, she asked, "Do you play?" She gestured toward the pool table with her cue.

Emma gave a single nod. "I do."

Daina watched her approach. "Just what I like to see. Confidence." She raised her eyebrows. "I'm not going to lose my shirt, am I?"

Emma casually crossed her arms. "Not unless you misplace it at some point."

Daina grinned. "Okay, well, choose your weapon."

They played for an hour, both of them easy in the presence of the other, before Daina felt in sudden need of a rest.

"Are you feeling all right?" Emma asked gently. "You look a little pale."

Daina smiled tiredly. "Yeah, I'm just fading. If you'll excuse me, I think I'm going to head upstairs. I need to lie down for a while."

"Do you need a hand up the stairs or—?"

Daina was touched by Emma's concern. "No, I'll be fine, thanks."

Emma seemed less than happy with that response, and so Daina relented.

"You can follow me up the stairs if you want, but I should be fine."

In the hall off the kitchen Daina again thanked Emma, and then retired to her room. With the air-conditioning on, the house was cool, but there was a fleece blanket folded at the foot of the bed. She spread it out, then carefully stretched out on the bed. Snuggled beneath the blanket, she fell asleep.

CHAPTER TWENTY

Emma returned to the basement after seeing Daina up the stairs. She turned off the stereo, dropped down onto the sofa, and turned on the TV with the volume muted. The room was comfortable, the atmosphere soothing; she was soon lost in her thoughts.

For once she wasn't berating herself. She was instead feeling rather pleased for comporting herself in a respectable, and respectful, manner. While it was no huge leap to do so, the situation she and Daina were in was unique. She warned herself not to become too friendly. The two of them had just spent a very pleasant hour together; she looked forward to more of the same. In fact, she was surprised and pleased at how thoroughly she had enjoyed Daina's company and vice versa. But that had only been one *hour.* She had no idea how long they would be restricted to such a confined space; it was only a matter of time before tensions arose. She wasn't kidding herself about that. She could only hope their time together was over long before that happened. Because once things started to unravel, she doubted she'd have a hope in hell of running any kind of damage control.

Emma knew she would like to get know Daina, wanted to get to know her, and doing so might not be too difficult. But it relied hugely on trust, and the current situation had already thrown up an obstacle that if left in place for too long, could prove insurmountable, destroying any trust Daina extended to her.

She frowned. If the deception was allowed to continue for too long, she would be in some very deep shit once the truth came out. The thought was troubling. Before it could take a strong hold, she shook her head impatiently, jolting herself out of her introspection. Turning her attention to the television, she reached for the remote, pushing any further thoughts to the back of her mind.

By nine that evening Emma, sitting outside by the pool with a book, was feeling just a little concerned that Daina hadn't made an appearance yet. Of course, it was entirely possible that she would sleep the whole night through, since she was still recuperating. Emma wasn't about to mount a twenty-four-hour watch. Daina was entirely capable of taking care of herself.

At a sound behind her, she glanced back. Daina was just stepping through the patio doors. She smiled and felt herself relax.

"Hey," Daina said. Her voice had a vaguely childish, I-just-woke-up quality to it.

Emma's smile broadened briefly. "Hey, yourself."

Daina's hair was damp and a bit tousled. She'd obviously showered, despite the somewhat drowsy look to her. She wore a baggy pair of black cargos and a white tank top with the Nike swoosh emblazoned across the front. Below that was some small print that Emma couldn't quite make out in the fading light.

Daina must have noticed her looking because she took a step closer and pulled the fabric out slightly. The small print read *Just Do Me*. Emma attempted to stifle her laugh and it came out as a snort.

"It's a slogan, not a suggestion," Daina said mildly.

Emma looked up, to see Daina grinning ever so slightly. "Ah. Thank you for pointing that out."

Daina gave her a nod and a wink. She reached for another one of the patio chairs and dragged it over.

"So, did you think I was going to sleep all night?" she asked as she sat down.

"It wouldn't have surprised me."

"Well, I probably would have, if I wasn't so hungry." Daina grinned and looked a little embarrassed. "My stomach woke me up."

"Right, you haven't eaten yet, have you?"

"Nope. But I need to wake up a little more first."

She attempted to stretch then, but groaned and made a face as she dropped her arms. "I'll be glad when I can actually stretch properly. I feel like a bloody wind-up toy that's been wound too tight." Abruptly, she moved to the edge of her seat. "You want to sit by the pool?" she asked, jerking her head in that direction.

"Sure."

They both rose, and without a word, took up positions diagonal to each other, the corner of the pool between them. Both dangled their feet in the water and as the sun set, their immediate area was illuminated warmly by the lights from the pool itself. It was a flattering light, Emma observed, at least so far as Daina was concerned. She was attractive to begin with, but the watery glow lent a softness to her features that was at odds with her usual look of intensity.

"So. How are you feeling?"

"I'm all right." Daina gave a dismissive shrug. "Still a bit tired, but that's to be expected, I guess." She splashed the water with her feet. "I'm looking forward to using this pool, but I can't until I get my staples out. And that doesn't happen until Monday."

"Will someone be coming here?"

"As far as I know. That's the information I was given, anyway." Another shrug. "I guess we'll see."

There followed a silence, which Emma found by no means uncomfortable.

"So how long have you been a cop?" The question was put forth very politely.

Emma did the math. "Seven years, thereabouts." She swirled her own feet lazily in the water.

"Oh, not that long."

"Well, I'm not that old," Emma stated mildly.

"How old are you?" Still polite, with no attempt to diffuse what could be construed as a nosy question, no if-you-don't-mind-my-asking tacked on.

"Thirty-one."

Daina nodded, without taking her eyes off Emma.

"You?" Emma raised her eyebrows, expressing her own polite interest.

"Twenty-eight."

With a nod of her own, Emma looked away, at the water.

"Do you like it?"

She glanced sidelong at Daina. "What, being thirty-one?"

Daina smiled gently. "No. Being a cop."

Emma nodded. "Yes." She shrugged, shook her head. "I don't have any complaints."

"Have you always wanted to be a cop?"

Emma considered. She shook her head. "I don't recall giving it any thought at all, up until shortly before I applied."

"Really?" Daina cocked her head. In the light from the pool, her eyes were a little less the color of ocean water, a little more the color of glacial ice. Her pupils were tiny black islands in the center. "You seem like a natural."

Emma frowned. "Why do you say that?"

"Well...I don't know. You just do." Daina took a moment to ponder, frowning. "You know, like...some guys just *look* like firefighters."

"So you're saying I look like a cop."

"No, I'm not saying *that*. I'm just saying—" She gave Emma one of those disconcerting up-and-down looks, then continued, "You're so comfortable in your skin, what you are just seems to naturally fit you."

Emma regarded her for a couple of moments. "'Comfortable in my skin,' huh?" she asked, a bit skeptically.

Daina smiled gently. "What do you do? In your spare time, I mean." Another one of those up-and-down looks. "Obviously you work out."

"Well, I run," Emma replied carefully. "I have a universal gym I work out on at home. And I practice jiu-jitsu."

Daina smiled and nodded with obvious satisfaction. "That's what it is. I thought it had to be something like that. That's cool. What belt?"

"First-degree black."

Daina raised her eyebrows briefly. "Wow. Scary. But cool."

"Scary?"

"Well, okay, maybe not scary as in *frightening*," Daina amended. "I guess maybe exciting is more what I meant."

As soon as she uttered the words, the look on her face indicated she regretted saying them at once. She cleared her throat before continuing, "It's just that you're a very attractive woman and who you are, what you are, you wear it so well, without any kind of arrogance." She shrugged, then added quietly, "You just don't see that every day." She lowered her gaze to the water.

The magnitude of the compliment was completely unexpected. "Thank you," Emma finally managed to say, trying to lend the words enough weight to convey more than just mere appreciation or acknowledgment.

She could see that Daina was somewhat discomfited, and it occurred to her that her worry about whether or not Daina continued to view her as a cop and nothing more was largely unnecessary. Attempting to get past the awkwardness of the moment, she ventured, in an easy, conversational tone, "So, how long have you been doing what you do?"

Daina raised her head. "What, performing? Ten years, or so."

"Ah. Not that long then," Emma observed.

Daina rewarded her with a small, amused smile. "Well, I'm not that old," she returned smoothly.

Emma mirrored the smile, and the moment was past. She was pleased. "I'm really not that familiar with your music," she admitted, "but what you were playing earlier was very... compelling."

"What I was playing earlier is not what I usually play," Daina quietly informed her. "I've been...experimenting."

"Oh. Well, I was thinking it didn't really sound...*country.* Not entirely."

"Yeah. Well." Daina glanced at her once, swiftly, then away. "I don't like to be pigeonholed."

Emma took in Daina's profile, tracing it against the backdrop of the house, committing it to memory. "Well, I'm no expert in these things," she said thoughtfully, "but I don't think you have to worry about that."

"Well then *you* should've been my manager," Daina said, her voice and expression suddenly weary, "because *she* thought what I was trying to do bordered on blasphemy."

"Oh, I didn't say it wasn't blasphemous," was Emma's bland response. "I just said you wouldn't have to worry about being pigeonholed."

Daina grinned. "Smart-ass," she muttered.

Emma gave her a quick, disarming smile. "I thought what you were playing was beautiful. What was it that your, uh, manager didn't like?"

With a sigh, Daina said, "Kendra is rather...hard-core country I guess you could say. She didn't like it when I strayed from *the formula.*" Daina raised her eyebrows, and made quotation marks in the air around the last two words. "She said it could only cause confusion and divided opinions. Which I'm sure is exactly what will happen." She shrugged dismissively. "But like I said, I don't like to be pigeonholed."

"Well," Emma said quietly, "I think you've got the right of it. You're the artist, you have creative license."

Daina contemplated her, then said softly, "Thank you. For understanding. And for actually saying that." She paused. "*No* one has ever said that, just come right out and said 'Hey, it's your music, you can do whatever you like.' I mean, I understand their concerns, my record label, Kendra, all of that, I do understand. I'm under contract, I'm supposed to be promoting this album; I'm the new kid on the block, don't fuck with the formula." She frowned, seeming troubled. "The thing is, I've played that other music before, when I lived here. I had a couple songs I'd throw out and they were always well received. I guess, though, they were just considered fancies of mine, nothing directional, so they weren't taken seriously."

She stared out at the length of the pool. "And now I *want* them to be taken seriously," she said, her voice soft but intense. She looked at Emma. "Because that *is* the direction I want to go in."

Emma said in a lowered voice as softly intense as Daina's had been, "Then go for it. It's your life. It's your music. Go for it."

Daina looked out across the pool once more. Then she met Emma's eyes with a wink and a smile. "I think I'm awake enough now to eat a sandwich or two."

Emma grinned and rose smoothly to her feet. "Come on then, hungry girl," she said, putting her hand out. "Let's get you fed."

CHAPTER TWENTY-ONE

Daina was surprised at how easily she and Emma slipped into a comfortable routine over the next few days.

Emma was always up first, Daina never more than an hour behind her. But while Emma's first stop in the morning was either the pool or the exercise room, Daina's was the coffeepot. She would sit at the dining room table drinking her coffee and reading the newspaper which was delivered every morning. Emma retrieved it from the driveway and left it on the table for her.

Finished with her workout, Emma would come into the kitchen, greet Daina with a smile that seemed almost shy, and a soft "Good morning." She would fix a cup of coffee the way she liked it, take one swallow, then head off to the shower. By the time she returned, Daina was sufficiently rejuvenated by her own coffee and ready for her shower. Afterward, Emma would make them both breakfast, Daina did the dishes, and Emma read the paper. The morning routine never varied.

Afternoons were generally spent apart, each doing her own thing. Evenings they would come together again and either combine their talents or attempt singly to fix dinner. Later, they would watch TV or play pool or involve themselves in some other activity. But the end of the day always found them together.

A week ago she would hardly have credited that they could tolerate each other's company for longer than two minutes. But it was now Wednesday, their fifth day together, and the camaraderie that had sprung up between them was holding and growing. They were different, to be sure, but apparently not so vastly different as perhaps either had at first believed.

Prior to the attempt on her life, Daina would not have been open to any level of introspection. But now, with nothing but time on her hands and little if any distraction, she found herself doing what she very rarely did: looking inside herself. She came to see that the bombing was one of those life-altering events she'd always heard about but had never experienced or even credited much. It had certainly made *her* sit up and pay attention, take stock of her life and herself, and realize that she was far from happy, that it was time to make some changes. She had already made some of those changes. Likely others would follow.

The imminent change of her musical direction was enormous and the possible repercussions were almost frightening to contemplate. But it was Emma who somehow reduced that fear with her calm analysis and unquestioning and unexpected support of her ideas, her clear understanding, and her genuine interest in and enjoyment of Daina's music. It was Emma who calmed her when she felt herself becoming fractious and tense, something no one else had ever been able to do. She had never met anyone like her. She couldn't help but be drawn to her. And couldn't help but be aware of the fact that she really knew very little about her. She wanted that to change. But it was a change she didn't know how to implement. And of all the changes she wanted to see happen, it was the one that truly unsettled her the most. And she had no idea why.

Wednesday evening found them both in the kitchen, preparing dinner in a companionable silence. Emma was fixing a salad, Daina a pasta dish of her mother's she was fervently hoping she could re-create perfectly. They were both startled to hear a loud *thump* from the living room. Their respective reactions were wholly different.

While the first words out of Daina's mouth were a tightly muttered "What the fuck was that?" not a word escaped Emma. She became as taut as a coiled spring. With one index finger, she motioned Daina to silence and patience.

Daina shushed and went as still as Emma, though she doubted her transformation into alertness was as beautiful or as deadly-seeming.

They stood that way for a full ten-second count before Emma turned to look at Daina. She made a single motion with her right hand: *Stay put.* She then turned, stepped into the hall, and was gone. A handful of seconds later she reappeared, gun in hand.

Daina immediately stiffened. The gun drove home the gravity of the situation in a way nothing else could have. Emma shot her a look as hard as flint, then turned and headed straight for the back door. Daina blinked, but stayed put. She heard Emma lock the door behind her.

After an interminable length of time there was a knock on the front door. Daina didn't move until she heard Emma call out, "It's all right, it's me."

She threw open the door to see Emma standing there, holding the screen door open with her left hand, the gun in her right lowered to her side.

It turned out that the thump was a robin flying full tilt into the living room window. It now lay in a little feathered heap in the planter running the length of that outside wall.

"Aw, poor thing," Daina commiserated. "Is it okay?"

Emma pushed her lower lip out thoughtfully. "Well, I don't know a lot about birds," she said slowly, "but that one doesn't look okay to me."

"What should we do with it?" Daina asked, still looking down at the stricken bird.

"'Do with it'? What do you mean *do with it*?"

Daina gave her a hard look. "What if it's still alive, just knocked out cold?" she asked of her, none too gently.

"Then I guess at some point, it'll wake up and...fly away. No?" Emma tacked on a hopeful note to the question.

"No, smart-ass," Daina admonished her with a light one-handed shove. "What if it can't fly?"

Emma seemed to consider this. She blinked. "Well, then I guess it could take the bus everywhere," she offered.

In spite of herself, Daina giggled. She was trying to be serious, but Emma's dry humor was hard to ignore. She fixed her with a scowl as she took a step down. "You're bad. Come on, I want to bring it in the house."

"*What?*"

The shock in Emma's voice stopped Daina in her tracks. "Well, yeah, it could be—"

"Oh, no," Emma cut her off firmly. "I'm sorry, but I have to insist, you are *not* bringing that bird into the house."

"What? Why not?" Daina was completely mystified by Emma's reaction. "It might still be alive, it might just be hurt."

"Yes, and then it'll wake up and probably start flying around the house. No. No way. I'm sorry." And Emma actually shuddered. She crossed her arms and assumed a no-nonsense look.

Daina looked at her with something like open-mouthed wonder but asked, with genuine concern, "Are you afraid of birds?"

"No," was Emma's firm response. "But I never developed an affinity for them. They freak me out."

"Well, but—"

"No, Daina, please? I'm serious. If this one's still alive and it freaks out in the house and starts flapping round, I'll have a heart attack or something, okay? I'm serious."

This was said with such sincerity and the plea, small though it was, was so obvious in Emma's eyes that Daina relented. Still, she couldn't keep the tiny grin off her face as she said, "Okay, I'm sorry, I didn't know." She paused. "A big, strong girl like you, who would've thought?"

Emma blushed. "Yes, well, now you know," was all she said.

"I'll just take it around back to the garage, okay?" Daina moved toward the crumpled little body and retrieved it from the flowerbed. Its head lolled back against her fingers as she lifted it.

"I don't think it's alive anyway." She said this sadly, looking back up at Emma.

"Ya think?" Emma responded dryly.

Daina gave her what she hoped was a dirty look and then headed off for the garbage cans lined up beside the garage. She lifted one of the lids. She didn't know for sure if the bird was dead and she didn't know how to check, but if it wasn't, she didn't want to just dump it in one of the garbage cans and close the lid on it. She opted for laying it on top of a garbage bag and setting the lid off to one side. If it *was* still alive, it would hopefully be able to fly away once it came to.

She headed back into the house, washed her hands in the bathroom, then returned to the kitchen. Emma looked up at her from where she was slicing mushrooms, then turned her attention back to her task. Daina felt a certain sadness steal over her. She'd only just begun thinking that Emma might be gay. She'd been watching her closely and thought that she was reading things correctly. But she couldn't be sure and it was messing with her head.

And then she had to laugh at herself, because really, what was she thinking? If Emma wasn't a lesbian, then she was off-limits. And if she was, she would still be off-limits if she wasn't single or, get this, she wasn't even interested in Daina. The thought caused her to snort out loud at her foolishness.

Emma glanced over at her. "What?"

Daina blinked. "Nothing," she said quickly. "I—nothing." She shook her head. *Idiot*, she reprimanded herself.

Emma was still looking at her.

"Do you want wine with dinner?" Daina asked brightly.

"Sure," Emma replied.

"Red?"

"Red is fine."

Daina rose to her feet to retrieve the wine and remove herself from Emma's scrutiny.

CHAPTER TWENTY-TWO

At eleven thirty that night, Emma closed the book she was reading. Straightening in the armchair, she told Daina she was going to check that the doors were locked and the alarms set.

"You know," Daina said thoughtfully, looking up from her guitar when Emma returned, "a prison disguised as a holiday resort is still a prison."

It could have been construed as an ignorant thing to say, but Emma only nodded.

"I know," she said quietly, "but try not to think of it that way."

Daina shrugged. "It just crosses my mind once in a while."

"Well, it's probably a good thing that it does, but I can understand how it can kind of spoil the fun."

Daina nodded and idly plucked a run of notes. Emma's

understanding was never expected and was therefore more surprising and pleasing as a result.

"Will you be all right?" Emma asked gently.

Daina was casual in her response, though Emma's concern never failed to move her. She nodded, a single, downward jerk. "You know it," she said simply, then raised her eyebrows. "Do you want me to put this aside?" she asked, making a gesture to indicate the guitar.

"No. Never. It's fine."

Never. It struck Daina that that was a rather odd thing to say. And yet, singularly beautiful. She eyed Emma steadily, then asked, "Are *you* all right?"

Emma smiled, more with her eyes than with her mouth. "Yes." The smile broadened momentarily. "Thank you." Then, "Goodnight, Daina."

"Goodnight, Emma."

Daina felt that small wave of sadness wash over her once more, but with a shake of her head quickly dispelled it and turned back to her music. She sat up for about an hour longer, working on the bridge in her song until she was finally satisfied, and returned her guitar to its case.

As she made her way down the hall to her own room she wondered what sort of fears or insecurities plagued Emma. Not that she'd been given any indication that Emma was so plagued. Emma was very good at keeping herself to herself. If she had any emotional baggage, she likely kept hers safely stowed out of sight in an overhead compartment somewhere, rarely taking it down or allowing anyone to see it. This was in stark contrast to those who would regularly assault you with theirs, whether they knew you or not. Daina had met her fair share of that type.

Readying herself for bed, she knew she wasn't going to get an answer to her question tonight, possibly not ever. She sighed, the soft, guttural purr sounding at the back of her throat. *Because really, who am I? I'm nobody, just some chick she was hired to protect. Get over yourself, Buchanan.*

She slipped beneath the covers, emptying her mind of any more questions. Still, it was awhile before she was able to fall asleep.

She was brutally awakened from a sound sleep by the piercing warble of an alarm going off in the house. She bolted upright and swung her feet over the edge of the bed. Her heart kicked into high gear and she felt her whole body engulfed in that sickening, prickly feeling of fear bordering on terror. But while her body was screaming *Run!* her brain was telling her to sit tight, just hang on a second.

It wasn't a smoke alarm, she knew that. She'd been present when Michaels had run through the alerts. And this particular one meant that someone had managed to gain entry to the house, or was currently in the process of it. But if that was the case, what had happened to the two other alarms that should have sounded, first the gate alarm, if it was breached, and second, the yard alarm, which was keyed to anything entering the yard that weighed over fifty pounds?

Horribly indecisive, aware on some level that she was shaking, and that only a handful of seconds had passed, she quickly crossed her room and slipped into the attached bathroom, closing the door behind her. She froze in the pitch-black, eyes widened enormously, dumbly rooted to the tiny area of floor she occupied. The alarm continued its almost deafening trill.

"Daina!" It was Emma, loud and clear over the sound of the alarm. The light in her bedroom came on. Her paralysis broke.

"Here!" she yelled out, and pulled the door open.

Bathed in the room's light, wearing boxers and a T-shirt, Emma had her gun in hand, muzzle pointing at the ceiling. Daina had never been so happy to see anyone. Emma's eyes flooded with relief at the sight of her. She put her left hand out. Daina took one step toward her, trembling.

The look of relief on Emma's face was replaced with one of concern and sympathy. She caught Daina's hand and brought her in. She put her mouth close to her ear, speaking over the alarm.

"It's okay, it was a false alarm, a short, I think." She leaned back to look into Daina's eyes. "Are you okay? My God, you're shaking like a leaf."

A false alarm. A short. Of course. Fuck. Had it been the real thing, she probably would have held together just fine. But this anticlimactic conclusion robbed her completely of fortitude. Between one breath and the next, Daina fell apart. She didn't even try to fight back the tears; she'd had enough, it was too much.

Emma's eyes widened in alarm. "Oh, hey now, come here," she said, and gently pulled Daina into her. She wrapped an arm around Daina's shaking shoulders.

Daina cried silently into the space between Emma's neck and shoulder. She didn't put her arms around her, just grasped the edges of Emma's T-shirt and held tight. Soon she felt herself calming. The tears continued to flow, but the urgency of the moment was leaving her. She shuddered and a shaky breath escaped her.

Emma pulled back slightly, her eyes searching Daina's as she said, "I have to go take care of that damn alarm, okay? Come here, sit on the bed." Emma stretched across to the dresser, then leaned in with a couple of Kleenex. "I'll be right back, okay? I promise."

When Emma returned, she was carrying the phone and was practically yelling into it. "No, the override isn't working, I tried it! Shut it off on your end! What?" And then she *was* yelling: "NO! YOUR END! SHUT IT DOWN!"

And mercifully, when Daina thought her nerves had just about had it, the alarm was silenced. Emma switched the phone off, placed both it and the gun on the bed, and sat down beside her.

"Are you all right?" She placed her hand on Daina's still trembling shoulder.

"Yeah," Daina managed to whisper. "Just scared the shit out of me."

"I know, me too. I'm sorry. I got here as fast as I could."

Daina breathed in shakily, raised her eyes to Emma's. "It's not your fault."

"Maybe not, but I still feel bad." Emma squeezed her shoulder lightly.

Daina nodded, tried to smile, but failed. She lowered her head and for several moments they sat like that, both in shorts and T-shirts, not saying a word, while she attempted to regain her scattered self.

And then the phone rang, making them both jump.

They looked at each other with strained smiles, and at that moment a gulf that had existed between them was bridged. Daina felt it immediately, and knew that Emma felt it too, for she reached to pick up the phone with her left hand, while her right arm she wrapped around Daina's shoulders once more. Daina leaned into her as she answered the phone.

A voice on the other end, indecipherable.

"Yes, we're okay."

A pause, as the voice spoke again.

"Yes, I understand the procedure, that's fine." Emma paused, then continued patiently, "No, I told you, I tried the override, it didn't work."

Another pause.

"No, everything else seems to be working. It was just the one."

As Emma continued her conversation with what Daina assumed to be the security company, she reflected that she had never really felt safe with anyone before, other than her parents. But with Emma, what had started out as little more than a vague awareness was now a very real, very tangible feeling. Emma, with her cool head, her sharp instincts, her quiet strength; yes, Daina felt safe with her. She'd known it from the beginning. The gun wasn't even a consideration. This woman seated next to her, with her arm around her, speaking in that mellow, mildly hypnotic voice, *this* was her safety. To hell with everything else right now.

"Okay, that's fine, send whoever," Emma was saying. "I'll be up." She disconnected.

"What?" Daina asked, lifting her chin the tiniest bit so she could see Emma's profile.

"Well, the cops are on their way; they should get here first, followed by a couple of techs to fix the problem. Considering it's the house alarm, it's a pretty big problem."

Daina suddenly shivered within the circle of Emma's arm.

"You're cold," Emma said gently, worriedly, drawing back ever so slightly.

"I think it's more nerves than anything." Daina straightened and felt Emma remove her arm.

"Well, I told them I'd wait up, we don't both have to."

"I think I'd like to wait up with you, if that's okay." Daina was more than a little unwilling to be alone at the moment.

Emma smiled. "Yes, of course, it's fine."

Daina stood, grateful her trembling had ceased. "I think I'm going to, uh…" She pointed toward the bathroom.

Emma smiled once more. "Sure," she said. "I'll be in the living room."

Daina watched her leave. Closing the bathroom door softly behind her, she leaned heavily against it. She sighed. And the thought and feeling that rose within her, she didn't even try to ignore or dispel: *Christ, I think I'm falling in love with her.*

Emma was sitting on the sofa, now wearing an oversized sweatshirt, with a folded fleece blanket in her lap. On the coffee table, along with the gun and the phone, sat two glasses of red wine. It was the same wine they'd shared over dinner. Daina smiled slightly and met Emma's look of gentle concern.

"I thought we could both use it," Emma told her, "all things considered."

"You thought right," Daina said ruefully. "Though a cigarette might've been *my* first choice."

Emma cocked her head. "I didn't know you smoked."

"I had to quit, as of a week and a half ago." She made her way around the coffee table and sat on the end of the sofa opposite Emma.

"Cold turkey?"

"The coldest."

"How's it going?"

Daina shrugged. "This is the first time I've felt like I really want one, like I need one. So I guess it's going well." She glanced at the blanket and cocked an eyebrow. "Are you gonna hog that all to yourself?"

"Well, I was," Emma returned easily, "but since you showed up..." She grinned, rose, and draped it around Daina's back and shoulders.

Enveloped in cozy softness, Daina grasped the edges and pulled it a little closer as Emma sat back down.

"Very nice," Daina said quietly. "Thank you."

"I turned the air-conditioning down as well, in case the cold takes over where your nerves leave off."

Daina was touched by Emma's continual thoughtfulness. She reached for her wineglass. Emma did the same. There were no words spoken, no attempt at a toast, no forced levity at a time when it would have been badly out of place. They drank their wine and sat quietly, Daina comfortable with the silence, Emma seeming to be, as well. There was something Daina *wanted* to say, but she was still far too rattled by what had happened to even attempt bringing it up. She needed to be calm and clear in her mind first, because what was troubling her needed to be addressed. But not hastily, nor in anger. And so they drank their wine and sat in silence.

The phone rang. Emma answered it, spoke briefly, then disconnected.

"Well, they're here; they're on their way in." She returned the phone and her half-empty wineglass to the coffee table. "I'm going to go out and speak to the officers. Did you want to join me?"

"No," Daina said, with a slight shake of her head. She didn't want to be around anyone else at the moment and felt no need to explain that. If she was required, they could come to her.

Emma was gone for the better part of an hour. During that time, Daina settled herself more comfortably on the sofa, lifting her feet off the floor and hugging her knees to her chest. She sipped at her wine and listened to the voices and footfalls carrying from the back hall and basement. She supposed she should be taking an interest, should involve herself in some way, but she tended to subscribe to the too-many-cooks-in-the-kitchen line of thought. She was confident Emma would tell her anything she needed to know.

By the time Emma finally rejoined her, after seeing the techs out (the cops had come and gone long ago), it was almost three in the morning. She perched on the far arm of the sofa.

"All fixed?" Daina asked.

"For now." Emma reached for her wineglass, took a sip. "They're coming back later this morning to run a full diagnostic. But it's working now. And that's what matters."

Daina nodded and hugged her knees closer. She inhaled deeply, held it a moment, before releasing her breath slowly, never once taking her eyes off Emma. "We need to talk," she said quietly.

"Okay." Emma's voice was calm, level. She lowered herself down to the sofa proper so she was facing Daina, her legs crossed, back straight. She returned Daina's look unwaveringly.

Daina caught her lower lip between her teeth. She swallowed. So softly she was almost whispering, she said, "That was bad, Emma. That was very bad."

And Emma, just as softly, said, "I know, and I'm sorry. I wasn't prepared for that and I should have been. I'm sorry."

Daina wasn't the least bit surprised that Emma knew what she was referring to. What surprised her was that Emma was willing to accept complete responsibility for the incident.

"Emma, no, I don't want you to apologize. I'm not blaming you; I don't want you blaming yourself. You might as well blame *me*, because *I* sure as hell didn't think of it. We both should have thought of it and had some kind of plan. Because *that*—" And here Daina made a sound that was supposed to be a bit of a laugh, but was too shaky to even come close, "—that was bad."

She took a swallow of her wine, to steady herself.

Emma regarded her calmly, then nodded slowly. "You're right, you're completely right." She shook her head, dropped her eyes. "I don't know what I was thinking." When she looked up, she met Daina's eyes and said, "I *should* be blaming you."

Daina's mouth dropped open in stunned surprise. A second

later, she saw Emma's mouth twitching humorously. Her jaw dropped even further, even as she felt herself starting to grin. "Oh, my God, you are so bad," she breathed, attempting to sound outraged, but failing completely.

"We'll think of a plan," Emma assured her. "We can do it right now, if you want. I'm up for it."

"So am I."

For another hour they brainstormed over a contingency plan in the event that a true threat should occur. And when they were done, and both were satisfied with what they had come up with, Daina glanced at her empty wineglass and decided she didn't want any more. She placed it on the coffee table and wrapped her arms around her knees once more. "So now what?" she asked quietly.

Emma shrugged. "Bedtime, I guess," she replied, just as quietly.

"Oh." Daina shook her head. "No, I can't," she said in a small voice. She hated the way she sounded, hated the obvious weakness, but was unable to deny it.

Emma didn't seem in the least surprised or troubled. "Okay," she said easily. She stood, reached for their wineglasses. "Just give me a minute, all right?"

Emma left the room and Daina stared fixedly at the fibers of the blanket covering her knees. She heard Emma go into the kitchen, then down the hall. A few minutes later she heard her returning, this time turning off lights as she came. And when she reached the living room, she made a *shooing* motion with her hand.

"Scootch over," she said in a mild, matter-of-fact way.

Daina moved forward to the edge of the sofa. And then she watched, with something almost like wonder, as Emma sat, then stretched herself out behind her.

"Now, come here." Still in that matter-of-fact voice. "And bring the blanket."

Daina knew now what Emma had in mind, and she could feel the little butterfly of fear in her chest quieting. Emma was up on one elbow and Daina lay down on her side beside her. The sofa and the blanket were big enough for two in this arrangement. Emma spread the blanket over them both. Daina rested her head on the plush sofa cushion.

"Okay?" Emma's voice was a soft vibration against her back.

"Yes." Daina's own voice was little more than a whisper.

She hadn't the slightest idea how Emma had known what she'd needed. But she'd known. It was uncanny, but overwhelmingly soothing at the same time.

"Now, I don't want this to become a habit," Emma spoke softly into her ear. "You're a big girl, you should be able to sleep on your own."

Daina laughed, but it was the lightest of exhalations.

Emma reached up, turned off the lamp beside the sofa. In the darkness, she slid down a bit, then draped her arm over Daina, her lean body fitting warmly against her. Daina felt hugely comforted and completely comfortable. She knew she could sleep this way.

And that was how they spent the remainder of the night.

CHAPTER TWENTY-THREE

When Emma woke up, the brightness of the sunlight suggested it was perhaps eight A.M. or so. Daina stirred. Emma remained as she was, her arm still draped over her, loath to move and disturb her if she was merely shifting and not waking. She felt a niggling sense of worry, and for the first time allowed herself to wonder what, in the grand scheme of things, the significance of the night's events might be. Considering that what she had done was completely unorthodox and unprecedented, it was foolish to think her actions would hold no significance whatsoever. Still, she could hope there would be no serious repercussions.

"Emma?" Daina whispered. "Are you awake?"

Emma smiled slightly. "Mmhmm."

A pause, then in a voice slightly above a whisper, "Did you sleep?"

Emma gave a slight shrug. "Sort of."

"I'm sorry."

"Don't be."

They kept their voices low, as if unwilling to disturb either the peace that surrounded them or the new and tenuous bond that had sprung up between them.

And then Daina said, "I can make coffee."

And Emma grinned. "I'll be sure to let the media know."

Her comment earned her an elbow in the ribs. "Brat," Daina muttered, and proceeded to sit up.

Emma raised herself up on her elbow. She tried to look contrite.

Daina glanced back, saw the look, and narrowed her eyes. "Oh, don't even," she said, with something like mild disgust, shaking her head but grinning at the same time. She rose to her feet.

Emma smiled and watched Daina walk away. She moved to a sitting position. *Well, I guess that means things are okay. That was easy.* She felt a little disbelieving that the transition had occurred so smoothly. Either Daina was a great actor or she was truly untroubled or unaffected by what had transpired.

Emma ran her fingers through her hair. *Okay, well, good. That's what I wanted, isn't it?* It was. Up until this very moment, she hadn't realized how much she'd wanted, *needed* things to be okay between them. She'd taken a huge risk without even realizing. It was unlike her and she didn't know what to think of that. And she didn't want to think of it, not right now, maybe not at all. *This might happen to be one of those things that either stands on its own, or doesn't.* Daina, it appeared, was willing to let it be the former. For that, Emma was grateful, relieved.

She glanced at the clock on the DVD player. Two minutes after eight. Stretching luxuriously, she reflected that four hours spent in the same position was not factory recommended. She was stiff, her muscles cramped and tight. A visit to the pool was definitely in order. She rolled her shoulders a couple of times and then stood, glancing through the cut-away into the kitchen. Daina, true to her word, was making coffee. Emma grinned.

Looking up at just that moment, Daina caught the grin. She paused between scoops of coffee, smiled ever so slightly and then resumed what she was doing. Emma grabbed the blanket from the sofa and headed down the hall to her room, changed into her swimsuit and threw on her bathrobe. Making her way back to the dining room, she slid open the patio doors. Daina was nowhere to be seen.

"Emma?" Daina stood at the far entranceway to the kitchen.

Emma turned away from the doors to face Daina more fully.

"I wanted to thank you for...well, for last night. This morning." Daina shrugged, shook her head. "Whatever. Just... thank you. What you did was probably the sweetest and most thoughtful thing anyone has ever done for me. I mean that. So...thank you."

Emma tilted her head fractionally. "You're welcome," she said gently, and said nothing more. As she stepped outside, it took a supreme effort not to look back; she could feel Daina's eyes boring into her back, had seen the disappointment in her less than satisfactory response.

For the next twenty minutes, she swam hard. The technicians were due shortly after nine; she intended to make it her business to know exactly what was going on with the alarm system. That meant she'd have to cut her swim short. She meant to make good use of the time she had. Her mind was mercifully blank; she didn't want to think. She cut through the water smoothly, forcefully, and felt her muscles limbering, loosening. She concentrated on nothing else. And when she gauged her time was up, she dove beneath the water's surface and swam the last ten yards underwater.

She surfaced a foot shy of the pool wall and exhaled forcibly. Gaining her feet in the shallow water, she wiped the water from her face and saw Daina crouching at the edge of the pool, eyes on her, her expression intent.

"What?" she asked, confused by the look on Daina's face.

Immediately, Daina's features relaxed. "Nothing," she said

calmly, and held out the cordless phone. "Telephone. It's your boss."

"My—? Oh." Emma realized she must be referring to Sergeant Michaels. "Thanks," she said, as Daina gave her the phone.

"Don't mention it," Daina said coolly, rose to her feet, turned and strode back to the house.

"Emma? Michaels." The sergeant's voice was clipped, businesslike. "I'm just calling to touch base. I realize I haven't called since Monday, but there hasn't been any reason to."

"I see."

Monday had been an interesting day, Emma remembered. Maintenance workers had shown up to do the yard work, staff had shown up to clean the house, and a nurse had shown up to remove Daina's staples. The nurse had also pulled Emma aside to advise her that while Daina was healing nicely, her complete recovery would take some time yet, and she was not to overexert herself. Emma had nodded solemnly at this, but inwardly had wondered at the degree of influence the nurse thought she had over Daina. A physiotherapist had also shown up for Daina, and every morning since. And, last but not least, Michaels had called and then made an appearance.

The reason for his visit had been, ostensibly, to check on them, ensure that they were comfortable, that they wanted for nothing. The *real* reason for his visit had been to pick up the lists of names they'd both been asked to provide. This was done surreptitiously, since neither was supposed to know that either had been asked to provide this. The subterfuge had rankled Emma; when he had come to her, she'd taken a certain uncharacteristic, mean-spirited pleasure in telling him she had nothing to give him, that she had come up completely blank. He surprised her by merely sighing and saying that Daina's attempt had proven just as fruitless. A worthwhile idea, he told her, but a dead end. She had been further pacified when she was made aware that Daina would be allowed to call her parents, via cell phone. The only problem with that came up when Daina realized that using her own cell phone was out of the question; the roaming charges would have been astronomical. Emma had solved that quandary by offering *her* cell phone. Everyone was happy.

"The investigation is pretty much at a standstill at this point," Michaels was saying now, "no leads, no fingerprints, nothing." He added, "We'd hoped, obviously, that the two of you would come up with something to shed some light, but..."

Emma said nothing, but wondered why he'd even bothered to mention it. She knew he wasn't trying to be an asshole, but the word still popped into her mind. She ran a hand over her face once more, removing droplets of water. She looked toward the house, but saw no sign of Daina.

"So...how're things?" Michaels asked into the silence.

"Everything's fine," Emma answered smoothly. She glanced up to see the contrail of an airplane sketched across the blue sky above her. She almost longed to be that far away, that removed from her current situation.

"You two are...getting along?" For the first time, he sounded hesitant.

Emma felt a stab of annoyance. She closed her eyes, shook her head and took a silent, deep breath.

"Everything's fine," she repeated, focusing once more on the gauzy trail left behind by the aircraft.

"Look, I'm sorry—"

"Don't." Hardening her voice, Emma dropped her eyes and looked off toward the backyard. "Don't apologize. I'm doing this because I have to. Not because I want to, or I think it's right." She spoke sharply and made an effort to rein herself in. "So don't apologize. I agreed to it. Leave it at that."

"Has she asked any questions? Are you—?"

Emma straightened abruptly. "*Don't*," she said tightly, clenching the phone. "You tell me what I need to know, I'll tell *you* what you need to know. In case you've forgotten, I am *not* on duty, so don't push me on this. Everything is fine. All right?"

"All right. Yes, okay, it's fine," he said quickly. He took a deep breath, then said, "I'll call you when I know anything. Take care."

She didn't respond, just disconnected and then stared at the phone, jaw clenched. With a fair deal of self-restraint, she carefully placed the phone a foot or so from the edge of the pool. Turning abruptly, she dove beneath the water's surface once more. Breaking through ten feet beyond, she swam an extra three laps in an effort to burn off her current frustration. It was a poor attempt to regain a measure of control that she felt was slipping from her like a handful of sand.

When she entered the house, clad once more in her robe, Daina looked up from where she sat at the dining room table, newspaper spread open before her, cup of coffee near at hand.

"That was short," she observed.

"What?" Emma's tone was sharper than she'd intended. She winced inwardly.

Daina narrowed her eyes ever so slightly. "Your swim," she clarified warily.

"Oh. Yeah. Well…" Emma pulled the screen door closed behind her. "The technicians are supposed to be here around nine. I thought I'd hang around them awhile, find out what happened with the alarm." Crossing the floor to the far counter, she replaced the phone in its cradle, then reached for a coffee mug in the cupboard above.

"Do I need to be there?" Daina asked.

Emma glanced over her shoulder and shrugged. "*I* probably shouldn't even be there. But I want to be." She reached for the coffeepot and filled her mug, saying, "If you want, I can keep you informed. Not that they wouldn't, but…"

She didn't finish her sentence. She realized what she was saying, what she was doing, assuming the role of cop, slipping into it automatically, naturally, when she had no need to be doing so. And suddenly, she could see why she was doing it, could even see why she'd responded to Daina in the manner that she had when Daina had thanked her for last night. She was trying to distance herself. Without even realizing it, the closer she and Daina became, the more she was pulling back, behind a cool façade and a wall of professionalism.

Briefly she squeezed her eyes shut and pressed her lips together in a tight, thin line. That feeling persisted of being pulled in four directions at once. She grabbed a teaspoon from the drawer, reached for the sugar bowl, and dumped a measure of sugar into her cup. She stirred it vigorously.

"You okay?" Daina asked, sounding wary once again.

Emma hesitated, then took a deep breath. "Yes," she said, stirring with somewhat less energy.

"Really." Daina's tone was flat, disbelieving.

Emma felt a smile tug at the corner of her mouth. She cast a look at Daina, one eyebrow lifted. "Why don't you just *say* bullshit, if that's what you're thinking?" she inquired mildly.

Daina, sitting back in her chair with her arms crossed, looked unperturbed. "Well, that would just be rude, now wouldn't it?" she returned, just as mildly.

Had Emma not been feeling so out of sorts, she would have laughed at that. As it was, her smile only quirked up a little further.

"Yes, it would be. Very." She turned her attention back to her coffee as she considered her next words. Replacing her mug on the counter, she rested her hands on either side of it. "No, I'm not okay," she said quietly, without turning. Having admitted it, she was left feeling a little bereft. It was a completely unwelcome feeling.

Daina asked gently, "Do you want to talk about it?"

Emma lowered her head slightly, staring at the counter, at nothing. "Not really, no." She was trying hard to block out the emotional uproar that had started in her head and heart. "But I know I have to," she finished quietly.

"Does this have something to do with Michaels' phone call? What did he want?"

Emma shot her a sharp look. "He didn't talk to you?"

A certain coldness stole over Daina's features. "Nope," she said, with a single shake of her head.

Emma's mouth opened in disbelief. She looked away from Daina, back to the counter. "Fuck," she muttered, stunned, disgusted.

"*You're* angry?"

Emma jerked her head around again.

"How do you think I feel?" Daina's tone didn't change, which drove the point home far more effectively.

This time Emma turned and moved a step toward her. "*That's why I'm angry*," she said firmly. "This is absolute bullshit."

"Well, I'm glad you feel the same way," Daina told her. "I mean, I took the call, he asked for you. What am I supposed to do, insist he speak to me? I'm not going to play that game."

"You shouldn't have to," Emma said. She glanced away briefly, then back. "I'm sorry."

"Don't, please." Daina's expression was pained. "Don't apologize for him."

Emma wasn't so sure that that was all that she was doing. But she couldn't let her mind go there at the moment because Daina was speaking once more.

"Honestly, I thought if there was something I needed to know, you'd tell me. So I kept my mouth shut."

Emma felt a horrible sinking sensation in her gut at those words, at the implicit trust so simply stated. And she thought, *This is it, I have to tell her, tell her everything*. And she actually opened her mouth to say what needed to be said.

And then the phone rang.

Emma automatically answered it, listened briefly and then hung up.

"It's the security company," she said, turning back to Daina. "They'll be here in fifteen minutes." She couldn't get into the conversation now. She knew there had to be no interruptions, in all fairness to Daina. "Can we...continue this conversation later?" she asked her. "And whatever you want to know, I'll tell you, okay?"

Daina blinked, looking perplexed. "Sure. Of course."

Emma nodded, relieved. She left to take her shower, not realizing that in this instance, sooner rather than later would have been better.

CHAPTER TWENTY-FOUR

The technicians' arrival coincided with the arrival of Daina's physiotherapist.

During the first half of the next hour Emma managed, for the most part, to avoid dwelling on the impending discussion. She could accomplish nothing by worrying about it. She could only hope that Daina would understand and accept her role and the reasons for her involvement. She had to admit to a certain amount of trepidation at the thought of coming out to her.

Emma was a private person and very protective of her privacy. She was afraid of doing the wrong thing for the right reasons, or the right thing for the wrong reasons. Her feelings for Daina and her feelings regarding her imminent disclosure warred with each other, creating a morass of confusion and consternation that made it difficult to concentrate on her reasons for hanging out with the techinicians.

After thirty minutes of listening to technical jargon and numerous tests of the alarm system, she gave up. She understood they were re-routing one of the circuits. As long as it worked the way it was supposed to, she didn't care to know more.

She made her way upstairs. Outdoors, poolside, Daina and her physiotherapist were working on muscle extension in Daina's left leg. Emma didn't allow her glance to linger. She headed to her room, gathered up an armload of laundry and headed back down to the basement. Quickly sorting through it, she felt something in the pocket of a pair of khakis and pulled out a folded sheet of paper. With a frown, she unfolded it. That damn letter. With a sigh of frustration, she tossed it onto the dryer. *Don't forget that*, she told herself sternly.

"Um, excuse me?" a voice spoke up behind her as she pushed the START button.

The tech she'd spoken to earlier was standing in the doorway. "I just wanted to let you know that we're going to implement a new security code," he said. "You're going to need to know what it is. Do you have a pen and paper?"

"Yes, upstairs," Emma said.

Once there, he wrote down the new code. They ran a test; it worked fine. With everything satisfactory, the two technicians left.

Emma glanced outside once more. Daina was still busy with the physiotherapist. Feeling the need for a bit of muscle extension herself, Emma made her way to the spare room with its exercise equipment. The treadmill would do nicely. She was already clad in shorts, T-shirt and running shoes, so she climbed on, fixed the settings and began to run. She sorely missed running outside and wondered how long their forced confinement would drag on for. Not too much longer, she hoped, because it was beginning to wear on her. Of course, even bothering to hope was utterly pointless and she abandoned that line of thought.

She wondered whether Daina had even considered the fact that Emma might be gay. The funny thing was, Daina could have just come right out and asked her, and she wouldn't have been surprised in the least. That seemed more Daina's style, really. Instead, she regarded Emma with a calm scrutiny that was creating a growing sense of unease within her. She was glad she'd decided to get everything out in the open. Anything was better than walking this emotional tightrope. As that thought settled in her mind, she realized the truth of it. She suddenly felt as if a weight had been lifted from her.

Yes, anything is better than this.

She continued with her run, hearing Daina moving about the house, but paying no attention. Fifteen minutes later she hit the cool down button. Finally, she stepped off the treadmill, did a few rudimentary stretches and left for the bathroom next door. She splashed water on her face, and after toweling herself dry, studied her reflection in the mirror. She inhaled deeply and exhaled slowly. *You can do this,* she told herself. *It's no big deal, you'll be fine.*

She left the bathroom and made her way to the kitchen. Daina was sitting in her customary place at the end of the dining room table, an elbow on the table, her cheek resting against her palm. She seemed to be reading something and didn't look up as Emma entered.

Emma went to the fridge and grabbed a bottle of water. She opened it and took a deep swallow as the fridge door swung shut with a soft thump.

At the sound, Daina looked up and the expression on her face froze Emma in her tracks. The look was cold and hard.

"Why are you here?" Daina asked flatly, point-blank.

Emma stared at her, dumbfounded, understanding the question, and yet not understanding it. "What?" she managed to ask, sounding as confused as she felt.

"*Why are you here?*" Enunciating each word this time, a definite edge to her voice, to her look.

Emma just blinked. She couldn't think of how to answer the question.

"Oh, you can't answer that? Well, then, let me change the

question." She grabbed the sheet of paper from the tabletop. Shoving the chair back, she got to her feet and advanced one step toward Emma. "What the *fuck* is this?" she demanded hotly, holding out the paper.

And Emma knew instantly what *this* was; it was the letter, that damning letter. *Oh, shit.* She couldn't even begin to condemn herself for her sloppiness. Placing the bottle of water off to the side, she tried to collect her thoughts.

"Okay, Daina, wait, listen," she began, one hand out in an effort to placate, "this isn't—this was *not* my idea. I argued against it, but Michaels thought—"

"*Michaels?*" Daina's tone was disparaging, disbelieving.

Emma realized her words sounded dangerously close to an attempt to shift blame, and Daina had caught it. Still, she pushed on. "Yes, Michaels," she asserted. "*He* thought the situation would be better served if—"

"*Fuck* you." Daina's voice rose an octave. She now sounded insulted as well as skeptical.

"No, *listen* to me," Emma said heatedly. "I am as much a part of this as you are. Did you read the letter, Daina? Did you read the fucking letter? *This* is what they came up with, to protect *both* of us. They didn't know what else to do, and Michaels said—"

"Fuck you," Daina said again, but this time she looked and sounded disgusted. Her tone held a note of finality. She flung the sheet of paper at Emma and stormed past her.

Emma stood, frozen, stunned into immobility. She watched the letter waft to the floor. Her gaze remained fixed on it until she heard Daina's bedroom door slam. She flinched. *What the hell just happened?*

She realized an instant later what a stupid question that was. What had happened was exactly what she had feared would happen, why she had been against Michaels' idea in the first place. At the thought of him she was filled with a sudden anger, sharp and searing.

You stupid, *cocksure bastard,* she thought, for the moment perfectly willing to heap all the blame on him. Before too many more moments had passed she saw how unfair that was. It was she who had violated Daina's trust, with little more effort than would have been required to just walk up and slap her in the face. It amounted to the same thing, really.

Nicely done, she snidely congratulated herself. Her eyes alighted once more on the sheet of paper. A surge of irritation flooded her. She snatched it up, and in a fit of pique, mashed the paper into a crude ball and flung it away from her. It struck the windowpane and bounced off to drop into the stainless steel kitchen sink. Too bad there wasn't a Garburator to finish the task of disposal properly.

She stalked across the kitchen to the patio doors. She needed to think, to decide how to proceed. She needed the space and freedom of the outdoors.

For the better part of an hour she paced. Being outside cleared her mind, the endless pacing occupied her physically. Eventually, she reached the verge of exhaustion. Her legs felt leaden, her mind, her thoughts, were thick and muddy.

Her concern for Daina drove her back into the house. She approached Daina's room with trepidation, summoning whatever courage and conviction she had left, and knocked politely, three times. Her heart rate had sped up, her mouth was suddenly dry. Swallowing, she waited a full count of ten, forcing herself into an attitude of relaxation that she didn't feel.

Receiving no response, she was loath to just leave it at that and walk away. She knocked again, but this time she spoke, saying, "Daina? Can we talk?"

"Don't," she heard from within. "Just go away, Emma. Leave me alone."

Daina's voice was calm, completely without rancor. It was utterly flat and cold, and the bluntness of her words sliced through Emma keenly. For the first time, she felt a thread of fear wend its way through her.

Four hours later Emma stood at the counter opposite the kitchen sink. She was now so worried and worn out, she felt physically ill. She trembled minutely, stricken with some sort of palsy, the cure for which sat behind a closed bedroom door down the hall. She held the phone in one hand. She had been just about to make a call, but then she had stalled, uncertain. She stared blindly through the cut-away into the living room.

"What are you doing?"

She started violently, heart lurching in her chest, and almost dropped the phone. She grabbed at it, regained her hold, and whirled to see Daina standing in the doorway.

"Jesus Christ, you scared the *shit* out of me!"

"I'm sorry," Daina said quietly, and then reiterated, "What are you doing?"

Emma was aware that her hand was shaking, that her whole being was shaking. She made a gesture with the phone. "I was... going to call Michaels," she said, deciding to tell the truth, incapable of any kind of deceit at this point. She couldn't read Daina's tone or expression. "I thought I'd see about...making some other arrangements, leave you to yourself—"

"Don't." Daina stepped forward. "Please." She reached to take the phone from Emma's hand.

Emma surrendered it, wondering at the look in Daina's eyes. "But, I thought—"

"That's the trouble, you know," Daina broke in gently. "You think too much."

Emma blinked and watched mutely as Daina moved to place the phone back in its cradle. She was paralyzed by her closeness.

Daina met her eyes once more. "There's something I need to say to you," she said quietly, intently. "But before I do, I need to ask you something."

The look in those clear blue eyes was troubled and searching, and Emma almost quailed before it. "What?" she whispered.

Daina shook her head once, in quick negation, more as if in dismissal of the question. And then her gaze sharpened. She took a half-step forward, reached up to slide her right hand to the back of Emma's neck and gently pulled her closer.

Emma's eyes widened as she realized Daina's intent. A moment later, she closed them, fearing her heart would stop. And at the first touch, the first soft, gentle pressure of Daina's lips on hers, she literally stopped breathing. She was aware of her heart pounding, aware of an almost subliminal heat rushing through her, aware of the cool touch of Daina's fingers, that those fingers trembled as she, herself, was still trembling. She was aware of everything and she was aware of nothing.

The kiss was tentative, questioning almost, in its tenderness. Emma did her best to provide an answer of some kind in return, hoping it was enough.

And when they parted, and she remembered to breathe, she looked at Daina and met a gaze that was completely calm.

"Don't ever keep anything that important from me again. Please," Daina whispered.

Emma could only nod. She could still feel Daina's lips on hers and she felt an almost dizzying mix of weakness and strength infusing her. Completely overwhelmed, she wasn't surprised in the least to realize she was going to cry.

CHAPTER TWENTY-FIVE

Daina watched the tears flood Emma's eyes and thought helplessly, *Oh, Christ, I've done it again.*

"Oh, hey, no," she said with some alarm. "No, no, no, come on, please, don't cry."

But it was useless. A person didn't stop crying simply because someone asked them to. Emma brought her hands up to cover her face, bowing her head. Her shoulders began to shake, yet she wept in complete silence.

It broke Daina's heart to witness this strong, brave woman reduced to tearful emotion. She, herself, was so emotionally ragged she was afraid she was going to start crying if Emma didn't stop. She grabbed a handful of tissues from a nearby

Kleenex box, then gently placed her hand on Emma's trembling shoulder.

"Hey, hey, come on, please, don't cry, okay?" She leaned in close, pleading softly. "It's okay, everything's okay, I've got some Kleenex, just don't cry, okay, 'cause if you don't stop, *I'm* gonna start, and then where will we be, huh?"

She ended with a shaky laugh, totally unfeigned, but her words seemed to have no effect. Emma continued to cry and actually began to turn away. Daina did the only other thing she could think of, which required no thought whatsoever.

"No, no, no, hey, come here," she said softly, taking a half step forward. She gently grasped Emma's arms, brought her back around, and pulling her in close, wrapped her arms around her. Emma, completely unresisting, draped her own arms over Daina's shoulders, lowered her head and wept into the curve of Daina's neck.

There was barely an inch difference in their height. It was a comfortable embrace. For the short while that it lasted, Daina felt she could hold onto Emma like this forever. She whispered a few words of comfort, stroked her hair a couple of times, but mainly just held her. Eventually, she felt the tension leaving Emma's body; her trembling eased, and her sniffling wound down.

"Okay?" she queried gently.

She felt Emma nod against her shoulder. She took a step back and Emma brought her hands up to wipe at her reddened eyes and tear-stained cheeks. Daina held up the Kleenex, which was accepted with a grateful smile. In the aftermath of her emotional outburst, Emma's beauty seemed almost ethereal.

"Better?" Daina asked.

Emma nodded. "Yes, much," she replied, though her voice was barely above a whisper, as if she might still be on slightly shaky ground.

"Come on then," Daina said, as gently as before.

She led Emma into the living room to the sofa. She leaned forward, resting her forearms on her knees, palms pressed together. She looked intently into Emma's brown eyes.

"We need to talk," she said softly.

And Emma nodded, calm now, focused, her own arms resting on her thighs, hands clasped together, fingers interlocked. "I know," she breathed, somewhat sadly. "I'm sorry."

"Don't," Daina said, quietly but firmly. "Don't be sorry. Don't apologize anymore. Just tell me what's going on, what's *been* going on."

And Emma did, haltingly at first, as if unsure of how her words would be received. But Daina listened calmly, attentively, without interrupting, and in the face of her patience Emma's narrative began to flow more smoothly.

She told of finding the letter (that *fucking letter*, she called it, causing Daina to smile ever so slightly), of how she'd delivered it to Michaels, how it was he who'd spelled out the implications of it because she hadn't made the connection. She told of the subsequent interview with the detective and the investigative team, and ruefully explained how she'd felt about her inadvertent coming out. Daina nodded with understanding and sympathy. She'd read the letter. Its blatant disclosure would have been difficult to deny or ignore in light of the circumstances.

Emma continued by telling of the phone call she'd received at her apartment, the subsequent arrangements Michaels had made, her own growing discomfort and disbelief toward her increased involvement. She became somewhat impassioned when she got to the part about Michaels' idea of the two of them cohabitating, but in the end it had seemed logical. And then Daina had circumvented the whole discussion by providing her own request and how could she refuse that? Yet it had all hinged on whether Daina was comfortable with the arrangement, if she agreed to it. Once it became clear that Daina was fine with it, Emma had no more arguments. She then stated how she'd had every intention of coming clean with Daina, that she had never felt comfortable or happy with the deception or her part in it, and how she had feared it could only turn out badly if allowed to continue.

Daina knew, as Emma did, that it very nearly had. She had listened to Emma's narration without a single outward reaction and had suffered her only real episode of outrage and indignation when Emma related the incident at the hospital cafeteria. She couldn't believe they had kept that from her, but she kept her fury in check, since it was really meant for Sergeant Michaels and the detectives, anyway.

The fact was, as she heard out her story, she'd exonerated Emma already. She had been thoughtful and careful in her telling, in her choice of words, and Daina had no reason to doubt her sincerity or question her motives. True, she could have backed out of the proceedings at any time and stuck by her principles, but even Daina could see how difficult it would have been to make such a decision. That she was in as much danger now as Daina was sobering and startling. It cast a whole new light on everything. Her respect and admiration for Emma was growing exponentially. Truth be told, she knew she was a little in awe of her, but that was probably something she was better off keeping to herself.

Emma leaned back into the sofa. "And that," she finished with a sigh, "brings us to here."

Daina nodded and looked down at her hands. She was silent for a while as she considered what she'd been told and what she already knew. The letter itself, and its revelation, had thrown her into a tailspin of confusion and consternation. She'd managed to put two and two together, recalling what the detective had said regarding a certain letter and a certain third party, and she had come up with... Emma. It all made sense now, but at the time, as she held the letter in her shaking hands and read it over twice in the laundry room with disbelieving eyes, nothing made sense. She had felt confused, betrayed and angry. She had confronted Emma, not out of a sense of righteousness, but as a result of a disorienting tangle of conflicting thoughts and emotions.

When she'd finally left her room, it was with a whole slew of questions, all jostling for first place in her attentions. In the end, that was what drove her from her room, the need for answers. She was unprepared for the sudden flood of emotion she'd experienced when she saw Emma at the counter. She suddenly knew she didn't want to lose this woman; she wanted her in her life. In light of that epiphany, all other questions and concerns were relegated to the back burner. The one she was left with, the only one of any importance at that moment, was whether Emma felt the same. Everything seemed to hinge on the answer to that one question.

But as she'd stood before Emma, the question, and her ability to ask it, had fled. There seemed no right way to ask it. And so, with the reckless courage that defined her nature, she had kissed her.

Daina raised her head. "So, all of this," she said, meeting Emma's eyes and spreading her hands in an inclusive gesture, "is simply because you saved my life."

Emma appeared to consider, then nodded. "Basically, yes."

Daina's eyebrows rose fractionally as she said, "Bet you'll think twice before doing *that* again."

And Emma smiled, that slow, incredible smile of hers.

Daina felt her insides weaken. Taking a deep breath, refocusing, she said, "Thank you for being honest, for telling me everything. It's bullshit, complete and utter bullshit," she went on, "but I know you know that. And we're both agreed on the fact that it could have been handled better, differently, so there's no point in ranting on here and I'm not going to." She paused. "I do have one question, though."

"Sure."

Cocking her head slightly, Daina asked, "Whose idea was it to keep your identity from me?"

Emma took a moment or two before replying carefully, "When I had my meeting that morning after finding the letter, I was asked if I was comfortable with the contents of the letter and my name being revealed to you. I gave them permission to disclose any information that would further the investigation. Other than that, I said I would prefer not to be brought into it. Then, when things escalated, I realized my personal feelings weren't important, and by *not* telling you, I could be compromising the investigation and your safety. But because the threat had shifted to include me and there were now two of us to protect, Michaels suggested I hold off telling you anything until he could be sure of getting us both somewhere safe."

Emma paused a moment, then continued. "I'm sorry, I guess that doesn't really answer your question, but…I don't think it was anyone's hard and fast intent to keep my identity a secret, per se. It just happened to work out that way. And I'm not making excuses for anyone, least of all myself, because I understood, and still do, that your safety comes before mine."

"What?" Daina stared, confused. "Okay, no, wait, what? How can you say that? That's not true."

Emma blinked. "Of course it is."

"No, it's *not*. What kind of crap is that? You're in as much danger as I am, you said so yourself. You're here for your protection as much as I am. I *know* you're not here as a cop or a bodyguard or anything like that, I'm not stupid. So don't give me that shit about my safety coming before yours because I'm not buying it." As she reached the end of her little tirade she realized with mild affront that Emma was looking at her with something like amusement. "What? What's so funny? I'm serious."

"No, no," Emma quickly countered. "I know, I'm not—I'm sorry, I'm not laughing, I—" She seemed to struggle with her words, her mouth open but nothing coming out. In the end, she just said quietly, "I just like the way you don't hold back. That's all."

"Oh. Well." Daina searched for something to say. "I've been told it's not my most endearing characteristic."

Emma smiled ever so slightly, but said nothing. She lowered her eyes.

Daina regarded her closely. She caught her lower lip between her teeth, thought briefly, then said, "Hey, um, I have one more question."

Emma looked up, met her eyes.

Daina hesitated. She licked her lips, swallowed, before finally asking, in a low voice, "Are we okay?"

Emma just looked at her for what seemed the longest time.

Daina waited.

And when Emma did answer, it was in a voice as low as Daina's had been. "Yes," she said. "Yes, we're okay."

She sat by the pool in near darkness, the immediate area lit only by the light from the pool itself. She was alone with only her thoughts and her guitar for company.

Daina guessed it was now sometime after ten. She had lost herself in her music, immersed herself in it, all the while longing to be with Emma, aching to be near her, but completely unsure of how to achieve that end. Things had changed between them, she had unwittingly initiated that change, and now she didn't know how to proceed.

She finished the song she was playing and didn't silence the strings. Instead, she allowed the notes to fade into the night.

"Hey."

She glanced over her shoulder to see Emma standing a few feet away. She wore a pair of loose-fitting casual pants and a sleeveless T-shirt. She was barefoot and had her hands in her pockets.

"Hi," Daina greeted her with a small smile.

"I love hearing you play," Emma said.

I love hearing you speak. "Thank you."

Emma stood there a few moments longer, then moved toward one of the other patio chairs. She carried it over to place it diagonal to Daina, and sat down. Leaning back, crossing one leg over the other, she rested her hands in her lap.

"Play me something," she requested softly, in a voice Daina had never heard her use before.

Daina studied her for a moment, then nodded. "Okay." And without even thinking, she began to play Fleetwood Mac's "Landslide." The look of pleasure that stole over Emma's face warmed her. *Maybe there's not a lot of things I can do. But I can do this.*

The song was soothing to play, soothing to sing. There was no need to embellish, no attempt to impress. She was a performer, but her audience consisted of one. Such intimacy begged subtlety, not swagger. And when she ended, allowing the notes to once more fade into the night, she looked out over the pool briefly, then shifted her glance over to Emma.

Emma's expression was difficult to read, but her words stilled the disquiet Daina was beginning to feel. "That was beautiful," she said. "Thank you."

Daina nodded once, but kept silent. Words somehow seemed superfluous.

Emma shifted, placing her hands on the seat of the chair, at her thighs. "I actually…came out to say goodnight," she told Daina softly.

Daina didn't move, nor give any sign of her disappointment. "Oh," she said.

"Can you…see to the alarm?"

"Of course."

Emma nodded, seemed to hesitate, then said, "So… goodnight, Daina." So soft now it was almost a whisper.

"Goodnight, Emma."

Daina watched her rise, turn and leave. She heard the screen door slide open as Emma let herself into the house, then slide shut behind her. And still Daina didn't move. She no longer felt like playing. She no longer felt like doing anything. And so she sat, unmoving, refusing to think, refusing to feel. Until finally she roused herself out of her self-induced stupor, put her guitar back into its case and headed for the house.

She let herself in, put her case off to the side, closed the doors, and in the semidarkness set the alarm on the lighted keypad. Guessing that Emma was already in bed, she turned, intending to make her quiet way to her own room.

Emma was leaning against the divider wall, her arms crossed, little more than a dark form across the way. As soon as Daina saw her, her heart began to pound. They stood that way for a handful of moments, not speaking, not moving.

Finally, Emma pushed off the wall and came toward her, and Daina could only watch her approach. And when Emma reached her, she didn't say a word, just raised her hands to cradle Daina's face, and kissed her.

Daina returned the kiss, her heart in her throat, her breath stalled in her lungs. Her head swam dizzyingly.

Emma slid one hand behind Daina's neck, the other she slipped around Daina's lower back, pulling her in close. Daina dropped her hands to Emma's waist, their bodies pressed together, and at the feeling of that lean body against hers, the slim waist beneath her hands, she inhaled with a soft, audible gasp.

The sound seemed to incite Emma. Her mouth on Daina's became insistent, demanding, hard. Daina responded as hungrily, as a flood of heat rushed through her, filled her.

It was Emma who broke the kiss; she buried her face into Daina's neck and wrapped her arms around her in a fierce embrace. Daina did likewise, her forehead on Emma's shoulder; they stood that way for some time, both of them trembling.

Emma lifted her chin, relaxed her hold, brought her hands up to Daina's shoulders. Her lips brushed over her ear, her breath warm, inciting shivers; her tongue circled the lobe, sending a current down her spine. Their mouths met again, gentler, calmer, and then once more at Daina's ear, Emma whispered, "I'm not sure—"

And Daina whispered, "I know."

Emma's hold on her briefly tightened, her breath left her in a rush; leaning back, she looked into Daina's eyes searchingly. Whatever she read there must have been answer enough, because she finally nodded, almost imperceptibly, and kissed Daina once more.

Then, with an air of shyness, she reached for Daina's hand, and without a word, led her down the hall.

In Daina's room they faced each other, the only light that of a three-quarter moon. In its almost ethereal glow, they slowly undressed each other. There was no rush; the world was on hold. Awkwardness, shyness, was overcome by kisses, touches, embraces. Garments were eased off them, slipped from them;

newly exposed flesh was greeted with soft lips, lingering tongues, gentle caresses. Skin alternately shivered and burned.

Daina was overcome with an awareness of a tenderness and sensitivity she'd never known existed in her. She pulled Emma onto the bed with her, aching to possess her, hungering to take her, but she capitulated to the fragility of the moment, of the woman, without hesitation.

Emma's mouth was on hers once more, soft, gentle, her tongue searching. Then she moved, to travel along the line of her jaw, to her neck, down to the curve of her shoulder. Daina turned her head, closed her eyes, allowing her hands to roam the smooth expanse of Emma's back. Emma's tongue, mouth and teeth dragged gently, teasingly, along the stretched skin between neck and shoulder, pulling a response from the muscles of Daina's lower belly, sending a shiver up her spine and scalp; a sound somewhere between a sigh and a moan escaped her.

Emma rose slightly above her, raising her head. Daina brought her hands forward to cover Emma's breasts with her palms, felt the nipples rise beneath them and reached to take one nipple in her mouth, a taut gem, glistening with the touch of her tongue. She felt Emma's chest expand with a sharp intake of breath. She sucked harder, flicked her tongue over the erect flesh and Emma whimpered, throwing her head back. With one hand she cupped the other breast, teasing that nipple to hardness with her thumb.

Lowering her head back to the pillow, she slid her free hand along the curve of Emma's side to her lower back. She positioned her thigh between Emma's legs and pressed against her. Emma responded with her own pressure and groaned, and the feel of heat and wetness on Daina's thigh wrenched her insides with a blinding, aching throb.

"Oh, dear *God*," she whispered brokenly, the words catching in her throat as she pressed into her again, feeling Emma slick on her thigh, pushing against her, an inarticulate sound escaping her.

Emma covered Daina's mouth with her own, harder, demanding, hungry. Daina buried her fingers in her hair, then ran them down her back, wanting, needing the length of that lean body against hers. She pulled down gently, but Emma resisted.

"I don't want to hurt you," she whispered.

"You won't," Daina said.

Emma lowered herself, Daina brought her arms around her, their bodies conformed, melded together. Emma let all her breath out in a shaky exhalation against Daina's neck and Daina felt a wave of intense possessiveness wash over her, through her. She tightened her hold, almost crushing Emma to her. Emma's arms slipped behind Daina's back, and Daina could feel Emma's heart against her own body, beating life. She herself had never felt so alive.

Emma moved and Daina released her to allow her to rise again, until she was poised once more above her, her body a slender, sculpted figure outlined in moonlight. She could see Emma's gaze drop down, traveling over her body; Emma then leaned back and allowed her hands to follow the path her eyes had taken, slim, tapered fingers raising shivers, awareness, as they traversed arms, ribs, belly, hips. Down her outer thighs, then velvet soft up her inner thighs; a gentle parting, followed by a delicate upward stroke.

Daina sighed, deep, trembling.

Another stroke upward, then down, and then she entered her and Daina uttered a single cry of intense pleasure. Emma withdrew slightly, slipped in deeper, and Daina moaned and raised her hips to meet her, and the motions were repeated for endless moments.

And then Emma withdrew gently, hovered over her, kissed her tenderly, and met her eyes, and the look Daina saw was hungry, almost pleading.

Daina whispered one word: "*Please.*"

Emma lowered her mouth once more to Daina's body and her tongue traced over her skin, exploring, testing, learning; around, over, and down, her breath hot, her lips soft; everywhere she touched she awakened a response, etched in fire. Lower, to her inner thighs, her tongue silken warmth, and Daina ached almost painfully. And at the first gentle, questing stroke, Daina arched her back and cried out wordlessly.

Emma's tongue caressed her, searched her, playing, tasting, never dwelling, hot velvet gliding over a wet path.

"Oh, God, *please*." The words were whispered, jagged and raw, all Daina could manage.

Emma's tongue stroked, slipped down and inside, stroked up again, circled, massaged, and Daina trembled and writhed, beyond simple need. Until Emma's lips enclosed, her attentions became more concentrated, her tongue flicking over and around, eliciting whimpers, a growing heat. Every muscle tensed in Daina's body, and finally her climax rocked through her, ripping her open. Emma was merciless in her delivery and Daina cried out, shameless in her release.

And as her body quieted, Emma slid up and held her once more in her arms.

Daina awoke, nestled against Emma, an arm draped over Emma's warm body. She lay quietly, listening to Emma breathe, knowing she still slept, knowing that her own ministrations had led in part to her peaceful repose.

She hadn't been able to stay her own hunger for Emma for long; making love to her had been one of the most singularly intense and satisfying experiences of her life.

Afterward, the only question Emma had asked was, "I didn't hurt you, did I?"

Daina shook her head. "No."

"I was worried. The nurse warned me that you weren't supposed to overexert yourself."

"Well," Daina stated mildly, struggling to keep the grin from her face, "unless you'd planned on chasing me around the bedroom, there was really no reason to worry." She arched an eyebrow. "I notice that didn't stop you, though."

"No, it didn't, did it?"

They'd dissolved into laughter, curling into each other. And slept.

Now that Daina was awake, her hunger had reawakened. And it would not be ignored.

She kissed Emma's shoulder blade, slid her hand up to cup her breast, teased the nipple erect with her thumb. She felt, heard, Emma's breath catch in her throat.

She rose slightly, kissed Emma's shoulder and shifted, applying gentle pressure with her arm to ease Emma over onto her back. The nipple she had teased to hardness she drew into her mouth, eliciting a helpless whimper of sound from Emma. She felt a deep, complex pull within the muscles of her own belly, and an accompanying ache even lower. She circled the erect nipple with her tongue, sucked on it. Emma uttered another one of those helpless sounds.

Daina ran a hand over Emma's ribs and down the flat belly, trying to divine her need through touch alone. Her mouth still at her breast, sensing, feeling rather than seeing, Emma opening herself up to her once more.

Daina slipped inside. *So wet, so damn beautiful.* She hovered over her, pressed against her, deeply into her. Their bodies moved together, unchoreographed, undisciplined, yet a dance all the same.

And when it ended, when the dance was complete, they slept once more.

CHAPTER TWENTY-SIX

The call came Saturday morning.

Emma had it in mind that morning to do what she should have done far earlier than this: familiarize Daina with a gun. Hers, to be precise. She considered the idea over breakfast and decided it was sound. She couldn't allow Daina to fire the weapon, since they weren't in a safe and restricted enough area, but she saw no harm in introducing her to its finer points.

She waited until Daina had finished doing the dishes, patiently reading the newspaper and drinking her coffee in the interim. She studied Daina, viewing her with a certain detachment, reminding herself that Daina was still largely an unknown entity. Emma found herself regularly slipping into her usual reserve, even when they were interacting closely. She seemed unable to free herself completely of her restraint.

As she eyed Daina, she was aware of a subtle, almost constant state of low-grade arousal permeating her. It was a completely alien sensation, and in the past forty-eight hours it had left her feeling breathless and somewhat shaky on more than one occasion. Their sexual connection was incredible, thrilling, unlike any she had ever experienced. The fact that they connected both mentally and emotionally should have soothed Emma's psyche. Instead, that level of comfort continued to elude her.

Daina turned and looked her way. Their eyes met. Emma's belly did a slow and complicated tumble. She ignored it.

"Do you have any experience with guns?" she asked casually.

Daina narrowed her eyes slightly. "No."

"Are you okay with them, you're not uncomfortable with them?" Emma pressed gently.

Lifting one shoulder in a shrug, Daina said, "As long as they're not pointing at me, I guess I'm okay with them."

Emma smiled, amused as ever by Daina's spark and attitude. She certainly didn't lack for courage or spirit. Not for the first time, Emma found herself wishing they could have met under different circumstances. Rising to her feet, pushing the chair back, she approached Daina, leaned in and kissed her fully on the mouth. Kissing Daina was like tasting candy for the first time. The wondrous shock and pleasure of it never faded.

"Can you meet me outside? I'll be there in a couple of minutes."

"Sure." Daina nodded once, unquestioning.

In her room, Emma retrieved the Glock from the bedside table drawer, balancing its weight in her right hand. Turning her wrist slightly, she allowed her gaze to settle on the weapon and then, with a sigh, she sat on the bed. She rested the barrel of the gun in the palm of her left hand, the grip held lightly in her right. She pondered the concern currently eating away at her. While their current setup had facilitated their coming together, they could not possibly continue in this way for much longer. The same circumstances that had brought them together could and most likely would tear them apart. The thought was an unhappy one, but the realist in her recognized the truth of it.

Also, Daina had just left a relationship. Emma had no idea what Daina's intentions were and it went against the very grain of her nature to dabble in anything even remotely resembling a long-term relationship, yet the prospect gave her an unexpected, and unwelcome, thrill. She wanted to be with Daina, wanted to get to know her, and while that want, that desire, was dizzying and discomfiting, it was not one she could deny.

She knew she should be discussing all of this with Daina. But Emma's particular skill, at least in past involvements, lay in discouraging attachments and expectations. She felt woefully ill-equipped to broach a discussion about anything resembling an ongoing relationship. She lacked the experience and the capability to bring up such an emotionally convoluted topic. *And*, she thought, with dismaying clarity, *I don't have the guts.*

The realization almost brought her to her knees. She was immediately engulfed in a wave of self-pity and self-loathing.

Fuck this, she thought, reaching out to slam the drawer of the bedside table shut. *Just fuck it*. She turned and strode from the bedroom.

"It's lighter than I expected," Daina said, holding the Glock. She turned it this way and that, studying it closely.

Emma let her take her time to get comfortable with the weapon, with the feel of it, and the concept of it. Even people who thought they were okay with guns, once they actually held one for the first time, simply couldn't abide it.

Emma watched Daina closely for any sign of abhorrence. Daina only seemed curious. She raised her arm and extended it slightly off to her right. She sighted down the barrel, keeping, Emma noted with approval, her finger barely on the trigger. She'd removed the loaded magazine and held it now in her own hand, but she'd explained to Daina that one of the features of the Glock was that its safety was in the trigger mechanism. Daina had obviously been paying attention. Even though there was no chance of firing a round, she was careful, and her caution was good to see.

"So, why now?" Daina asked, lowering her arm and turning her head to look at Emma.

"I should have done it sooner," Emma replied, "but now seemed as good a time as any." She paused, then added, "In case you need to use it. In case something happens to me."

Daina said nothing to this; her expression and the look in her eyes remained unchanged. Emma approved of this, as well. The full reality of their shared predicament was staring them both in the face. Now was not the time to dispute the potential danger of it. Had Daina tried to do so, Emma's estimation of her would have dropped a notch or two.

She held out the magazine and Daina took it from her. She studied it with as much interest as she had the gun. Emma smiled.

"There are fifteen rounds in a magazine," she explained. She removed one of the bullets. "Obviously, we can't have you shooting up the neighborhood, so you're going to have to settle for just looking at the bullets and not firing them."

Daina gave a little snort of laughter, but took the bullet and turned it over and around in her fingers. Handing it back, she watched as Emma replaced it in the magazine. Emma then showed her how to insert and eject the clip, and how to rack the slide to chamber a round, which Daina seemed to take great pleasure in. Finally, placing the magazine on the patio table, she instructed her in the proper marksman pose and explained how it was important to squeeze the trigger, not pull on it.

Standing slightly off to the side, she viewed Daina critically. Under her breath Daina was uttering, "BANG!" in a steady, unending barrage.

Emma grinned and came up behind her. "Hit anything yet?" she asked dryly.

"Give me back that magazine and maybe I would."

"We can visit a firing range when we're out of here, if you'd like." Emma moved closer to stand at Daina's back.

"I'd like that. I might be good at it, you know."

"I wouldn't doubt it. You *look* good."

"Oh, yeah?"

"Yeah." Emma reached out and placed her hands lightly on Daina's shoulders. "Just…drop your arms a bit, spread your legs a little more, and relax."

Daina made a small *huh* sound of amusement. "That sounds more than a little provocative, Constable," she chided lightly.

Her mouth at her ear, Emma said, in a lowered voice, "I know." And she slid her hands off Daina's shoulders, down her sides, to her hips. She kissed Daina's neck, circled with her tongue, while she slipped her hands beneath the fabric of her T-shirt. She pulled her back against her, one hand on Daina's belly, the other traveling up to her breast which she briefly cupped, then began to massage.

Daina's breath caught audibly in her throat; Emma felt the abdominal muscles contract beneath her hand. Daina exhaled, a bit raggedly. "Do all of your students get this treatment?" she breathed.

"No," Emma replied in that same low voice. She gently caught Daina's nipple between her thumb and forefinger, rolling it, teasing it to hardness. "Just the ones that turn me on."

Extracting the gun from Daina's hand, she placed it on the table. She ran her tongue along Daina's neck, bit her gently, eliciting a moan. At the same time, she slid her left hand down past the waistband of her nylon track pants, and lower, to the elastic of her soft cotton briefs. She slipped past, traveling unerringly down, aching to touch her, hungry to feel her.

And in her pocket, her cell phone rang.

"Damn," Emma whispered. "I'm sorry."

Emma released her, retrieved her phone from her pocket, and glanced at the caller ID. It read Restricted Number. She was surprised to discover it was Sergeant Michaels. Keeping her voice level, she inquired, "Hey, Sarge, why are you calling my cell?"

"Because I tried the house phone and there was no answer," he replied.

"Oh. Well, we're outside. I guess we didn't hear it."

"Well, then I'm glad you had your cell on you, because I have some good news. I'll keep it brief, since this is hardly a secure line, but we've made an arrest. Early this morning we nabbed a guy, got a full confession from him—"

"Sarge?" Emma interrupted him calmly. "Hang on a second." Handing Daina the phone, she said, "It's for you."

Emma stepped past her to retrieve the gun and magazine and headed for the house, leaving Daina to deal with the call that should have been hers anyway. If Michaels refused to speak to Daina, Emma would force him to. Perhaps it wasn't her place, but she found it ridiculous and annoying that he continually chose to speak to her over Daina. She knew *why* he did, but that wasn't the point. And if they *had* made an arrest, Daina was the one who should be hearing about it first.

She put away the breakfast dishes, washed out the coffeepot and wiped down the counters. She could still see Daina outside, still on the phone. She left the kitchen for her room. She placed the gun on the dresser and sat on the bed. Now that she and Daina would be able to leave the house and rejoin the real world, would they continue seeing each other, or would Daina depart, go back to Nashville, carry on with her musical career? Was this just a sexual interlude for her, for them both, or did it actually mean something to Daina? She didn't know and knew she hadn't the courage to ask. She barely had the courage to admit to herself that it meant something to her. She despised herself for her weakness.

It occurred to her, and not for the first time, that she was in way over her head. She had neither the skills nor the experience to deal with something that was undoubtedly the best thing that had ever happened to her. *How pathetic*, she thought, shaking her head.

She was jerked out of her reverie by the sound of Daina's voice calling her from the kitchen. "In here," she called back and sat up a little straighter.

A couple of seconds later, Daina stood in her doorway, cell phone in hand, looking more than a little put out.

"Would you mind telling me what that was all about?" she demanded.

"What?"

"*That*," Daina said impatiently, jerking her thumb back in

the direction she'd just come. "You drop the ball in my lap and then just walk away? What the hell was that?"

Emma frowned in return, puzzled by the need for an explanation. "I thought he should be talking to you, so I handed him over."

Daina gave her a hard look. "Well, you could've given me a heads-up, don't you think? I had no idea what was going on and he was more than a little pissed off to be suddenly talking to me instead of you."

With a vague shrug, Emma said, "I guess I thought he'd figure it out soon enough."

Daina frowned and squinted at her. "I'm not talking about *him*, Emma, I'm talking about *me*."

Emma just looked at her, certain she was missing the point.

"Did it ever occur to you," Daina went on, visibly exasperated, "that I might not know what you're thinking, what you're doing? Did it ever occur to you that I might not be on the same page as you?"

And still Emma just looked at her, at a loss as to how to respond.

"Well, obviously not," Daina said, spreading her hands in frustration.

"No, I—" Emma began, then realized she had no defense. Daina's expression was openly curious and impatient, but Emma blinked and closed her mouth on her own protests.

"Okay, look," Daina finally said, seeming to realize that nothing else was forthcoming from Emma's camp. She exhaled forcibly and adopted a patient expression. Taking another step into the room, she said, "You need to start…communicating with me, Emma, because I don't know what you're thinking, what you're feeling, and I—" She gestured helplessly. "—I can't do this, Emma, I can't. I'm not a bloody mindreader."

And still, Emma could think of nothing to say. She didn't know how to rectify the situation and felt paralyzed by her own inadequacies.

"Jesus, Emma, would you say *something*, at least?"

Emma blurted out the first thing that came to mind. "What did Michaels have to say?"

Daina blinked rapidly a few times, obviously thrown, but she rallied and responded, "Well, among other things, they've arrested someone and we can leave here. Today. We can go."

"Oh." She hadn't expected such an abrupt conclusion.

"That's it? *Oh*? That's all you can come up with?" Daina sounded vexed. Rather expansively, she asked, "Did you…maybe want to…*do* something? Maybe make plans to go for that drink? We haven't done *that*, yet."

Emma briefly considered. "No, we haven't, have we?" She recalled her surprise at that unexpected request. It seemed as if it had happened eons ago. "We can, certainly, if you'd like."

Daina inclined her head slightly, in a thoughtful manner. And then, with care, she asked, "You don't…think we've gotten ahead of ourselves, do you?"

So much for not being a mind reader. She felt a little off-balance now that the subject was suddenly out in the open. She inhaled deeply, filled with some unnamed emotion. Exhaling, she finally found the words she needed. "No, I—I don't think we have."

Daina eyed her briefly. "Okay, well, good." She added, "Because I *would* like to go out with you."

Emma's response was automatic. "I'd like that, too," she said, though she felt as if a shift had occurred between them, the significance of which she'd missed. "That would be nice."

Daina's eyes narrowed almost imperceptibly as she cocked her head once more. "No, Emma," she said carefully. "I mean, I'd like to go out with you."

Emma blinked. And then blinked again.

"I'd like to *date* you," Daina clarified gently, though she seemed a trifle amused.

Emma went completely still, even as her mouth opened to form a soundless *Oh*. Struggling to overcome her paralysis, it was still a few moments before she was able to get the word out. "Oh," she said.

Daina raised her eyebrows, and a sound escaped her that could have been a laugh. And then, dropping her brows into a frown, she asked warily, "Is that a good 'Oh' or a bad 'Oh'?"

Emma's eyes widened. "It—no, it's good," she said quickly, and groaned inwardly. *Christ, I am so in*ept.

Daina, still eyeing her closely, asked carefully, "So...you'd like to continue seeing me?"

Emma knew it was she who was making this far more difficult than it ought to have been. She was aware that she felt shaken, that inwardly she was quaking, not because she didn't want this, but because she wanted it so badly. As much as she was afraid of what she was about to reach for, she was even more afraid to not reach at all. She strove to find steadier ground. Feeling light-headed and a little bit unsure of herself, she said, just as carefully, "Yes, I would like to continue seeing you, Daina."

Daina's watchful expression softened and a smile touched her eyes and the corners of her mouth. "All right then," she said, almost under her breath. Suddenly seeming to realize she was still in possession of Emma's cell phone, she held it out. "Here."

Emma reached to take it, murmured, "Thank you." She leaned to place it on the dresser.

"Emma?"

"Yes?" Emma fervently hoped that if Daina were about to ask another question it would be one she could answer without struggle.

And in that same lowered voice, Daina asked, "May I... make love to you?"

Emma's belly did that slow, complicated tumble. She swallowed. "Yes," she answered simply, quietly.

Daina nodded. "Good," she whispered. "Because I really want to." She leaned forward, placed her hands on Emma's shoulders, and gently forced her back onto the bed.

And when she had undressed them both, Daina loved her, as only Daina could.

It was only then that Emma, surrendering herself to the exquisite pleasure of her attentions, realized what that unnamed emotion that had filled her earlier was.

It was hope.

CHAPTER TWENTY-SEVEN

"So what did Michaels have to say about the arrest?" Emma asked, reaching to take Daina's guitar case from her to load into the Explorer along with the rest of their belongings.

"Oh, shit!" Daina exclaimed with a grimace. "I forgot to tell you. He wanted you to call him back."

"Did he say it was urgent?"

"No." Daina shook her head and shrugged. "He just…asked that you call him back."

"Oh. Okay, well—"

"I'm sorry, I…got distracted." Daina leaned against the side of the Explorer, crossed her arms and flashed Emma a guilty little half-smirk.

The two of them had decided to take a quick shower, where they had ended up making love yet again. Emma was astounded at her appetite, shocked that she felt a continual hunger for Daina, even now. Seeing Daina leaning against the side of the vehicle, wearing that smirk, made Emma want to grab hold of her and just...take her. Right there, against the side of the truck. A throb of sexual hunger coursed through her and she was shocked anew. *God, I'm depraved.*

"You're not...angry, are you?"

"No, not at all. He's just going to have to wait, though, until I get you home. Your parents must be positively antsy by now."

"Yeah, I think my mom's in a bit of a state," Daina stated ruefully.

"Well, I would be too, if you were my daughter." Closing the door of the Explorer, Emma turned to face her. "As it is, seeing you standing there like that," and she gave Daina a deliberate up-and-down look, "is putting *me* in a bit of a state."

Daina's crooked little grin made an appearance. "Oh, really?"

"Yes, really," Emma returned mildly. Leaning forward, she pressed her lips to Daina's in a soft kiss that quickly deepened. Her hunger, always so close to the surface, was raging once more. Daina moaned through her open mouth as Emma kissed her with an almost feverish intensity. Then, abruptly, she broke the kiss; she wrapped her arms around Daina, pulled her tightly against her. "God, I could take you right here," she uttered in a choked voice.

"I'd let you," was Daina's own hoarse response. Her hands gripped firmly at Emma's waist.

Emma's belly flip-flopped, and she exhaled raggedly. "It's not very romantic," she pointed out.

"I don't care."

Emma laughed, breathlessly. "You're as depraved as I am," she said, running her hands all over Daina's back.

"You mean that in a good way, right?"

And with that, they both laughed. Emma pulled back reluctantly.

"It's also not very timely," she said. "We really should get you home."

"Yeah, you're right," Daina admitted. She looked into Emma's eyes. "You drive me crazy, you know that?"

Emma quirked her mouth up in a little grin. "You mean that in a good way, right?"

Daina laughed and collapsed against her.

Reaching with one hand, Emma tilted her chin up. "Ditto," she said softly, and kissed her. "Now let's go. Before we become permanent fixtures around here."

During the drive, Daina filled Emma in on the particulars of her conversation with Sergeant Michaels. "So, that guy they arrested, it happened right in front of my parents' house, at about two this morning."

"Oh! Jesus."

"Yeah, I was a little bothered by that, too. They'd placed an unmarked car in the area, just up the street, to keep the house under surveillance. They didn't tell my parents because they didn't want anything to be given away. We Buchanans are *notorious* for not being able to keep secrets, you know."

Emma glanced over, amused.

"Anyway, I'm not going to bitch about that," Daina went on with a dismissive wave of her hand. "So, this guy drives past my parents' house at about one this morning, just kind of cruises past in this van, and the cops are watching, but he doesn't stop. Just goes on by. An hour later, the same van does another drive-by. This time, the cops stop him. Apparently, this guy put up a fight. So they restrained him and searched him and his vehicle."

Continuing to stare out the windshield, Daina said, "They found a bunch of stuff. A copy of my album, a dozen photos of me from that night, a couple of promo posters, even a copy of that letter, though why he'd carry that around is beyond me. Oh! And let's not forget the gun he was carrying."

Emma snapped her head around. Daina stared straight ahead.

"This may sound like a stupid question," Emma said, "but what was he doing there?"

"Actually, it's not a stupid question," Daina replied calmly. "He said he was going to force me to come to him since obviously I had gone into hiding, and he'd missed his chance once already. He wasn't about to let that happen again. So he came to my parents' house. Now there's a scary thought, huh?"

Emma had to agree, it was a very scary thought.

Daina turned, fixing her gaze on Emma. She looked and sounded weary all of a sudden. "He just...gave up. I mean, they caught him with all that stuff, what was he going to do, deny it? Well, I guess he could have, but he didn't. He confessed. To everything."

"Do you need to corroborate his story? Did Michaels say anything about that?"

"He did. And I did. Not that there was any reason, really, to doubt the guy."

"Why is that?"

Daina didn't answer immediately. Emma glanced over at her and saw that her gaze had become unfocused. She didn't seem to have heard the question, just stared out somewhere past the steering wheel. Emma allowed a handful of moments to pass; she looked over a couple of times before finally prompting gently, "Daina?"

Daina blinked twice, came back into herself. She turned her head away. She sighed very deeply.

"Because," she said heavily, as if the very words that she was about to speak were weighing her down, "he's the husband of a woman I was involved with three years ago."

Emma remained outwardly impassive and responded in her usual fashion. "Oh," she said.

Daina gave a light snort, sounding more bemused than anything. "Yeah. 'Oh,'" she muttered. In the same heavily weighted manner, she added, "I didn't know she was married. I wouldn't have gone there if I had."

Emma glanced at her. "I'm not judging you, Daina," she stated, very gently.

Daina blinked, then dropped her gaze. "Maybe I'm judging myself."

"You shouldn't. You didn't know."

Daina was silent, obviously thinking that over. "You know, it's funny," she finally said, "I haven't even thought of it, of her, in all this time. We were together maybe two months, from May to July. When she told me she was married, I ended it. Just like that. I left town two weeks later. And that was it. I never saw her again, I never spoke to her again. I never thought of her again. But now I'm on this…major guilt trip." She shrugged and shook her head as if her reaction puzzled her.

"The fact that her husband is trying to kill you probably has a lot to do with that," Emma said mildly, though not unkindly.

Daina gave her a brief, humorless smile. "Yeah, I guess."

And though Emma already knew the answer to her next question, still she asked, gently, "She fell in love with you, didn't she?"

Daina's "Yeah" was flat, unemotional. She quickly followed it up with a derisive laugh. "So *she* said."

Emma arched an eyebrow. "You didn't believe her?" She didn't need to ask if Daina's feelings had been reciprocal.

"It didn't matter. That sounds harsh, I guess, but…she told me she was in love with me *after* she told me she was married. The one basically canceled the other out."

Emma nodded, seeing her point. She mulled over what she'd been told so far, then glanced over. "You said it's been, what, three years since you had this affair?"

"Well, I wouldn't…call it an *affair.*"

They had arrived at the end of suburbia and the beginning of the city proper. Pulling up at a stop sign, Emma looked at Daina with a kind expression. "I'm not going to argue semantics, honey. I'm just trying to do the math."

Daina visibly clamped down on her emotions. "Yes, it's been three years."

Waiting her turn to proceed through the intersection, Emma kept an eye on approaching traffic as she asked, "So why did it take him so long to finally come after you?"

"Michaels said that she'd only just told him three weeks ago. She told me she wouldn't ever tell him. I remember I made a point of asking, because this is exactly what I was hoping to avoid. But I guess three years is a long time for some people to keep something like that a secret."

"So why tell him now? Why, after all this time? Just because you were due to show up in town?"

"Apparently she was trying to save their marriage."

"Excuse me?" Emma shot Daina a look of disbelief, blowing a perfect opportunity to cross the intersection. "Wouldn't confessing to an affair have the opposite effect?"

Daina looked pained, perhaps at Emma's insistence on using the word *affair*. "Apparently," she supplied with exaggerated care, "they'd been having problems for a while. He said she was trying to come clean with him."

"I'm guessing that didn't go over so well."

Seeing another break in traffic, Emma took advantage of it. She tossed another glance Daina's way. "So, this...what's her name?"

"Cathy. Cathy Marks."

"This Cathy...she's been carrying a torch for you all this time, is that it?"

"*What?* What makes you say that?"

Emma briefly pondered her reasons. "Why would she finally tell him about the two of you right before you're due to show up here? Why now? Was she trying to save her marriage or end it? Maybe she told him just to force the issue, so she could decide one way or the other how to proceed. Or maybe—" Emma suddenly bit down on her words. The thought that had occurred to her was disturbing, almost too disturbing to give voice to.

"What?" Daina asked.

Emma didn't reply, but she was frowning deeply, troubled in the extreme.

"What?" Daina's voice had sharpened.

"Maybe," Emma continued slowly, cautioning herself to speak with delicacy, "this is the outcome she was hoping for."

"Excuse me?"

"Maybe this is as much her vendetta as it is his." She glanced over quickly, once, as she added carefully, "Am I right in assuming you, uh, broke her heart?"

Daina's face clouded up in consternation and confusion. "Well...I guess, yeah, but—Christ, that was three years ago! There's no *way*—"

"Daina, don't ever think people will behave in the way you expect them to. It doesn't work that way. People don't work that way. She may not have been that forgiving."

Daina said nothing in response, but Emma knew her mind was working. She allowed the silence to stretch for a few moments before breaking in with, "Can I...ask another question?"

"Sure."

"The wife. Where is she in all of this?"

"It's funny you should ask that." Daina sounded a little snide. "She left. Once this guy had gotten the full story from her about us, he says he flipped, became extremely jealous, started making threats...which caused her to freak on him, and she just...took off."

"That's it? She just...took off?"

"Yeah," Daina said rather testily. "That kinda pisses on your parade, doesn't it?"

"So where did she go?"

Out of the corner of her eye, she saw Daina shrug. "He doesn't know. Neither does your sergeant or your detectives. They can't find her. She has a sister in B.C. somewhere, but she hasn't turned up there. No one knows where she is."

"Is she a suspect?"

Daina took a deep breath and exhaled through her mouth. "According to Michaels, and I quote, 'In light of her husband's confession, Cathy Marks may not be considered culpable for what has transpired. She will, however, continue to be viewed as an accessory, until further evidence presents itself to suggest otherwise.' Unquote."

Emma looked over at her, impressed. "You have good recollection skills."

"This is not just another pretty face," Daina replied, her expression severe, then gave her a little smirk.

Emma grinned back. As she maneuvered her way through traffic she said thoughtfully, "So she's just disappeared then, right?"

"Right."

"And this doesn't strike you as strange?"

"No, but *you're* starting to," Daina fired back. "Maybe she's squeamish, maybe the thought of him killing me didn't sit that well with her, I don't know; how the hell do I know what's strange and what isn't? If she's carrying a torch for me maybe it makes sense for her to take off, don't you think?"

"Actually, no, I don't," Emma replied mildly. "If she's still into you, it would make sense if she hung around to prevent anything from happening to you by warning you, or the police, or someone. But she hasn't done that." She favored Daina with a sidelong glance. "She's just…disappeared. Why? Where did she go?"

"Is it really that important, Emma? I mean, Christ, I just want this over with. What difference does it make where she went, as long as she's not around here?"

Emma tried to think of a tactful way to say what was on her mind. "Well, what if—and this is just a thought, okay?—but what if he's responsible for her…absence?"

"Oh, Jesus, Emma." Daina looked and sounded frankly disbelieving. "Are you serious?"

Emma opened her mouth to say "dead serious," decided that was probably a poor choice of words, and instead just said, "Yes, I am."

"Okay, fine, so…what? What if he is? He's been arrested, she's nowhere to be found. What does this have to do with me? You're creeping me out here. I don't want to think about this shit, Emma. I just want this to be over with. I don't want to think about some crazy chick running around carrying a torch for me, and her crazier husband who wants to kill me and maybe killed her and God knows what the hell else. Oh, and let's not forget the fact that your life was threatened too."

"I haven't forgotten," Emma said quietly.

"Well, neither have I, okay? I haven't forgotten any of it, but I want to, dammit. I don't want to sit here and speculate and wonder and worry. And you are just speculating, right?"

"As I've said."

"Are you going to mention any of this to Michaels?"

"If he hasn't already thought of it."

"Good. Throw it in his lap. Don't throw it in mine. As far as I'm concerned, this thing is over. Kaput. *Tout fini.* Done like dinner. Over and out. Roger, dodger."

Emma looked over at her with raised eyebrows. Daina burst out laughing. Emma was glad to hear it.

"See? You've made *me* crazy. Nice." Daina laughed a little more.

"I'm sorry." Emma shrugged. "And who knows? She might still show up. Torch and all." She said this completely straight-faced as they came to a stop at a red light.

Daina narrowed her eyes as Emma looked over at her. Daina's expression of mock disgust almost made her grin. She held it back.

"You're bad. I don't even know why I talk to you."

"Well, when you figure that out, you'll let me know, won't you?" Emma tipped her a teasing wink.

Daina shook her head, in a long-suffering manner. "Just drive."

Grinning, Emma did as she was told.

CHAPTER TWENTY-EIGHT

"Oh, great," Daina muttered. They had just rounded the curve of the crescent her parents lived on.

Emma pulled up to the curb and they surveyed the scene half a block away. There were four reporters, along with two cameramen and two photographers. Daina was to be treated to both newspaper and television coverage, it seemed. *Lovely.*

"I'd like to know how the bastards knew I was coming here."

"Your parents?" Emma suggested.

"No, not a chance." While her parents were staunch supporters of her musical career, they detested the media attention that occasionally went along with it. They would never have alerted the press to their daughter's homecoming.

"Although," she added in afterthought, "it's strange they didn't call to warn me about this."

Emma shifted and reached into her pocket. Withdrawing her cell phone, she quickly glanced at the screen. She pressed a button and the phone beeped. Raising her eyes to Daina, she flashed her a guilty smile.

"Oops," she said, holding the phone out as if in offering. "I must have turned it off earlier without even realizing it."

"Ah." Daina took the phone from her. Two missed calls, one from her parents. There was no accompanying voice mail.

"Well, at least they tried," she said, handing the phone back. "Sorry."

Daina waved the apology away. "Don't worry about it. It's not like we could have avoided this."

Holding the cell phone slightly aloft, Emma said, "This is probably how they found out, by the way."

"What do you mean?"

"Cell phone scanners. They scan the frequencies used by cell phones."

"Those things exist?"

Emma nodded.

"Jesus. No wonder Michaels was trying to cut our conversation short. Here I thought he was just being a jerk."

"He knew it might not be secure."

Daina shook her head, bemused, and then jerked her thumb toward the cell. "There's another call on there, by the way."

"Probably him," Emma said, as she returned the phone to her pocket.

"Persistent little bugger, isn't he?"

"He's not all that bad," was Emma's quiet response.

"If you say so. But I'm certainly not his biggest fan at the moment." She wasn't ready to forgive the sergeant for withholding information. "Any suggestions on how to deal with *this* situation?"

"Well, I'd offer my professional services but as you can see, I'm hardly dressed for the occasion." Emma made a slight hand gesture to indicate her casual attire.

"Too bad. Seeing you in uniform would be a fine visual treat."

Emma gave a light laugh, a slight shake of her head. "What is it with lesbians and women in uniform? Besides," and here her tone and expression softened, "you've already seen me in uniform."

"What?" Daina frowned. "No, I haven't."

"Yes, you have."

Daina's frown deepened. "No, I haven't, Emma," she stated firmly. "I'm pretty sure that's something I would remember."

Emma's patient smile briefly quirked up in amusement, then faded as she said gently, "Backstage. The night of the concert. You were just about to go on."

Daina's memory of that night was practically nonexistent. Still, she cast her mind back to the point in time Emma was referring to. For several moments, there was nothing. And then…

"Oh my God," she breathed, locking eyes with the woman seated next to her. "That was *you.*"

"That was me," Emma confirmed softly.

Daina's mouth had fallen open, as the image that flooded her mind gained cohesiveness, that of the startlingly good-looking female cop standing just beyond her, staring, as she had turned, strapping on her guitar.

"You smiled at me," Emma said, in that same, soft voice.

Daina refocused on her. "Of course I *smiled* at you. I couldn't get over how fucking *hot* you were."

Emma blushed. Daina was touched by her unexpected reaction. She studied her for a few moments, appraisingly, wondering at the complexities of this woman who affected her like no other ever had.

"And then you ran away," she said with a puzzled frown.

"I didn't run away," Emma immediately protested, causing Daina to smile ever so slightly. "I may have left in a hurry, but—"

"You ran away." Daina's tone brooked no argument.

Emma grudgingly admitted, "Okay, I ran away. But I was supposed to be working, not gawking."

"You weren't gawking," Daina responded charitably.

"Oh, no, I was gawking. You know damn well I was gawking."

Daina grinned. "Okay, yeah, you were. But it was sweet."

"And that's so the effect I was striving for."

Again, Daina eyed her appraisingly.

Emma lifted her brows in an inquisitive manner. "What?" she asked.

"Nothing. You're beautiful," Daina said simply.

Emma blushed once more, lowering her eyes. Daina marveled that anyone as self-confident, as self-assured as Emma, could be thrown so completely by a compliment. Keeping her tone light, she said, "So, do you want to stay in the car while I deal with these clowns, or do you want to join me on the front page of tomorrow's news?"

"If it's all the same to you, I think I'll stay in the car." And then she assumed a thoughtful look and added, "Although, this *would* be a perfect opportunity for me to tell them about your coffee-making skills."

Daina fixed her with her best facsimile of a dirty look. Before she could say a word, though, Emma held up a hand to stop her.

"I know," she said, her mouth twitching with suppressed good humor. "Just drive."

Daina saw her parents framed in the big bay window of the living room, looking out anxiously. She glanced at Emma as the SUV came to a stop halfway up the length of the driveway. "I won't be long," she assured her.

"I'll be here," Emma told her with a single nod.

Daina spared a moment to wave reassuringly to her parents, who waved in return, now all smiles. She then directed her attention to the small group converging on her. Most of their questions were basic run-of-the-mill stuff, dealing with her recovery and the interrupted tour. No one seemed privy to the fact that there was more to it than that, which was fine with her. If they thought she'd been in the hospital all this time, she wasn't about to indicate otherwise. She kept her answers brief, succinct, and congratulated herself for her poise and politeness.

Then a woman from the group spoke up, saying, "Ms. Buchanan, it's come to this reporter's attention that there's been an arrest made in relation to the bombing the night of your concert. Also, that the individual arrested is, in fact, the husband of a woman you were involved with a few years ago. Can you confirm this?"

Surprised and annoyed, and noting the ripple of interest that went through the rest of the group at these words, Daina fixed her gaze on the woman. She was just removing a pair of mirror-lens sunglasses, stepping out from behind another reporter. Daina recognized her immediately: Tamara Blake, from the *Winnipeg Sun*, whose blonde, girl-next-door good looks masked a nasty personality. She'd had more than a few encounters with the woman, both professionally and personally.

Deeply closeted, Tamara Blake often surreptitiously visited the gay bars; she'd slip in while it was extremely busy, and slip out sometimes alone, sometimes not. Daina had seen her on more than one occasion in just such a setting, leaning almost too casually against the bar, eyes scanning the patrons intently, looking just a little too hungry. While Daina had lived in Winnipeg, Tamara had covered a couple of her performances. Her reviews had been tepid, unimpressed. She had also, without fail, propositioned her any time they'd both been in the bars and been summarily refused each and every time. She'd always taken the rebuffs in good humor, as if they were temporary, subject to change. But Daina had never once said yes, not only because Tamara was a fairly disagreeable piece of work, though that wasn't always a major consideration if a night of rough-and-tumble sex was all one was after, but mainly, because Tamara was a reporter. Daina didn't believe in sleeping with the press.

Tamara was looking back at her with a wolfish grin, obviously inordinately pleased with herself.

"No comment," Daina said dispassionately.

The reporter raised an eyebrow, and without missing a beat, smoothly ventured, "It's also been rumored that you've fired your manager. Does this mean that your personal relationship with her has been terminated as well?"

Daina favored her with a measured look. "And that's pertinent how?" she asked, somewhat testily. The question irked her. The woman had obviously been doing her homework and while she may not have spoken to Kendra personally, she'd certainly spoken to somebody in the know.

The thought of Kendra effectively severed the thin tether she was keeping on her patience. "All right, people, that's it, playtime is over. You can see yourselves off the property, I'm sure."

She raked the bunch of them with a meaningful look to ensure there were no misunderstandings. As one, the group began to disperse, Tamara Blake and her photographer among them. Though Daina bore her no animosity, the woman was tenacious and rather unpleasant to be around. She was relieved to have her depart so readily.

She ensured that everyone was truly on their way, and then made a sudden decision. With a quick, hang-on-a-second gesture to her parents, she went back to the Explorer. She opened the door.

Emma sat in a relaxed pose, left hand resting on her left thigh, her right draped casually at the wrist over the steering wheel. She wore a coolly expectant look.

Daina felt a brief flutter in her belly at the sight of her. "Hey," she said.

"Hey, yourself. How did it go?"

"Fine. Nothing I couldn't handle."

"That's good to hear."

A flicker of movement in the direction of the house caught Daina's eye and her glance strayed momentarily. Her parents, she saw, had just stepped outside, obviously having discerned that the coast was clear. "I was wondering if you might like to meet my parents?" she asked evenly.

"I'd like that very much."

Daina felt herself relax and was surprised. Obviously, the meeting she had just proposed mattered more to her than she'd realized. And she felt, for the first time in her life, that somehow, in some way, her future was inextricably entwined with another person's. It was a diaphanous concept. She reached for Emma's hand. "All right then," she said simply.

Emma abandoned her relaxed pose, extricating her lean frame from behind the steering wheel to join Daina on the asphalt drive. Fingers interlocked, they stepped back from the Explorer, pivoting slightly so Emma could close the door.

And there, at the rear bumper of the vehicle, stood Tamara Blake.

"Well, I guess this answers my last question, wouldn't you say?" She looked positively gleeful as she glanced between the two of them.

"Oh, for Christ's sake, I thought you'd left," Daina grumbled, not even trying to hide her annoyance. Wondering where the photographer had gotten to, she took a moment to lean back and flash another hang-on gesture toward her parents on the front step.

"What, and miss this?" Tamara was saying. "I'm glad I didn't." She then directed her attention at Emma. "Hello, *Constable*," she greeted her in a sardonic tone.

"Tamara," Emma returned, icily polite.

Daina blinked at this little exchange. Clearly the two of them knew each other, but it didn't seem to be a very friendly association.

"Actually," the reporter said, once again addressing Daina, "I stayed behind because I had another question for you. Completely off the record."

Daina gave her a dubious look. "'Off the record,' huh?"

"Yes. I was *going* to ask if you'd seen any more of Constable Kirby here since the night she saved your life. Judging by your coziness, I'm guessing the answer to that is a resounding yes."

Daina eyed the reporter with contempt.

"Anyway, as I said, that's completely off the record." Tamara glanced between the two of them once more, holding her hands out as if to set them at ease. "But I'm glad my curiosity has been satisfied." And then she added with an obvious smirk, "You make a cute couple, by the way. For what it's worth."

She made as if to turn away, then turned back, saying, "Oh, and Emma? If you ever want to hook up again, look me up. I really enjoyed that first time."

Daina narrowed her eyes.

Tamara made a face and snapped her fingers, as if suddenly remembering something. "Oh, no, wait, that's right. I forgot. You never fuck the same woman twice, isn't that what you told me? Jeez, I'm sorry, what was I thinking?" And that wolfish grin reappeared.

Daina shot a quick glance at Emma. Her jaw was set, her profile stony, her eyes fixed on the now-departing figure of Tamara Blake.

"Anyway, you two have fun, take care. Oh, and Daina? Good luck. With everything." With a final smirk and a wave, she turned and headed for her car.

Surprised, appalled, and amused all at once, Daina cast another look at Emma. "You slept with her?"

Her eyes cold flint, Emma said, "*That* is none of your business. Don't even go there."

The rebuke stung, and Daina immediately flushed hotly. She jerked her eyes away, dropping her chin. With a slow nod, she acknowledged, "You're right." Looking up, she added quietly, "But just for the record? I don't care."

Her lips pressed into a thin line, her own color heightened, Emma favored her with a wary, scrutinizing look.

"Really. I don't."

The tension slowly left Emma's body. Her expression, her eyes, lost their intensity. She nodded. "Okay," she said finally.

She gently squeezed Emma's hand. "Will you come with me now? Or do you want to do this some other time?"

Emma took a deep breath, seeming to gather herself together. "No, it's fine," she said. "I'm fine."

Daina, searching the depths of those brown eyes, suddenly felt there was one more thing that needed to be said, something she hadn't planned on, but maybe that was best. "Hey," she said, keeping her voice close to an undertone. Simply and quietly, she stated, "I love you."

Emma blinked. Her pupils briefly dilated, her eyes widened

and her expression slackened. Her lips parted slightly as her mouth opened in mute surprise.

Wanting her words to stand on their own, and her feelings as well, Daina gave a tug on Emma's hand. She took a step back. "Now, come on," she coaxed gently. "Before my parents think I fell into a black hole or something."

CHAPTER TWENTY-NINE

Feeling a little unwound after Daina's unexpected revelation, Emma was completely unprepared for her charming and disarming parents.

She briefly observed their emotional reunion before discreetly turning her head to look off in the direction of the street. Her gaze wandered over the few cars parked several yards apart beneath the elms that lined the crescent. The sun and light breeze that riffled through the leaves created a shifting dappled effect on everything below. When her eyes caught what seemed like a flicker of movement from the interior of one of the cars, her attention was immediately drawn back. Her gaze sharpened, focused on the windshield of a green Sunfire where she thought she'd seen the motion. But the changing light pattern made it impossible to clearly distinguish anything from this distance. A moment later Daina called out to her.

"Mom, Dad," Daina said, as Emma came to a stop before them, "I'd like you to meet Emma Kirby." To Emma, she said, "Emma, my parents, Marlene and Steve."

"*Constable* Emma Kirby?" Marlene Buchanan asked.

Emma gave a slight nod. "Yes, ma'am."

Marlene's smile broadened. "It's wonderful to finally meet you," she said, and stepping forward, unhesitatingly put her arms around Emma in a hug. "You're as beautiful as I thought you'd be."

The warm greeting was more than she expected and she was thrown a little off balance, both physically and emotionally. Still, she recovered her wits and equilibrium sufficiently enough to return the embrace, though a bit awkwardly. "Thank you," she managed to reply, and as they parted, added, "It's wonderful to meet you, as well."

Steve Buchanan stepped forward, hand outstretched. "Constable Kirby, it's a pleasure to meet you."

Emma grasped his hand, shook it firmly. "Mine as well. But please, call me Emma."

"Emma, then." He smiled, then sobered. "Let me just say that you are more than welcome in our home and in our hearts."

Deeply touched, Emma murmured, "Thank you." She glanced over in Daina's direction, to find her looking at her. As their eyes met, Daina gave her one of those little grins of hers, but for once it wasn't that which caused her breath to falter. If she'd had any doubt about Daina's feelings for her, it was banished by the look in her eyes, so clear and shining it was breathtaking. Emma had never been subjected to such a look, had never really expected to be the recipient of such a look. "Maybe we should get your things out of the car," she suggested, attempting to find more solid footing in the banal.

"I'll help with that," Steve Buchanan offered immediately. "Would you care to join us for a beer afterward, Emma?"

Daina sputtered laughter. "Dad," she said, sounding mildly scandalized, "it's barely noon."

Emma merely grinned at the invitation. "Sure," she accepted. "It's five o'clock somewhere."

Daina's father laughed out loud. "I like this girl, Daina. Where did you find her?"

"I didn't," Daina said, with a half-smile. She met Emma's eyes once more. "She found me."

Emma held Daina's look for a moment, then regretfully tore her gaze away. It would be all too easy to lose herself in those incredible eyes, but now was hardly the time or the place. She looked toward her parents and was a little discomfited to notice they were both beaming at her. It occurred to her that it wouldn't take a rocket scientist to figure out there was something going on between her and Daina.

"Shall we?" she suggested to Daina's father.

"Lead the way," he said with a nod.

Gratefully, Emma turned away to retrieve Daina's belongings from the Explorer.

"So, I guess what your mother and I would like to know," Steve Buchanan broached, speaking to Daina, "is if the danger to you is well and truly past."

The four of them were arranged casually around a large wrought-iron patio table with a smooth glass top and pebbled undersurface. They were seated on cushioned chairs, and all four were nursing a Corona with a slice of fresh lime. Emma opted to remain silent; she indicated with a nod that Daina go ahead and answer.

"From what I've been told," Daina said, "the guy they've arrested gave a full confession. The police seem satisfied with that. So yes, I guess that means it's over."

"And what about you? Are you satisfied with that?"

"Well, yeah, why wouldn't I be?"

"I'm just asking. I want to know that you're comfortable, that you feel safe."

"I feel safe, Dad, I do. The police have got the guy. That's what matters to me." Daina took a swallow of beer.

Steve looked at Emma. "And are *you* satisfied with that?"

Emma realized she wasn't satisfied with the general consensus, but she didn't want to say so, since she couldn't really explain, even to herself, why. The Buchanans may have clued in to the fact that she and their daughter were involved in some way, but she wasn't entirely certain they knew the role she had been playing.

She said, a little shortly, "You know, I'm actually a little out of the loop myself. Daina knows more about that right now than I do."

Steve and Marlene frowned. Emma realized her words had come off sounding very lame, almost like an attempt to palm the whole issue off onto Daina. Instantly, she was ashamed and annoyed, ashamed of her behavior, annoyed that her behavior had put her on the spot. Daina was looking at her a little askance.

Emma sighed. "Do they know anything of the situation we just left behind?" she asked Daina gently. "Have you told them anything?"

Daina shook her head.

"What do we need to know?" Steve asked.

"Everything." Emma then launched into a telling of the events that had led to this particular point in time, so they would understand her reluctance and her inability to give them any kind of a solid, objective answer. She left out the interview with the investigative team, deeming it irrelevant, and she left out the little exposé Daina had recently supplied, out of sheer respect. When she was done, she took a sip of her beer, enjoying the tang of the lime.

"And so why was this guy after *you*?" Steve asked, point-blank.

Emma was fast coming to see where Daina had come by her forthrightness. "Well," she replied with her usual mildness, returning her bottle to the tabletop, "he was after *me* because I had the audacity to save your daughter's life. And I guess, after his initial attempt failed, he viewed my further intervention as interference."

Emma was able to guess what was coming next and Steve Buchanan did not disappoint.

"And why was he after you?" he asked Daina.

Emma once more reached for her beer, shifting her eyes briefly in Daina's direction to see her sag and drop her chin. Emma sympathized as she took a short pull on the Corona; the answer to that question was not one she would want to have to provide to anyone.

After a few moments of silence, Daina finally just murmured, "Because I...had an affair...with his wife."

"Oh, Daina," her mother said softly, sadly.

Emma suddenly felt very uncomfortable, very out of place. She gave Daina a pointed look. "You know, I should really call the sergeant back."

Daina looked hugely grateful for the interruption, even though it had been for Emma's benefit, not hers. "Did you want to use the house phone?"

"Uh, sure, if that's all right."

Daina nodded and pushed her chair back. "I'll show you where it is."

Emma knew this was completely unnecessary, but she understood Daina's desire to remove herself, even if only for a short time.

In the kitchen, Daina indicated the phone on the counter. "You can use that one."

"Thanks."

Daina started to turn away, but Emma stopped her, saying, "By the way, I think I owe you an apology."

"For what?"

"I was very short with you earlier. That was uncalled for."

"What? No, Emma, you had every right; that was none of my business."

"Well," Emma shrugged. "Maybe it was, maybe it wasn't. Regardless, I didn't have to react that way and I shouldn't have. I'm sorry."

Daina eyed her keenly. "Okay, I accept your apology, if that's what you need me to do. But I want to repeat what I said earlier: *I don't care.* Your past is your business; it's got nothing to do with me. I don't know why you would think that I care, or why this is an issue for you. And I can see that it is, so don't tell me it's not.

But I'm telling you, it's not important to me. You are important to me, not who you've slept with, when, where, why or how many times. I don't care. Okay?"

After a momentary pause, Emma said, "Yes, okay."

"Good." Daina smiled. "Make your phone call. I'll be outside." And she turned and left.

Emma called the sergeant's number; after two rings, his voice mail informed her he was away from his desk. She left a message and replaced the phone in its charger, wondering why he'd wanted to speak to her in the first place. If it was just to recap what he'd told Daina, it couldn't be that pressing. She pulled her cell out of her pocket to ensure it was on, made a mental note that the battery was low, slipped it back and headed outside once more.

At the sound of the screen door closing behind her, all three Buchanans looked her way. Grouped together as they were, the family resemblance was so clear it was almost startling. She settled her eyes on Daina, who watched her approach. *I could do a hell of a lot worse than have her to love me, but I certainly could not do any better.*

"How did it go?" Daina asked.

"He wasn't there. I left a message." She slipped into her seat, reached for her beer. The bottle was sweating in the afternoon heat; as she brought it to her lips, the condensation dripped to splash darkly on her jeans. She wished she'd worn shorts. But she was carrying her weapon, and the ankle holster was more comfortable than wearing the gun at her back.

"Is he gone for the day or—?"

Emma swallowed, shook her head. "No, just away from his desk. We'll connect."

"Lucky you."

She smiled good-naturedly.

"Do you work weekends, Emma?" Marlene asked.

"I do, yes. You can't get away from it. That and shift work, you just…accept it. I don't mind, most of the time. I like my job."

"Your parents must be very proud of you," Marlene stated innocuously.

Emma froze. Marlene's words caught her completely off

guard. A moment later, she was astonished when, calmly and without rancor, she heard herself saying, "My family disowned me when I was nineteen."

The shock on the faces of the three of them struck her an almost physical blow.

"Oh, my God, I'm so sorry." Marlene's voice was almost a whisper.

Daina only stared at her silently.

Steve Buchanan said, "It's none of my business, I know, but *why*, for God's sake?"

Emma considered a moment, then said, with a slight shrug, "I came out to them." She added, "I'm not going to say I made the mistake of coming out to them, because I don't feel that it *was* a mistake, regardless of what happened. But my father couldn't abide it. He was the one who ordered me out of the house. The others, my mother and sisters, just…went along." She shrugged again, a tiny shift of her shoulder. "I haven't contacted them since. Or vice versa."

She was surprised by her little speech, surprised she had managed to pull off a casualness she did not entirely feel. Slightly shaken, she reached for her beer, took a deep swallow past the lump forming in her throat. The action allowed her to regain a measure of her composure.

"That's so…cruel," Marlene said softly.

"What kind of a man would do that," Steve asked, sounding more puzzled than outraged, "just drive his own daughter away, his own flesh and blood, because of who she is?"

"Dad, not everyone sees things that way," Daina pointed out quietly. "Not everyone is like you and Mom." She looked back at Emma. Her expression was sweet and kind. There was no evidence of pity; Emma could not have stood that.

"My father was a good man," Emma said to Steve. "I idolized him." She realized she was speaking of him in the past tense. *That* hurt her, but she didn't know, hadn't thought of a way to refer to him, since she did it so rarely. "There was a strength in him that I loved, that I admired. Not a physical strength, though he certainly was a strong man, but a mental strength, like steel, like…titanium, that made you think he could stand up to anything, face anything, and never back down."

Emma thought she was coming dangerously close to babbling, but speaking in this way felt cathartic. She'd never really done so and she would never have brought it up on her own, at least not in this company, under these circumstances. Yet it didn't feel wrong or out of place to speak of it now.

"It's in you," Daina suddenly spoke up. "That's you."

Emma looked at her in surprise.

"That strength, it's in you," Daina repeated, and smiled slightly, just a corner of her mouth lifting. "Only it's...different. Softer."

"I could never be that unyielding, that unaccepting. And though I recognize his faults, I don't fault him for them."

Daina returned her look thoughtfully.

"Well, then you're a better person than he is," Steve opined.

"No," Emma immediately returned, with a shake of her head, "just different. That's all."

"Well, then, here's to being different," Daina said, holding her bottle aloft and smiling.

The four of them clinked the necks of their bottles together, in a toast to echo Daina's salute. They spent the next fifteen or twenty minutes in idle conversation, interrupted once by a quick trip to the garage so Steve could show Emma his workshop. Daina seemed to find this highly amusing and laughed, shaking her head.

"What?" Emma gave her a puzzled look, as she rose to her feet to follow Steve.

"That's hallowed ground. He never takes anyone in there." Daina winked at her. "Consider yourself special."

Later, back at the table, Emma glanced at her watch. "I should really be going," she announced regretfully. "There are things I need to attend to."

"Will you come back?" Marlene asked as they all stood, chairs sliding back almost soundlessly on the smooth deck surface.

"Yes, I'd like to, very much."

"How about tonight then? Join us for dinner."

Emma grinned, unable to stop herself. Glancing at Daina, she wasn't at all surprised to see she was amused all over again. "Sure," she said to Marlene, "that would be wonderful. Thank you."

"Seven o'clock?"

"Seven o'clock." Emma nodded. "It's been a pleasure to meet you both." She was again embraced by Marlene, again shook Steve's hand.

"I'll walk you to the car," Daina said.

Stopping before the SUV, Emma leaned back against the grille, reaching to take Daina's hands in hers. "They're wonderful."

Daina smiled. "They think you are."

Emma cocked her head. "How do you know that?"

"I know."

Emma searched her eyes, as blue and as deep as an uncharted ocean, eyes that anchored her even when she lost herself in them. She knew, with sudden clarity, that this was it, the time and the place. "I love you," she said, calmly, with utter certainty, words she'd never said to any other woman. The sheer simplicity and beauty of the statement caused a shiver to race through her.

Daina never lost her smile. "I know," she said.

Her response made Emma smile in return. Daina's eyes shone, and Emma was possessed of a delicious want, a need to kiss her. Then, somewhere behind her, in the driveway, she heard a sound. Daina's eyes shifted past Emma, over her shoulder; a second later, her face visibly paled with shock.

Alarmed, Emma craned her own head around. And when she saw who stood in the driveway, her own shock felt on a level with Daina's. And then it was gone, replaced with a sudden concern as Daina, without a word, slipped her hands out of her grasp and stalked forward. Emma turned as she went past.

She thought she could not have been more surprised than she was by the sight of the woman standing, alone, in the driveway. She was wrong. Because as Daina approached her, she addressed the woman in a tight, challenging voice and the name she used caused Emma's mouth to drop slightly open with incredulity.

"What the fuck are you doing here, Cathy?"

CHAPTER THIRTY

Between one moment and the next, Emma went from open-mouthed surprise to cold and calculated reserve. Her gaze sharpened, narrowed, focused on the woman; her nerves hummed and sang in warning, and her muscles tensed.

Without knowing precisely why she did it, aware only on some level that she must, she smoothly raised her left leg, placed the ball of her foot on the Explorer's bumper, and removed her gun from the ankle holster. With fluid precision she racked the slide, chambered a round. Balancing herself lightly on both feet, she then leaned against the hood, deceptively casual. It had taken her all of six seconds to do this. She never once took her eyes off the woman standing in the driveway.

So this *is Cathy Marks. How interesting.* Though the woman looked quite unremarkable and nonthreatening, uncertain and perhaps shy, there was a certain vague air of belligerence, a knife's edge of attitude in the set of her thin, pale lips, and in the almost sly way her eyes traveled up and down and over Daina as she approached, that set her further on her guard.

"Hello, Daina," Cathy Marks casually greeted Daina. "It's good to see you."

Daina came to a stop about five feet from her, without blocking Emma's view. A good thing, since Emma didn't want to reveal the fact that she had her weapon in hand.

"Answer my question," Daina demanded tightly. "What are you doing here?"

Cathy looked past Daina, toward Emma. "Hello, Emma," she called to her, sounding coolly offhand, friendly even.

Emma retained her icy composure, her cold, contemplative expression. She didn't return the greeting. She saw Daina angle her head almost imperceptibly and knew she was puzzled, wondering at the connection between the two of them. She'd have to explain that. Despite Daina's claim about not caring about Emma's past, it was a foregone conclusion that she would *want* to know, at least the facts, if not the details. Especially in light of what was currently taking place.

If she had ever known the woman's name, she had long since forgotten it. No doubt they had introduced themselves that night in the bar three years ago. But Emma had ever eschewed the use of names, preferring her choice of partner for the night to remain anonymous. It didn't always work out that way; some women had issues with anonymous sex. This woman, she recalled, had had issues of another sort entirely.

It had been a very warm night in September. The whole month of September had been unseasonably warm. She'd gone to the bar, Swank, with her best friend Nikki and her partner Samantha. It was a rare night out for the three of them. They were her preferred company, but she didn't often get to spend time with them. That night she devoted her attention to them, laughing, drinking, conversing. On the periphery of her awareness, the rest of the bar was a living, breathing animal, constantly shifting, moving. Halfway through the night, she realized she was being watched. Infrequently, when Nikki and Sam left the table, to dance or get another drink, she casually surveyed the room at large and always she noted the slim, young-looking redhead who eyed her intently from the far end of the bar.

Emma had always appreciated and been flattered by such attention. She and her world were not sacrosanct. This time proved to be no exception. She considered, as she always did, whether to acknowledge the attention. It had been her intention this night to spend her time with her friends. But it was her friends who actually released her.

Returning from a trip to the bathroom, Nikki said casually to her, "You have an admirer."

"I know," Emma replied quietly.

"Only one?" Sam had asked, playfully mocking. "How sad."

Emma chose not to dignify this with a response.

"So what do you think?" Nikki asked.

Emma knew what she was asking. "She's nice," she said, in her usual understated way. Then added thoughtfully, "She looks straight."

"Yeah, well, so do you," Nikki pointed out smoothly.

"Fuck you," Emma tossed back good-naturedly, even though she knew it was true. Nikki had once ventured that it was Emma's lack of stereotypical attributes that attracted women to her. Emma chose to believe the reason was not quite so prosaic as that. "I'm spending the night with the two of you."

"If *you're* spending the night with *us*, *we* need to talk." Sam gave Nikki a pointed look.

Emma grinned.

In the end, the two of them had encouraged her, and in the end, Emma approached the young woman. Spent some time with her, chatted with her, warmed to her. Bought her a drink, danced with her, forgotten her name; kissed her once, twice, and extended an invitation. And been accepted. She had gone to her friends without ever once introducing the woman to them and explained she would be leaving. They weren't surprised.

And in the car, not hers, since she wasn't driving, the young woman turned to her. "We can't go to my place," she announced, seeming tense. "My roommate is home."

Emma had looked at her, and in that moment, had overridden one of her other basic rules: Never take a woman to her own place. Her hormones had overridden her common sense. The woman in question was young, hot, more than *nice*. It was a no-brainer. Later, she had time to reflect that she hadn't been thinking with her brain at all.

There was a quiet kind of desperation to the girl, to her attentions, her hunger, that at first excited Emma. Soon, though, that excitement waned, and her arousal dissipated as she became aware just how desperate the girl appeared to be. The girl came hard and fast, almost against her will, it seemed. And immediately after, burst into tears.

Flummoxed, feeling she had severely misstepped, misread, misjudged what had always been for her a relatively simple exercise, she hadn't known how to comfort the girl. And that seemed to infuriate her.

"Fuck you!" she'd cried, actually had screamed in a high-pitched breathless way. "Fuck you, you're just like her, you don't love me! Fuck you!"

Any thought of comforting fled, to be replaced with a sad kind of perusal. Obviously, the girl was carrying a torch for someone, was probably on the rebound. "Look," she started to say gently, "I'm sorry. I think, maybe—"

"You're not sorry!" the girl had snarled.

And before Emma even knew what was happening, the girl whipped one thin arm back and around, striking Emma an open-handed blow against her face, so solid, so forcefully, her head rocked.

Stunned, her cheek and ear stinging painfully, Emma felt a rage suffuse her, had felt for the first time in her life that she might actually hit another woman in anger. Swallowing down the heat of her fury, she said coldly, unmindful of her nakedness, "I want you to leave. Now."

"Or what? You'll arrest me?" was the snide retort. "Yeah, sure, what-the-fuck-ever."

Emma's apartment walls were adorned with artwork and educational certificates and diplomas. Some of the latter denoted her occupation. Obviously, the girl had seen them. Her attitude was shocking in its brazenness.

"Leave," Emma repeated, and this time her teeth met and her upper lip lifted threateningly. "Now." She grabbed the girl's clothing. "Get dressed." She threw the clothing at her.

"You're just like her, you know that?" The words were spat at her hotly, vehemently. "All you fucking dykes are the same, you're fucking *whores*."

"Yeah, sure, what-the-fuck-ever," Emma returned icily, in a cutting parody of the girl's own words. She gathered her own clothes and dressed quickly.

And then the girl had started crying again and Emma, completely nonplussed, had to literally haul her off the bed, insist she dress, and escort her out to the front entrance. Mind whirling, she had returned to her suite, blasting herself for being an idiot. She could still taste the girl on her lips. She went to the bathroom and showered for what seemed an eternity in an attempt to be rid of her essence.

And now, that very same girl stood in the driveway, looking at her almost defiantly.

"I came to tell you I'm sorry," Cathy Marks said, finally shifting her eyes from Emma and answering Daina's question. "I came to tell you I had nothing to do with all of this, and I'm sorry for what's happened."

Emma could see Daina's spine was rigid with tension.

"And so what are you *doing* here?" Daina demanded yet again, as if the explanation already supplied had not appeased her.

Emma didn't know what kind of dynamics had defined Daina's relationship with Cathy Marks. She only knew that what she was seeing right now looked like an incendiary fuse waiting for a lighted match. Her hand flexed ever so slightly over the grip of the Glock. The muscles in her back and shoulders corresponded.

"Tell her why you're here," she advised Cathy evenly. She herself couldn't fathom why the woman had shown up. She only knew she wanted that dreadful tension to leave Daina's body.

Cathy shot Emma a look that was laced with anger, hatred. "I want to talk to you alone," she said to Daina. Her voice, completely at odds with the look she had directed at Emma, was soft, subtly pleading.

Daina was having none of it. "This is as alone as it gets. Talk."

Cathy looked back and forth between Daina and Emma. Finally, she said, all in a rush, "Okay. Okay, this, I want to tell you this: I had nothing to do with any of this, this whole thing, it wasn't me. It was him. I knew about it, but I wasn't involved. Never, I would never—if maybe you thought—I would never hurt you. I wasn't even here, he did it all on his own. I only just got back into town today, to these messages, telling me he'd been arrested, could I contact the police. I'm on my way there now, I don't even know what for. I wouldn't do this, not to you I wouldn't. I wanted to tell you. Okay? I wanted to tell you."

There followed an infinitesimal pause, all it took, apparently, for Daina to process the information. And then she said, with a coldness Emma had only heard from her once before, "Fine. You've told me. Now get the fuck out of here."

Cathy's face blanched, fell. "But...Daina..." Her mouth and throat worked, as she struggled with what she wanted to say. "I...Jesus, I..."

"Don't," Daina interrupted harshly, and she no longer sounded cold. Now she sounded hot, angry. Emma watched as she dropped her chin and shook her head in tight negation.

"But...I love you...can't you..." Cathy's voice was small, shocked, lost.

Daina, just in the act of turning away, whirled, and Emma

could read the fury in her posture. "Don't!" she cried, even more harshly. "Just fucking *don't!*"

Emma tensed, shifted.

Cathy Marks visibly recoiled, stepping back a foot.

"I never asked you to and I don't *want* you to!" Daina rasped. "Okay? Is that clear enough for you? Don't! Just *leave!*"

Whatever the look on Daina's face, Emma was not privy to it. She did note that Cathy blanched further and then, swiftly shooting Emma another one of those hate-filled looks, she turned and stumbled down the driveway to the street, began to run toward the green Sunfire.

Emma remembered that flicker of motion within that Sunfire that she had dismissed, and she chastised herself for a fool. And then, her attention was only for Daina, who had turned, head down, and was coming back to her. She quickly ejected the round in the chamber, dumped it into her pocket, placed the gun in the waistband of her jeans. She stepped forward to take Daina into her arms. Distantly, she was aware of the Sunfire starting up and accelerating away.

"Hey," she said, wrapping her arms around her, pulling her in. "Hey." Trying to comfort, because Daina was crying now, though Emma hadn't a clue as to why.

Daina gripped her with a fierceness that almost unbalanced her. "I'm sorry," she said, muffling her words into Emma's shoulder. "I love you. I'm sorry."

"You're sorry you love me?" She opted for comical confusion, trying to lighten the mood because the emotional outpouring was so unsettling.

"No!" Daina made a sound, a cross between a cough and a laugh. She gently punched Emma's arm. "No." Her blue eyes swam in pools of tears. "What the fuck was that? She can't do that, did she think she could just bulldoze her way in, that I'd just *let* her in? How could she *do* that?" She blinked and her tears ran, joining the others on her cheeks.

Emma suddenly understood: Daina felt violated. Violation did not always occur on a physical level.

"You're right," she soothed. "You're completely right. She

can't just expect to insinuate herself into your life. She has to be invited. Somehow."

Daina's tears seemed to have slowed. Emma brushed away those that remained. She briefly considered how best to say what she felt needed to be said. In the end, hoping Daina would understand, she could only ask, "Do you remember when I gave you my phone number?"

Daina nodded. "Yes." A second passed, then two. And then Emma saw the light of comprehension dawn. "Ohhh."

"It was a small thing," Emma said with a shrug. "Yet maybe not so small."

"No," Daina agreed.

Emma fixed her with an unwavering look. "I love you," she said quietly. "And I want you."

Daina opened her mouth to speak.

"No, please, just…listen, okay?"

And Emma fell silent. She had never been in a position where her words counted for so much. She felt as if they were precious, fragile, that she had to deliver them with extreme care. "I've never had what I have with you. And walking away from someone is the easiest thing in the world for me. I never let anyone in close."

She paused, stared into those blue orbs that patiently reflected her own image. "But you, I haven't walked away from you. And you are so close I feel you, here—" she touched the spot above her heart, "—inside me. I want you, like I've never wanted anyone, anything, in my life. Beside you, everything pales in comparison. There's a whole world that wouldn't exist without you." She dropped her voice, afraid she had said too much, afraid it wasn't enough. "I want that world. It scares the hell out of me, but I want it, Daina. I want it."

Daina just looked at her. Emma trembled somewhere deep inside. And then Daina opened her mouth once again to speak, and what she said was, "Oh my." And she pulled herself in to Emma, and Emma clutched her tightly. And thought, *Oh my, indeed.*

They sat in the Explorer, the air-conditioning on to escape the heat. The Glock sat, like some weird ornament, on the dash where Emma had placed it.

"Was I in danger?" Daina asked, giving the gun a significant look.

"I didn't know. I was taking precautions."

"That was a bit of a tense scene, I guess," Daina said carefully, eyes on her now, as if looking for something.

Emma nodded. "It was."

"Did you…think you might…have to shoot her?" This was asked even more carefully.

Emma guessed that Daina was a little shaken by the fact that she'd drawn her weapon, which was understandable. "I didn't know," she replied, just as carefully. "I had no idea why she was here, and you were pretty freaked out. I was just taking precautions. It was automatic."

Daina seemed to consider this. Her expression changed to a frown. She met Emma's eyes once more, and asked bluntly, "Why does she hate you so much?"

The question surprised Emma. Daina didn't miss much. "I don't think it's personal. She doesn't even know me. I think, honestly, she probably hates everyone, if hate is the right word to use. She seems to be very angry and very lost. She was when I met her as well." This last she added deliberately.

Daina said nothing. She just waited.

"That was three years ago," Emma went on. "Sometime in September." She saw Daina's eyes widen slightly at this, and could guess as to the reason. She continued. "I picked her up in a bar. A one-night stand." She grinned ruefully, humorlessly. "Not even that, a couple of hours. She was…hugely angry, very hurt. I figured out pretty quickly she was carrying a torch for someone."

Daina's breath escaped her in a light huff. "Me," she said quietly.

Emma nodded. "It makes sense. The timing is right. But I didn't know her name. Or I'd forgotten it. Whichever. I wasn't able to put anything together until just now, when I saw her face."

After a moment's silence, Daina, with a wary look, ventured, "Did you—?"

Emma tried not to grin, was mostly successful. "Did I sleep with her?" She angled her head in acknowledgment. "After a fashion." At Daina's puzzled look, she clarified. "It was...one-sided. She got more out of it than I did, I'm sure." She paused, then added, almost as an afterthought, "She hit me."

Daina gaped. "She *hit* you?"

"Yeah." Again the rueful grin. "Just hauled off and whacked me. Hard. She was spitting mad. I almost hit her back, I was so shocked. Instead I told her to leave. Which she eventually did, but not before tearing into me, screaming at me, 'You're just like her, you don't love me, you're just like her.' I had no clue who she was talking about—"

"Me," Daina said again, this time with a note of recognition, resignation.

Emma angled her head once more, lowering her eyelids in agreement. "She was so...*resentful*. Like there was something I should have been doing that I wasn't. I didn't get it. I'd only just met her. It was just for one night, I'd been clear on that. But somewhere, somehow, I made a mistake. And it got messy."

"I don't think I want to hear any more." Daina sounded edgy, unhappy.

"There's nothing more to tell. I never saw her again." Emma shrugged. "I made a mistake. I never repeated it."

Daina gave her a curious look. "What was your mistake?"

Returning her look calmly, Emma replied, after a moment's contemplation, "I have a few...self-imposed rules. I've made it a habit not to go against them."

"Rules are made to be broken," Daina said.

"Some rules. Under some circumstances," Emma allowed.

It took a moment before Daina's eyes once more lighted with understanding. "Ah," she said, and smiled. "Giving me your number."

Emma returned her look steadily, only nodding once in acknowledgment.

"Well, I'm glad you're not inflexible." Daina's tone and expression bordered on coy.

Emma grinned ever so slightly. "I never claimed to be," she returned mildly.

"No. But you're very good at keeping yourself to yourself. It's...challenging."

To this, Emma said nothing.

"You've been with a lot of women," Daina said.

Emma narrowed her eyes slightly, tensing as if bracing herself.

"I don't expect you to talk about it," Daina went on easily, gently. "I don't really care."

"So why ask?"

"I'm not asking."

Emma regarded her thoughtfully for a few moments. Then, finally, quietly, she said, "Yes."

Daina's eyes and mouth hinted at a smile, a serious smile, not amused. "Thank you."

"For?"

"You know," was all Daina said.

A part of Emma refused to presume that she did. But another part of her answered, obliquely, *For this, that, everything.* She held Daina's eyes for a moment, and the moment stretched out. And then, hating herself for saying it, but needing to all the same, she said, "I don't know if I can do this. You and me. I don't know—"

Daina surprised her, by pointing out gently, "You already are."

With a startled blink, Emma realized she was right.

"I understand why you would say that," Daina continued. "Or at least I think I do. Based on what you've shared, about your family, I think I understand."

Emma wasn't entirely sure that she did, but the fact that she made the effort made all the difference.

"You need to go," Daina said matter-of-factly.

"Yes. I'm sorry."

"Don't be. Just hurry back. I don't know what it's like to miss you." Daina smiled. "I might not like it much."

With an answering smile, Emma told her, "I'll be here at seven, if not sooner. Shall I bring wine?"

"They have a fondness for a nice merlot."

"A merlot it is, then."

"Kiss me," Daina said, suddenly intent.

Emma leaned across and kissed her, and as ever, was shocked by the feelings aroused.

Abruptly, Daina broke the kiss and pulled away. Her eyes were wide, her chest rising and falling visibly. "Hurry back, okay?" She let herself out of the vehicle, slamming the door behind her.

Emma watched, a little numbly, as she dashed away up the walk, up the steps and into the house. She took a deep breath, reholstered the Glock, and left the Buchanan residence.

CHAPTER THIRTY-ONE

She let herself into her apartment, and the cool air, carrying the familiar, albeit slightly stale, scents of her home rushed toward her, as if in greeting. She moved to open wide the sliding glass doors to her balcony. She didn't mind the fact that the air outside was hot and muggy; judging by the storm clouds she'd seen building off to the west, it would freshen soon.

She stood for a while, staring out the screen, past her balcony, to the park beyond. It was empty. As empty as her apartment. The thought struck her, hard. She'd never considered her apartment empty before. But now it seemed as if the very room mocked her; the furniture, the appliances, the framed prints and diplomas on the walls, the paint on the walls, all seemed to mock her, to jeer at her: *You thought this was a home? Think again. This is just dead space. Dead space in need of filling.*

Daina could fill this space. Daina could fill a world. The lack of her here, a place she'd never been, space she'd never occupied, was almost painful.

Christ, when did I become so maudlin?

She unpacked first, and dumped everything on the floor in the laundry room. Even though most of it was clean, she was possessed of an irrational urge to rewash everything. Foolish maybe, but she didn't really care.

She checked the answering machine. Seven messages, none from Michaels. She sorted through her mail which she'd retrieved from her almost overflowing mailbox on the way up. In the haste of the relocation, she hadn't thought to arrange for someone to collect it. Good thing she'd only been gone for a week.

It felt distinctly odd to be alone; she'd become so accustomed to Daina's presence, she kept half-expecting to see or hear her. Soothing herself with the thought that she would see her later, she stretched out on the sofa; the muggy afternoon heat had begun to permeate the apartment and she felt herself getting drowsy.

When she awoke, she looked at her watch and was surprised to see she'd slept for two hours. It was now after five. And she still hadn't heard back from Michaels. She wondered if he knew Cathy Marks was in town, or if Cathy Marks had made it to the station to see her husband after the sergeant had left. The thought of the woman was troubling.

It was only as she was folding her laundry on her bed that the question she hadn't considered, hadn't asked, suddenly popped into her head. She froze, right in the middle of folding a T-shirt. *How had Cathy Marks known where to find Daina, how had she known that Daina would be there, at her parents', at that time?* Emma stared, unseeing, at the shirt held loosely in her hands.

"How could she have known that?" she asked herself, under her breath. A half-formed thought filled her mind, sickening her, worrying her, frightening her: Cathy Marks could not have known, unless—

The phone rang, startling her. Her heart, already pounding

rather violently, slammed in her chest. She convulsively dropped the shirt on the bed, reached for the cordless handset on the night table.

Emma was vastly relieved to hear Daina's voice. "Hey, sweetheart, hi."

"Oh, I *do* like the sound of that," Daina said, and Emma could hear the smile in her voice.

Her own smile faded, as she asked, "Are you okay?"

"Yeah. Just missing you. A *lot*." A pause, then, "Why?"

Emma sat down on the bed. She ventured carefully, "Did you tell Michaels that you were planning on going to your parent's once we left the house?"

"It came up. I didn't tell him, he guessed. Or assumed. Whichever." Judging by her tone, Daina still harbored residual feelings of resentment. "He wanted to know if I'd be here if he needed to contact me. Why?"

Michaels would not have released that information, Emma knew. This had nothing to do with him, or anyone else on the police force. That sickening, worried feeling in her gut intensified.

"And you didn't tell anyone else?" she asked, though the question was purely rhetorical.

"Who would I tell?" Daina now sounded a little impatient. "Emma—"

"I need you to ask your parents something, honey," she interrupted, rising restlessly to her feet, sharpening her tone, "and I need you to ask them right now."

"Okay—"

"Ask them if anyone called today, questioning your whereabouts, or if you were expected there anytime soon. Will you do that, please?"

"Yeah, of course. Hang on." Daina no longer sounded impatient. She'd caught the urgency in Emma's voice. She took the phone with her as she went to find Steve and Marlene. Emma heard muted voices. When she came back on the line, Daina sounded calm. "Emma? No, nobody called. They were home all morning and nobody called. Babe, what's going on?"

Babe. No one had ever called her that before.

"I need you to do something else now. Go and look out at the street and see if there's a green Sunfire anywhere in the area, but *don't leave the house* and try not to make yourself visible."

"Okay. We have blinds, no problem." There was a pause, during which Emma's pulse thumped loudly in her ears. Daina came back on, said, "Okay, no, there's no green Sunfire. Isn't that what Cathy was driving? Why am I looking for Cathy's car?" Daina was still calm, but her voice was hard and sharp, like cut glass.

"Because a question occurred to me that I don't have the answer to," she replied, her voice level but hurried now. "How did she know that you were going to be there?"

Silence on the other end.

"I hadn't thought of that," Daina admitted quietly.

"Neither did I. Not until just now. I don't know if it's relevant, but I'm not taking any chances. I want you to lock the doors, stay in the house. I'm coming over."

"Okay, but—shouldn't we call the police? If—"

"Michaels hasn't called me back. I don't know where he is or how to get hold of him." Emma grabbed her gun and ankle holster. "The police won't come. She's not a suspect, they have her husband in custody, and she hasn't done anything wrong." She was fastening her holster, her foot resting on the bed, trying not to hurry, thinking fast, trying not to make any mistakes. She jammed her gun in. "They might if I call them, but I can get there faster anyway. Wait for me." She was striding down the hall now, for her shoes, her keys.

"Okay." And then, quietly, fiercely, "I love you."

And Emma took a moment to smile. "I love *you.* Now let me go," she said gently.

At the door, she pulled on a pair of New Balance running shoes, swept up the keys and her cell phone from the shelving unit to her left, stuffed the phone in her pocket, and opened the door.

"Hello, Emma."

A blur of movement in her peripheral vision, an arm whipping up and across, the hand gripping something brown, shiny. She never even had time to react. The brown, shiny object connected brutally with the curve of her forehead where it blended into her brow, she *felt* her brow split, pain and light exploded in her head as she reeled, and then she was falling, and everything faded into nothing.

CHAPTER THIRTY-TWO

Daina locked all the doors and didn't leave the house. She told her parents about Emma's worry, which was now her worry, and which then became their worry. She told them that Emma was on her way over. They were visibly relieved to hear this.

And then she sat down to wait. Not patiently, since patience had never been one of her strong points. Every once in a while she went to stand at the window to peer through the blinds. She looked for a green Sunfire, didn't see one. She looked for anything out of the ordinary, saw nothing.

The minutes passed, agonizingly slow. She felt herself becoming anxious, caught herself glancing at the phone, found herself unable to sit at all, and began to pace, to the window and back, over and over. She told herself not to worry, but worried anyway. She told herself to stop pacing, stop going to the window, but couldn't seem to. She continued to wait.

Ten minutes past Emma's anticipated arrival time, her resolve snapped. She grabbed for the cordless phone on the coffee table, punched in Emma's home number. She waited, listened, breathing through her mouth. It rang and rang, until the answering machine picked up. She disconnected, then thought to call the cell phone, only to pause and blink stupidly.

"Shit," she muttered. She didn't know the number, had never called it. For a protracted moment, her mind went completely blank. And then she remembered and she strode to the kitchen where her parents were pretending to drink coffee. They looked up, somewhat anxiously.

"I need Emma's cell phone number," she said without preamble.

"Oh!" Her mother visibly started, then hurriedly crossed to the fridge. She plucked a slip of paper from behind a sunflower magnet, handed it over.

Daina glanced at the number on the slip as she entered it on the keypad; the cell phone rang four times before the voice mail kicked in, and again she disconnected without leaving a message. She looked at her parents.

"I can't get ahold of her," she told them quietly. "I don't know where she is. I don't know what to do."

From the way they looked back at her, it was obvious they didn't know what to do either. She turned away, to stare out the patio doors. *She told me to wait for her. She told me not to leave the house. I'll wait. I won't leave. Not yet*, she thought grimly.

It was the phone that brought her around. Its unusually strident and sharp tone sliced through the fog and agony in her head with all the delicacy of a ripsaw. She grimaced, half-aware, but still half-floundering in some thick, soupy darkness that was like mud filling her brain. Her grimace caused a line of fiery pain to burn its way across her left brow to the temple;

tears immediately squeezed out between her tightly closed eyelids. The pain was as effective as a slap in the face. Complete awareness flowed into her, over her. She became aware of the feel of the nap of the carpet against the left side of her face, became aware she was lying on her left side, that there was a horribly uncomfortable, hot, knife's edge of pain burning across her shoulders, between her shoulder blades.

She gamely tried to move, to relieve the pain, tried to open her eyes at the same time. For a moment, she could do neither, and she felt a wave of panic engulf her. A moment later, her right eye popped open; her left seemed glued shut. And then it, too, opened, but only to a slit. At the same time, she realized, with renewed panic, that she had been bound, her arms wrenched behind her back, her ankles tight together.

What the FUCK! her brain hollered.

And then, above and slightly behind her, she heard, "Well, that gives the term 'wake-up call' a whole new meaning, now doesn't it?"

Emma stiffened, went absolutely still. She recognized the voice. And suddenly she knew what had happened, what *was* happening. The near-wild, panicky fire heating her blood disappeared, to be replaced with the chilling cold of ice water. She heard a soft *thump*, as of someone landing lightly on the carpeted floor, then heard approaching, whispering footfalls.

The phone had ceased ringing; the answering machine had picked up, but there had been no message. Now, in her left pocket, where it pressed painfully into her hip, her cell phone began to ring. And she knew instantly it was Daina, because Emma was late and hadn't called, and now Daina was worried. These thoughts were wiped from her mind as a shadow fell across her, and sneakers and jeans-clad legs appeared before her. She tried to raise her head, felt the carpet, sticky and wet, resist, then give, felt a bolt of pain blast through her head, snake down her back and across her shoulders. Her vision shimmered, grayed. *Concussion. I think I have a concussion.*

She blinked, trying to focus, and lowered her head to a more comfortable angle. And then a figure crouched before her.

"Don't get up on my account," Cathy Marks told her blandly.

The cell phone stopped ringing. Emma's ears continued to. She was feeling vaguely nauseous; she fought against it, fought against the black tide that was at the edge of her awareness which threatened to swamp her and pull her back under.

"You're a popular girl," Cathy said. "Phones ringing all over the place."

"It's called having a life," Emma muttered acerbically. "Maybe you should get one." If it *was* Daina calling, she didn't want this woman clueing in to the fact. Cathy Marks swam before her, then solidified, sharpened. Emma could see her little comment hadn't exactly pleased Cathy. But she seemed calm enough. She could also see the gun she held, an older .38, dangling from one hand, between her knees. This, then, was what she had been struck with. A second later, she remembered her own gun, but immediately knew it had been taken from her. Obviously, from the way her ankles were bound, the Glock had been discovered and removed.

Cathy must have seen her eyes fix on the .38, must have known what she was thinking. "If you're wondering about your gun, it's up there." She jerked a thumb back in the direction of the tiered shelving unit.

She spoke in an easy, conversational tone, seemed utterly calm, utterly serene, and was so obviously utterly unstable.

"What are you planning on doing?" Emma asked, not because she couldn't guess but because she could; she wanted to stall the woman, give Daina time to realize Emma had been seriously detained and to call the police. With a story, *any* story, to get them there, to protect her. She shifted slightly as she asked the question, exploring her restrictions, feeling the bonds on her wrists and ankles rub painfully. They were excruciatingly tight.

Cathy scuttled back a few feet. "You know what I'm planning," she said shortly.

Emma's back and shoulders were beginning to ache now, to say nothing of her head. "Okay then, why?" She shifted again, rolled back slightly, only to come up against the sofa. Well, she could rest against that for now. It wasn't very comfortable, but the discomfort kept her alert.

"Why?" Cathy shrugged. "Because."

"*Because?* What are you, ten?" Emma looked at her with disgust and disbelief. "Because. What the fuck is that?"

"I don't have to explain myself to you," was the cold response. "You're lucky you're still alive. And that I have to go."

"Wait!" Emma jerked with alarm, then calmed herself. "Wait. So this was all you, right? Even though you said it wasn't, it was, right?"

"Very good, Constable."

"So what about your husband?"

A vague look of annoyance crossed Cathy's face. "I handled him completely wrong. When I knew Daina was coming to the city, it gave me an idea. So I told him about her, told him I loved her, I wanted a divorce. I wanted it set in motion before she came to town. I wanted to be with her, thought I would be. I was stupid. He wouldn't give me a divorce. Just kept saying he loved me, that I belonged with him. And I couldn't just *leave*, where would I go, what would I do? And then he threatened me with an infidelity suit. And I was screwed. I couldn't afford that; he and I both knew it. I kept thinking there has to be a way, I can be with her, I just have to think of a way. And then I'd think of how she left me, and pretty soon I couldn't think of anything else. I loved her, I told her I loved her, but that didn't matter to her. Her and her high and mighty 'I refuse to be a part of this' shit. Like she was so innocent. And then she hightailed it out of here, didn't say goodbye or anything, just fucked off and left me behind to pick up the pieces."

Cathy was speaking blandly, with very little emphasis on her words or in her tone. Emma was finding it hard to retain a continued level of alertness in the face of such monotony. She shifted once more; pain thumped through her head, scorched her eyeballs, wicked down her back, across her shoulders. *Instant alert*, she thought sarcastically. She felt her nausea rising again. She clenched her jaw, swallowed against it.

"So I made a deal with him. Take her out of the picture. With her gone, I wouldn't want to leave him. I didn't think he'd actually go for it, but he did. He was all for it. Go figure. He started making all these plans. And then just like that," Cathy snapped her fingers, startling Emma with the sudden action, "I was in. I couldn't think of anything else. So we started planning together. It was easy after that. He's an electronics tech and, conveniently, he's also the light and sound man for the concert hall; he can do amazing things with wires and switches and timers and such. The bomb was his idea, but he sold me on it pretty quick. It was perfect. And for the concert that night they had brought in their own people. He had no affiliation with the show that night at all. His name never came up. It was so simple. And it almost worked."

Cathy paused, and for the first time a flash of emotion lit up her voice, her eyes. "Except for you," she said tightly. "And you have been getting in the way ever since. When she was in the hospital, I had him follow you, to find out what floor she was on. He found out, but he couldn't get to her. I understand he took his frustrations out on you."

Emma said nothing.

"And then you both disappeared. I knew the only way to get you out of hiding was to make it safe for you. So I told him what to do. He did it. I told him not to worry, I'd get him out. He believed me. Like I'd actually do that. What an idiot." Cathy shook her head. "All I had to was wait. And not for very long. It was easy. Getting this gun was harder." She waggled the gun briefly, and then her eyes narrowed, sharpened. "And I've been practicing. So don't think I'm a complete novice."

Again, Emma said nothing.

"I actually did try to give her a chance to redeem herself, when I showed up today. That was a stupid move. Considering how it turned out, I shouldn't have wasted my time. But I thought, well, at least give her the chance. I didn't have the gun with me then or I would have shot her right there. Bitch. What a fucking bitch." Cathy shook her head with obvious disgust. And then she abruptly stood. "And now, if you'll excuse me, I have to go."

Emma jerked with surprise. "Wait. What about me?" she asked, wanting to stall the woman as long as possible.

Cathy looked down at her. "You don't get it, do you? I don't care about you, I never did. It was him who wanted you dead.

Two dykes with one stone, he said. He thought that was funny. You were a rotten fuck, and you've been nothing but a pain in the ass since, but I don't really care about you. But just so you know, once I'm finished with her, I do intend to come back." She held up Emma's key chain, jingled it. And then she turned, shoving the gun into the back of her pants and pulling her shirt over it so it was out of sight. She left the apartment without another word or a backward glance.

CHAPTER THIRTY-THREE

During the time that Daina waited, she almost wore a path in the plush carpeting of the living room with her endless pacing. She did not want to think of, or dwell on, the myriad possible scenarios that could be delaying Emma, but she couldn't help herself. The thoughts were making her feel ill. Almost all of them ended with Emma broken and bleeding, somewhere she would never find her, could never get to her.

Finally, when she could stand it no longer, she stalked into the kitchen and grabbed the phone book from the shelf.

"Daina, what are you doing?" her father asked, rising to his feet and moving toward her.

"Looking for something," she muttered tightly. Her entire

body felt like an overstretched steel cable, taut and thrumming and so terribly close to the breaking point.

"What are you looking for?"

"Her address," she rasped through clenched teeth. She felt herself beginning to shake.

"What?"

"Her address!" Daina's voice rose, as she slammed her fist down on the phone book. "*Her address!* I don't know her fucking address!" And then she started to cry, in anger, in despair, in shame. "I'm in love with her and I don't know her address! I don't know where she lives!" Tears poured down her face. "How pathetic is *that*?"

Steve Buchanan pulled her into his arms and soothed her, and she held tightly to him for all of thirty seconds, sobbing uncontrollably, before she gently disengaged herself from his arms. She glanced once more at the phone book listing, and then slammed it shut.

"Fremont Avenue, where the hell is Fremont Avenue?" she murmured, wiping at her eyes.

"Daina, you are not going there." Her father stepped toward her, one step. "She told you to stay here, not to leave."

"Yeah, well, she's not here, she was supposed to come to me," Daina reminded him sharply. "Obviously, something's happened. So I'm going to her."

"Daina, listen to yourself. That makes no sense."

Daina knew he was right, it made no sense at all, but it was better than sitting here waiting.

"She could be anywhere between here and there," he pointed out.

"Fremont is on the other end of the city, in the south end," her mother provided, though whether as a way to help or as a deterrent, Daina couldn't tell.

"Well then, what am I supposed to do?" she flared at her father. "What do you suggest?"

"Call the police," he told her.

"Call the police," her mother echoed firmly.

She is *the police!* Daina felt like screaming. Instead, she clenched her teeth and asked, in tightly clipped words, "And tell them *what*, exactly? That my girlfriend is late? That she *thinks* I might be in danger, but she's not sure? That the woman whose *husband* tried to kill me might also be trying to kill me, but we don't *know* for certain? Is *that* what I'm supposed to say? Because it's the truth, isn't it?"

"Tell them anything, anything at all to get them here," her father advised. "Emma's not here, and she's out of touch. If she can't get here to protect you, she would want somebody here who could. Call the police."

And Daina realized he was right, that his reasoning made all the sense in the world, and she was ashamed of her irrational behavior. She stared at him for a moment; he stared back. Finally she nodded and reached for the phone. That was when she heard it, all three of them heard it: footsteps running up the walk, up the steps. And then, pounding on the front door.

Daina whirled and dashed through the living room, filled with a relief so huge it threatened to overwhelm her. She reached the front door, unlocked it, yanked it open without hesitation.

"Emma, Jesus—!" she began.

She saw Cathy Marks first, saw the gun in her hand second.

"Is this where she was heading off to?" Cathy inquired mildly.

It was only after Cathy had left that Emma saw what she'd missed earlier. On the floor, a few feet away, lay a bundle of what looked like multicolored rope. Emma raised her head, tried unsuccessfully to ignore the pain, and looked hard at the bundle. At first, she couldn't make out what it was. And then it hit her: bungee tie-downs. All of them a foot long. *Oh, dear God, is* that *what she tied me with?*

The pain was incredible as she shifted, swung her legs forward and craned her neck to see...bungee cord, wrapped around her ankles. A surge of elation filled her and then another, as she flexed her wrists and felt an infinitesimal give. Bungee cord. The cords themselves were wrapped hideously tight and were cutting and burning cruelly into her; the metal hooks attached to the ends of them were digging into her flesh like icepicks.

With a sense of vicious euphoria, she spared a moment to glance at the clock on the wall in the kitchen directly opposite her: five fifty-four P.M. She began to work at freeing her wrists, shifting over onto her right shoulder, almost banging her head on the floor. The movement caused pain to flash through her skull like lightning, a wave of nausea clutched her gut, and she whimpered and swallowed and tried not to hurry, but knew that she had to. She worked her wrists back and forth almost frantically, pulling, stretching, twisting; she broke out in a light sweat.

Panting, trying to calm herself, she felt the nausea rising and tried to fight it down. She lifted her head and tried to roll onto her knees, pulling her wrists as wide apart as she could, which was only a centimeter, if that, and twisting at the same time. It was the impetus she'd required because, suddenly, her right hand slipped free with almost ridiculous ease, and she was shaking the cord off, shifting position, reaching back to free her legs, kicking them free. And as she rose up on her knees, she felt like laughing in triumph. But the sudden change in elevation was too much for her. A solid wall of black slammed into her; she passed out, dropping unceremoniously back to the carpet.

At Cathy's words, Daina tore her eyes away from the compact weapon in her hand and glared at her with barely controlled fury.

"Where is she?" she demanded hotly. "What have you done? What the *fuck* have you done?"

"Relax. She's fine. So far," Cathy assured her. Her eyes were odd-looking, glassy, almost seeming unfocused. Her voice was bizarrely, disconcertingly mild. "She may have a concussion. I hit her pretty hard, but other than that, she's okay."

"Where is she?" Daina took a threatening step forward, oblivious to the danger to herself.

Cathy chose to remind her of it, brutally. Her eyes suddenly lost their glassy look. She took a step back, raised the gun and pointed it at Daina's forehead. Her eyes were sharp, focused. Daina retreated that one step back in shock and surprise.

"I could kill you right now," Cathy told her, losing her conversational tone. Her voice was cold and brittle, her words ice. "And if you move one more step, I will."

Daina blinked. "What do you want?" she asked, managing to dredge up the words somehow, though her throat felt constricted with fear.

"You. I want you." The conversational tone was back. "Step outside."

Daina hesitated.

"Now!" Once again cold, brittle.

Daina had never been in the presence of madness, had never been face-to-face with it, but she had no doubt about Cathy Marks. She stepped out onto the concrete landing of the front steps. Cathy backed down one step to give her room. And then looked past her. At the same time, Steve Buchanan called, "Daina? What's going on?"

"Ah, ah, ah, no one else comes out." Cathy spoke over Daina's shoulder. "If you do, I will shoot you. Don't think that I won't. I'd rather not, only because it's so damn inconvenient, but I will if I have to." She focused again on Daina. "Close the door, Daina. If they follow, they're dead. You might want to impress that upon them."

Daina did as she was told, calling out, "Dad, don't come out. She's not kidding. Stay in the house." She pulled the door shut, let the screen door swing back.

"I imagine they're going to call the police, which means I don't have much time," Cathy said thoughtfully. The gun was now pointing deliberately at Daina's abdomen.

"What do you want, Cathy? Why are you doing this?"

"I want what you want." Cathy seemed surprised. "I want to be happy. Do you want to see your girlfriend? I bet that would make *you* happy. I'll take you to her. In fact, I insist. You know, it's really rather ironic that the two of you ended up together." Cathy's voice made the abrupt switch to hardness once more. "Move it, now, down to the car."

Holy Christ, she's completely whacked. And because she had no choice, Daina obeyed. She walked slightly ahead of Cathy, terrifyingly aware of the gun pointed at her, of the cold, almost detached determination of the woman wielding that gun. She thought of Emma, and prayed that she was okay. As they walked quickly across the lawn to the street, she absently noted that there was a storm building, that it would break upon them very shortly. Distantly, she heard the sound of squealing tires far down the street. *Someone in a hurry,* she thought distractedly. They reached the Sunfire and Cathy stepped aside.

"Open the door," she ordered.

Daina did. On the seat were a handful of multicolored bungee cords.

"Bring them out."

She did as she was told. She held the cords loosely in one hand. Cathy stepped forward, between her and the car, and took them from her. And then she frowned. "Shit," she muttered.

Daina realized what the problem was: how to tie Daina up without relinquishing control of the gun. It made for a pretty problem. A second later, she became aware of the sound of an engine gunning down the crescent. Cathy heard it, too, and they both looked to see a huge, black pickup truck roaring down the street toward them.

CHAPTER THIRTY-FOUR

Once again, it was the sound of the phone ringing that dragged Emma back to consciousness. She wrenched her eyes open, the sound of the phone tearing through her tortured head, jangling her nerve endings, setting off her nausea once more. She was on her stomach, flat out, and oh, Jesus, her head hurt, and the trilling phone only exacerbated it. She struggled to her knees, pushing up with her hands, fighting valiantly against the urge to vomit out her guts onto the carpet. Her eyes weren't working properly; she blinked several times, rapidly, trying to focus. The phone rang once more and then the answering machine picked up.

Suddenly sure it was Daina calling, she lurched to her feet, stumbled backward and slammed into the corner of the shelving unit. She cried out as pain lanced, then radiated through her lower back. She managed to keep her feet and scrabbled around, reaching for the phone as the answering blurb on her machine rattled off. A second later, it wasn't Daina's voice that filled her ears, but Perry's.

"Hey, Emma, it's Perry, it's, um, five fifty-seven—"

She latched onto that: five fifty-seven. She'd only been out a couple of minutes this time.

"—and I was in the neighborhood, so I thought—"

She ceased listening, just grabbed for the phone, pressed the Talk button as she brought it up; the deafening screech of feedback filled her ear, her head, and she almost dropped the phone. "God*dammit!*" she muttered, almost crying. "Perry, wait, hang on!" She reached for the answering machine, turned it off, while in her ear, Perry was saying, "Emma, are you there?"

She sagged back against the shelving. "Yeah, I'm here." Her voice was breathless, strained.

"You're home, hey, what—?"

She started to slide down to the floor, caught herself, pulled herself back up. "Perry, where are you?" she broke in, forcing herself to sound calm, to remain calm. Panic now would undo her.

"Uh, at the top of your street. Are you okay? I was just—"

"Perry, I need your help. Now." She bit the words off, spat them out. "Come to my apartment. I'll meet you downstairs."

"Okay. I'm there in twenty seconds."

She reached for her gun. Released the magazine, checked to ensure it was loaded, slapped it back in. She didn't bother holstering it. She was afraid if she tried to bend over, she might pass out again. She pushed off the shelving unit carefully, tried her first steps, swayed drunkenly, halted to steady herself and tried again. This time worked better. Her legs obeyed her brain, and she managed to stumble to the door. She pulled it open, threw it wide and made her unsteady way down the hall. Behind her, the door sighed shut on its pneumatic hinge and locked with a soft *click*.

She used the guardrail bordering the stairwell for support, being careful not to look over the side, afraid of vertigo, even though she was only on the second floor. Her head pounded a steady rhythm as she walked carefully to the stairs. The stairs were wide and well spaced. She managed them, barely. She reached the first landing and now she could feel herself strengthening, steadying. She descended the next risers with less difficulty.

She reached the foyer and there was Perry, on the other side of the glass door, staring in at her, wide-eyed. She approached the door with relative smoothness, caught sight of her reflection in the glass and saw her bruised, bloodied and damaged face. *Have to take care of that*, she thought, as she leaned toward the door, rested her weight against it, and released the latch. Perry pulled the door open, unbalancing her. She practically fell into his arms.

"Emma! Jesus, what—?"

She shook him off, shook off his concern. "Let's go." She was already pushing past him.

He was right behind her, his hand brushing against her back, touching her elbow. "Which hospital?"

"No hospital," she told him shortly, shaking off his hand.

She knew she looked a terrible sight, knew she'd have to explain that, and why they weren't going to the hospital. She told him as much as she could, as quickly as she could. She stuck to the facts, refused to embellish. In his truck, a huge Dodge Ram 4x4, she ended by saying, "She's going to kill her. We have maybe fifteen minutes."

"Jesus, no pressure, huh?" He grinned tightly, grimly. "Don't worry. I can do it. Hang on." He threw the truck into gear and floored it.

She was thrown back in her seat and the world skewed momentarily. Quickly regaining her equilibrium, she reached into her pocket for her cell phone, asking at the same time, "Are you carrying?"

"Yeah. Glove box." His voice was as tight and grim as his grin had been.

She opened the glove box one-handed, reached for the

Glock, a twin to the one trapped beneath her leg on the seat. She thrust it toward him. He shoved it in his pants without a word. She hit the speed dial on her phone for 911. As she raised the phone to her ear, the sky was suddenly lit up by a flash of lightning. The storm she'd been expecting was on its way to becoming a reality.

As she waited to be connected, she heard a bleep in her ear. *What the hell?* She glanced at the screen, saw the warning message Battery Very Low, and cursed herself for a dozen kinds of fool. She pressed the phone tightly to her ear, as Perry drove very fast, very well, through the city streets. When the dispatcher came on the line, Emma steeled herself to absolute calm.

"Listen to me carefully. This is Constable Emma Kirby, with the Winnipeg City Police Department—" The *bleep* sounded again. She ignored it, and rattled off her badge number. "There is an emergency situation at 27 Descartes Crescent, a woman with a gun. She has targeted—" And then her phone died.

"Mother*fucker!*" she exclaimed, and hurled the useless device to the floorboards.

"Emma, Jesus—!" Perry shot her a quick startled look.

"My fucking phone died!"

"So use mine! Jesus, calm down!" He gestured to the car phone, under the dash.

Taking a deep breath and forcing herself to relax, she reached for it, called 911 again. The dispatcher quickly assured her that emergency units had been dispatched to the address she had given, based on the information already provided. Could she please provide more details, though, in case something more was needed? Emma did so, explaining the situation quickly, succinctly. She only hung up when she was certain that all possible emergency units were on their way.

She glanced at the dashboard clock. Eight minutes had passed. Cathy had, what, a five-minute lead? *Shit, we're running out of time.* The woman couldn't possibly drive any faster than Perry, who was careening in and out of traffic, smoothly, competently. Still, Emma's heart and gut clenched with tightly controlled near-panic. The sky lit up, flashes of lightning illuminating the dark swollen-looking clouds' innards and underbellies with building, blinding intensity.

She raised the phone again, to call the Buchanan residence. With something close to despair, she realized she didn't know the number. *Directory assistance, call directory.* She did so, as they hurtled through the city of Winnipeg; the traffic and scenery whizzing by made her feel slightly dizzy.

The operator came on line; Emma quickly identified herself and her emergency. And when the connection was made, the sound that filled Emma's ear was the *dah-dah-dah* of a busy signal.

"Shall I try again?" the operator asked.

"Yes, until we get through," Emma told her, willing herself to patience. "It's a matter of life or death."

Perry suddenly slammed on the brakes as a car veered to get out of their way. Emma was thrown forward, caught by her shoulder harness, and jerked back sharply.

"I'm not much good to her dead, Perry," she muttered dryly, a bit of herself coming back. Her head ached tremendously.

"Sorry. That wasn't my fault." He shot her a shamefaced grin as he roared the truck back into the flow. A few seconds later, he glanced over once more, at her face. "You're a mess," he observed, none too tactfully.

"Gee, Perry, thanks."

Emma wondered why the Buchanan's line was busy, hoped there was no ominous reason for it. She still had time; she knew she still had time. As she waited, she pulled down the window visor before her with its inlaid mirror and lights. Looking at herself, she could see she was, indeed, a mess. The two-inch gash over her brow was a clean split, and had already clotted over, but it had bled excessively, as head wounds will. There was a fair amount of dried blood on her face and neck and ear; there was some caked in her hair. The wound itself was puffy and bruised, and her left eye was swollen, though not entirely shut.

"What did she hit you with?" Perry asked, with a sideways glance.

"The butt of a .38." She heard the operator still trying to get through.

"Ouch."

"Yeah, just a little."

They drove, or rather raced, in silence for a while. Emma was impressed with his driving. Simply for something to say, feeling a need to talk, she asked, "Why don't you drive like this in the cruiser?"

"Because you won't let me," he shot back with a grin.

She almost grinned in return, but couldn't quite do it, her heart wasn't in it. He seemed to notice her difficulty.

"So, do you love her?" he asked, and his voice was gentle.

"Yes, Perry, I do." And oh God, it felt so good to say it. "I love her very much. I don't know how that's possible, after only a couple of weeks, but I do."

"Anything is possible," he said.

And she looked at him, surprised and grateful. But she couldn't say anything, because in her ear the phone was ringing and she jerked. The phone was answered by a male voice, Steve Buchanan's voice, and she spoke urgently. "Steve, it's Emma, listen, I'm—"

"Emma, thank God," he broke in, sounding calm and agitated at the same time. "Some woman showed up, she has a gun, she came for Daina—"

The words filled Emma with desperation. She shoved it brutally aside, kept her focus. "Are they still there, Steve?" she barked. "What's going on?"

"They're going to the car, the gun is pointed at Daina, we were told not—"

She'd heard enough. They were less than a minute away. Perry had made phenomenal time. "Listen to me, Steve. You and Marlene need to get somewhere safe—the basement, go to the basement, don't come up until someone calls you—"

"But—"

"Do it!" she snapped. "There are guns, there might be gunfire. I've called the police and—"

"We called, too," he told her.

It explained the busy signal. "Good, now get to the basement, Steve. Now! We're almost there."

And then Steve said something that almost broke her heart. "Save her, Emma, please. Save her."

Oh, God, I'm trying *to.* "Get to the basement," she ordered, and disconnected.

And then they were pulling into the crescent with a scream of brakes, and then a squeal of tires as Perry accelerated into the curve. And as she reached for her gun, automatically chambering a round, she saw, half a block away, Daina and Cathy beside the Sunfire. And she saw how close they had cut it, and in a flash of lightning that lit up the air like a strobe, she saw something else as well: she saw Cathy shift, step into the space between the open door and the car, and then the two of them seemed to stand in a moment of indecision, confusion. And in a split second of clarity, lit by another flash of lightning, she saw the one thing which might make a difference. And she said, coldly, "Ram it, Perry."

"What?" He sounded startled.

"Ram it," she repeated, because she could see it and it could work.

A second later, she saw both Daina and Cathy look their way, heads raised and eyes widened identically.

And then Perry must have seen what she saw. "Hang on," he said tightly.

She fumbled with her right hand to find the button to retract the window, glanced down, found it. And as the window rolled down, and they hurtled forward, she leaned out and bellowed, "Daina, *MOVE!*"

And as she watched, Daina moved. She recoiled from Cathy as if burned, slid, lost her footing on the grass, regained it, spun around and began to run.

CHAPTER THIRTY-FIVE

Emma saw Daina begin to run and felt fiercely proud. She slipped back into the cab as Perry pulled the wheel sharply to the left, was braking, crying out "Hang on!" again. She braced herself as best she could, as the truck bumper clipped the outside left of the Sunfire's bumper. The compact vehicle jumped and slammed into the curb. The open passenger door swung violently, connecting with Cathy Marks.

Then Emma was caught up in a startling blur of fabric and cornstarch as the airbags deployed. She fought with the airbag, Glock gripped tightly, as she reached to release her seat-belt.

Perry was just a little faster. He freed himself, threw his door open, leaped out onto the pavement.

Cathy Marks had apparently only been clipped. She was rising to her feet on the grass bordering the street. The car stood between her and them, and nothing stood between her and Daina. She saw Cathy raise her head, turn to look after Daina.

Flash of lightning. Surreal. Everything felt surreal all of a sudden.

Emma released her seat-belt, fought back the airbag, threw her door open.

Flash of lightning. Low rumble of thunder.

Perry was at the front of the truck. "Hey!" he called out, bringing his weapon up to bear. "Police! Don't move!"

Emma saw it clearly: Cathy glancing around, looking almost irritated, raising her gun, and without hesitation, firing twice. There was less than ten feet separating them. The reports were loud, startling. Perry spun, staggered, looking surprised as he went down without a sound. Emma's shock encompassed a world, but she looked away, slipped to the pavement, and saw Cathy turn. Daina had skidded to a halt on the lawn at the sound of the gunshots, halfway to her parents house. Her eyes were huge.

"Daina, *run!*" Emma was squeezing her way through the space between the vehicles, trying to bring her weapon up and over; she lost her balance, as well as a second or two.

Daina turned away at the sound of Emma's voice, just as Cathy started to move forward.

By the time Emma managed to bring her weapon up, Cathy was between her and Daina; it was too risky to shoot.

Another flash of lightning, brightening the entire sky.

Emma saw Cathy raise the .38 and fire at the same time Daina turned. She missed. Daina was running again. Cathy broke into a run after her. Emma finally cleared the vehicles, sprinted after them both. She couldn't shoot, couldn't take that chance. She could only run, hope to intercept. Perry was down, wounded, and she couldn't spare a second to check on him.

Lightning continued to rip open the skies. Thunder boomed much closer.

Daina had reached the front steps, was climbing them. She reached the top riser, grabbed the screen door handle, flung it wide, grasped the knob of the inside door.

Emma strained to cover the vast frontage of the Buchanan yard. Cathy had closed the distance between her and Daina to less than fifty feet. Emma was rapidly closing in on Cathy. And then Cathy halted, lifted the .38, and took aim. Standing as she was at the top of the stairs, Daina made a perfect target. Firing her own weapon was simply not an option. Emma did the only thing she could: she ran straight at Cathy.

But, oh God, she was too slow, still too far, and she heard Cathy fire three shots in rapid succession just as Daina managed to get the door open; Daina cried out, jerked violently to the right, pitched forward through the opening door.

Emma's horror was absolute. So was her rage. She slammed into Cathy from behind, a full body check, her shoulder a battering ram. Cathy was propelled several feet forward; her breath was knocked from her in a startled *oof!* The shock and force of the collision unbalanced Emma. She stumbled, felt herself falling, but her reflexes and training kicked in and she managed a tuck and roll. She regained her feet smoothly, easily. She'd held onto her gun; gripping it tightly, she spun in Cathy's direction like some feral cat, hot and wild and deadly.

Cathy, struggling to roll from her back onto her side, had managed to hold onto her weapon. Incredibly, she was actually bringing the .38 up.

"Don't," Emma told her, striding forward, arm outstretched, Glock in hand, aimed directly at her. "Drop it." She didn't recognize the sound of her own voice.

"Fuck you," Cathy wheezed out breathlessly, swinging the .38 in Emma's direction.

Emma fired from seven feet away without missing a step or breaking stride, a single shot that took Cathy in the chest. Cathy bucked and slammed back onto the lawn. The gun tumbled from her hand. Emma covered the remaining distance with her same long stride and kicked the weapon away. She shoved her own gun into her pants at the small of her back. And then she turned and glanced down.

Cathy lay as she had fallen, arms at her sides, bent at the elbows, hands in the air, clenching and unclenching spasmodically. Her shirtfront was darkening with blood. She was pale, getting paler, and her eyes were huge, round, staring. Her mouth worked soundlessly. A wheezing, whistling sound came from her. A flash of lightning bathed the scene, revealed the spittle flecked with red gathering on her lips. A lung shot, if not more. Glocks fired soft-nosed rounds which mushroomed on impact; they rarely left an exit wound.

Emma noted this all in the space of a couple of seconds. She felt nothing, thought nothing. She glimpsed her key ring hanging half out of the woman's jeans. "I'd like my keys back," she said tonelessly, and bent and hooked them with a finger. Pocketing them, she turned her back, coldly uncaring, and made a run for the house.

Daina lay half in, half out of the house, her legs caught between the screen door and the doorjamb. She was struggling to free her legs, kicking weakly, whimpering. Emma gently opened the door, secured it with the attachment on the hinge. The sight of the blood soaking her shirt, her beige shorts, the carpeting beneath her, caused her heart to lurch and constrict with sharp fear, her throat to close up. Stepping over her, over the threshold, she called out loudly, hoarsely, "Steve! Marlene!" She sank to her knees at Daina's side.

"Emma?" Daina's voice was small, scared, confused.

"I'm here, honey." Emma leaned over, looked into blue eyes that were now wide with surprise and vague incomprehension. She grasped the hand that was grabbing for her. "It's okay, I'm here." Managing to sound calm, when she felt anything but.

She registered the sound of hurrying footfalls on stairs.

"It hurts," Daina whispered. "Oh, fuck, it hurts." And she started to cry.

"I know, honey, I know," Emma soothed her, squeezing her hand, brushing a palm over her brow. "Let me take a look, okay? Try to stay still, try to stay calm."

Distantly, she heard the wail of sirens. She quickly ran her eyes and hands over Daina, pulled up her shirt to reveal a single gunshot wound in her right side; the bullet had entered her lower back, punched out through her lower belly about an inch or so higher. It was a clean shot, but there was no way of knowing what it might have hit on the way through. It was bleeding profusely.

She glanced around for something, anything, to use as a compress. Spying a flannel jacket in the closet straight ahead, she yanked it off its metal hanger which went *whanging* off somewhere, and folded the jacket roughly.

"This is going to hurt, sweetheart," she warned Daina. She gently eased Daina toward her, rolling her slightly forward onto her hip. She pressed the wad of fabric firmly against her back.

Daina shrieked thinly. Emma tried not to flinch. Behind her, she heard Marlene Buchanan cry out, "Oh, my God! Daina!"

Steve and Marlene looked as shocked and horrified as Emma felt. Marlene was turning white. Emma fixed her with a stern look. "Don't you fall apart on me. She needs you. *I* need you. Get me some towels, hand towels, from the bathroom. Can you do that?"

Marlene nodded, eyes on Emma.

"Good. Go. Now."

Daina's breath was panting out of her. Her eyes were squeezed tightly shut. She was becoming pale.

"Daina?"

Daina opened her eyes, blinked rapidly. "Yeah?"

"I'm going to lay you back down, okay? It might hurt again, but your weight will help with the compress."

Daina gave a tight little nod. Emma slowly lowered her so her back was again on the floor, this time with the flannel jacket acting as compress beneath her. Daina winced, but lay still.

"Okay?" Emma asked, reaching for her hand, gently squeezing it.

Daina nodded, squeezed back. "Okay."

Marlene appeared with the towels. Emma grabbed two. Daina's belly was slick with blood, so much blood it was almost as if someone had upended a can of paint on her. Emma placed the towels over the exit wound. "Steve, get down here," she said calmly.

Steve dropped to his knees beside her. She glanced at him; he was almost as white as his wife.

"Hold out your hands."

They were steady. He seemed focused, controlled.

"Press here," she told him. "Gently, but firmly."

He placed a hand where she indicated and applied pressure. He flinched visibly when Daina cried out once more.

"I know it hurts, sweetheart, I'm sorry." Emma leaned over, made eye contact with her. "I'm really sorry, but I need you to be calm, okay? Can you do that? Just slow your breathing down." Daina's breath was rushing in and out of her in short, sharp gasps. "Try to calm yourself. I know it hurts, but the ambulance is coming and I need you to stay awake and stay calm, okay?"

Daina squeezed her eyes shut, nodded, whispered, "Okay." A tear leaked past her eyelid, slipped down her cheek.

"That's my girl," Emma said, and her voice shook slightly. She brushed the tear away. "Marlene," she said, strengthening her voice with an effort, "I need you down here, I need you to talk to her, about anything, just talk to her, keep her awake, alert, calm." The danger of Daina slipping into shock now was very real, very present. "I need to check on my partner, he was shot—"

"Your partner is fine," she heard from outside, and she whipped her head around, to see Perry coming slowly up the steps, swaying slightly, backlit by flashes of lightning. The sound of sirens was very close.

"Jesus, Perry!" Emma rose, grabbed another couple of towels. She and Marlene traded places.

She reached Perry's side just as he sat heavily on the top step. His entire left side was drenched with blood, and his left arm hung uselessly. He held it tight against his body with his right hand.

"How bad?" she asked gently, kneeling beside him.

"Two in the shoulder. Shattered it, I think. I can't really feel anything."

She reached to open the top buttons of his shirt, eased the fabric aside, surveyed the bloody ruin of his shoulder. It looked very bad. She pressed the towels against the injury to stem the blood flow. He hissed sharply. "Okay, *that* hurts."

"I'm sorry. Here, hold these," she told him.

He looked pretty gray, but he was alert. Jerking his head back in Daina's direction, he asked, "How is she?"

"Single gunshot wound. Lower abdomen." She pressed her lips briefly together, shook her head. "I don't know. She's bleeding a lot." She swallowed, hard.

"Go to her," he said gently. "I'm all right."

"What about her?" Emma thrust her chin in Cathy's direction. A flash of lightning illuminated her still form.

"She's dead." The words fell like cold stones from his lips.

A crack of thunder punctuated the news. She realized the sirens had ceased; red flashing lights now filled the area. The minutes it had taken them to get there had seemed like hours.

And then, behind her, Marlene's voice, brittle with anxiety and fear, called out, "Emma!"

She shot to her feet, dashed back inside.

Marlene looked at her, eyes wide. "She's fading in and out. She won't stay awake."

Emma knelt, lifted Daina's head, cradled it. Her eyes were closed, her muscles slack, her breathing shallow. "Daina? Honey? Wake up, it's me, Emma." She spoke in a strong, sure voice, to penetrate the depths Daina was sinking into. She shook her gently, patted her cheek. "Daina, come on now, wake up, sweetheart. Wake *up*."

Daina eyelids fluttered, opened. Her pupils were tiny, black pinheads. She was going into shock. Emma glanced quickly at the towels Steve continued to hold firmly in place. They were darkly sodden.

"Hey, you," she said, looking back at Daina, forcing a smile. "Stay awake, okay, stay with me. The ambulance is here." She could hear the noise and bustle of the EMTs. Mercifully, the sirens had been turned off. "You're going to be fine, just fine. Just hang on, don't—" *leave me*, she almost said, and she felt herself beginning to shake, felt a sob threatening to tear loose from her chest, and she fought it all back, "—don't give up, Daina, stay with me, okay?"

Daina blinked slowly; tears leaked from the corners of both eyes. "Did you get her?" she whispered.

Emma had to lean close to hear her. "Yes, I got her."

Daina managed a faint, fleeting smile. "Good. Fucking bitch shot me." She spoke with a trace of her usual fire.

Emma smiled, leaned forward, kissed Daina's forehead, and saw tears, her own tears, fall onto Daina's face, to mix with hers. And then she felt Daina suddenly relax in her arms, and with alarm, she looked to see her eyes had rolled back and her eyelids were closing. And she cried, hoarsely, "No, Daina, no! Wake *up*, stay with me, *please...*"

The EMTs were there then, and she had to get out of their way. Steve and Marlene stood back with her, while all around them the air was lit with red, washed in the red of flashing emergency lights. And she looked down to see her hands were covered in red, washed in the red of Daina's blood. And she remembered the night—*had it only been two weeks ago?*—when her hands had been similarly awash in Daina's blood, when she had saved her as she lay bleeding her life out, and she had a terrible, frightening feeling that this time she hadn't saved her, couldn't save her. She had tried, dear God, she had tried, but she was desperately afraid that this time she had failed.

She stood helplessly off to the side, watching the EMTs attend to Daina. Glancing outside, she saw two more ministering to Perry. Three police officers converged, surrounded Cathy Marks' body, then looked toward the house. One of them broke away, heading for the house and she thought, *Ah*, in a distant kind of way, *I'll have to answer some questions.* A moment later, another EMT was in her face, insisting she be looked at. She suffered through it, suffered through the few preliminary questions asked by the cop, surrendered her gun and her ID badge. It was protocol; she'd fired her weapon, shot someone. She relinquished both freely. And all the while, she wondered why it all had had to happen. But it was pointless to wonder; she didn't have an answer. She knew she never would. Some questions just didn't have answers.

She watched Daina being lifted onto a stretcher, watched as they prepared to bear her terribly pale, still form away. She felt as she had that first night she had borne witness to this exact same scene. She felt herself disassociating, felt disconnected, raw inside, altered. She felt as if she would fracture where she stood, that she would shatter into a thousand little pieces and those pieces would never quite fit together as they had, that the events of this day, this night would change her utterly. Without even realizing it, she began to shake.

Outside, it began to rain.

EPILOGUE

She sat on the edge of the bed, stiff, unmoving, still as glass, feeling just as fragile. Her eyes were wide, blank, staring at the wall three and a half feet in front of her, not seeing it. Her hands were folded in her lap, her feet on the floor, ankles together. The only discernable movement was the slow and steady rising and falling of her chest as she breathed; inhale, exhale, inhale, exhale. Automatic, life sustaining. No thought required at all. Which was a good thing; coherent, cohesive thought eluded her. Her mind was as blank as the white wall before her. No shape, no contour, empty, flat.

She was dressed in black: black dress, black hose, black pumps. A black sweater was draped over her shoulders. It was one of the few occasions when she would wear a dress; normally she eschewed them, considering them somewhat impractical. But for certain events, she felt that a dress was a more appropriate choice of outfit, that it denoted a measure of respect in specific instances: civic functions, weddings, funerals. The sweater around her shoulders was warm, almost uncomfortably so, but she knew she would be grateful for it later. The temperature had dropped in the last week. Summer was fading into fall. It made much more sense to wear dresses in the summer.

She'd been present when they'd turned off the life-support, though she hadn't wanted to be. But her attendance, her presence, had been requested, almost expected, and she hadn't the willpower to refuse. But it had felt all wrong, she had felt horribly out of place, as if she were someone in a play, an extra who'd been scripted in at the last minute, with no speaking lines, no real reason for being there, except to stand off to the sidelines and bear witness to the event. And, in reality, that was the part she had played; when it was over, and the time of death given in a hushed tone and dutifully written down, she had silently turned away from the others present, and had strode stiffly, swiftly from the room.

The cause of death, as she understood it, had been a brain embolism. The words reverberated through her mind as her long stride carried her from the hospital. *Brain embolism.* Such a complicated word for such a simple thing. A clot, which had cut off the flow of blood to the brain, starving it of oxygen, killing it. She couldn't quite grasp it, or accept it. She gave up trying. She left the hospital without a backward glance.

She'd received a phone call later that evening. The funeral would be two days hence. Again, her attendance was requested. Again, she hadn't the willpower to refuse. She agreed, though she hated funerals. On the few occasions she'd had to attend one, she had always felt uncomfortable, restless. But she had suffered through them because it was the respectful thing to do.

This funeral, however, was different. She'd never lost anyone close to her before. And while she'd been denied the chance to get to know the deceased as well as she would have liked, as well as she would have wanted, still, there was a history there. She could not turn her back on that. She may have felt deeply troubled in regard to the loss, confused, torn, saddened, but she also knew where her duty lay, her responsibility.

And so she sat, perfectly still, in her bedroom, and the funeral was in an hour and she had to get to the funeral home, but she couldn't move. She could only sit and breathe and stare.

She heard a sound then, a soft knock at her door, and then the even softer tread of footsteps across the carpet. She registered an approaching figure, also dressed in black, in her peripheral vision: black slacks, black silk shirt, black dress shoes. She didn't turn her head, didn't look. It was only when the figure stood before her, and then crouched at her knees and said gently, "Hey, you," that she tore her eyes away from the wall.

"Hey, yourself," she greeted Daina softly, with a trace of a smile.

Daina covered her hands with her own, looking up into Emma's face, her eyes a startling sapphire blue. Emma stared into them, saw herself reflected in them.

"How are you feeling?" Daina asked.

"I don't know," she answered honestly, because she truly didn't know how she felt. "I mean, he was my father, I should be feeling something, but—I don't know."

"Do you still want to go?"

"Want to? No, not really. But I should. Maybe—" She paused, considering. "Maybe I need to." She lifted one shoulder in a vague shrug.

Daina nodded, seemingly more in acknowledgment than agreement. "Do you still want me to go with you?" The question was voiced in a considerate, thoughtful manner.

Emma smiled. "Yes. I want you with me. Always."

It was more of an answer than was required and she knew it. Daina obviously knew it, as well. She nodded again, then lowered her head to rest her cheek on Emma's knee.

"How are *you* feeling?" Emma asked, lifting a hand to gently run her fingers through Daina's hair. It was longer now, not short and spiky like it had been.

"I'm fine."

"You're sure?"

A slight movement against her knee, a nod beneath her fingertips. "I'm sure."

It had been four weeks since that night at the Buchanan home. Daina had spent eight days of those four weeks in the hospital. Already taxed from her initial injuries, her body had barely been able to withstand the brutal shock of the second assault. She had become tachycardic, due to the massive blood loss, as her heart valiantly strained to keep her alive. Eventually, she had been stabilized with the help of blood transfusions, and she'd undergone emergency surgery to resection her perforated intestine and to remove her right kidney, which had been irreparably damaged by the bullet.

That first night Emma had spent at the hospital, getting coffee for herself and Daina's parents, sitting and talking quietly and worrying with them.

"You're blaming yourself, aren't you?" Steve asked at one point, as the three of them sat anxiously awaiting word on the outcome of the surgery. It had already been three hours.

"Shouldn't I?" Emma had asked, somewhat bitterly. She sat with her head lowered, hands clasped between her knees.

"No, you shouldn't," he replied firmly. "No more than I should, or Marlene, or Daina, herself. This is nobody's fault. Shit happens, as they say. Based on what you've told us, nobody could have foreseen this."

She knew he spoke the truth. But that didn't ease the ache in her heart, the palpable fear and despair that she hadn't done enough and that Daina would pay the price for her shortsightedness. He spoke the truth, but what good was that truth when the woman that they loved lay down the hall on a surgical table fighting for her life?

"Do you know what she said to us, when you left this afternoon?" Marlene asked quietly, gently.

Emma could only shake her bowed head.

"She said 'That's the woman I'm going to marry.'"

Emma raised her head, startled, dumbfounded. "She said that?"

Both Marlene and Steve nodded.

"She said that you were her sanctuary. That she'd never felt safer than she did when she was with you." Marlene's eyes met Emma's without blinking. They were a paler shade of Daina's.

Emma hadn't wanted to hear those words, had felt ripped open and scoured raw at the sound of them, at the knowledge that she hadn't kept Daina safe, had failed utterly to do so. Steve must have seen the look on her face, must have read it for what it was, her absolute refusal to entertain the notion that she had done everything she could, that nothing else she might have done would have changed the outcome in the slightest.

"Now, you listen to me, young lady," he began, and Emma, despite herself, had smiled inwardly at that. "My daughter is *alive* because of you, twice over, and she is *happy*, because of you. If you want to beat yourself up over *could-haves* and *should-haves*, you go right ahead. But you're wrong to do so and I, for one, will not help you do so."

She had sat motionless for several moments, allowing the words to sink in. And then she had stood. "Excuse me," she said politely, and had left the waiting room, blinded by a sudden flow of scalding tears.

After stepping outside and sobbing almost wildly into her hands, crouched against a brick wall, she had eventually managed to rein in her emotions. She ended up prowling the halls restlessly. It was there that she had run into Sergeant Michaels, heading down the hall she was pacing.

"Emma, there you are. How are you?"

She gave him a cursory, automatic response.

He'd blinked, asked after Daina.

"She's in surgery."

"Is it bad?"

Emma shrugged. "It could be worse, I suppose." Her lower jaw clenched and the muscle there jumped, belying the mildness of her tone.

There was a brief silence, then he asked, "Have you been to see Perry?"

She looked at him sharply. "He's out of surgery?"

"Fifteen minutes ago. He's okay, though how much use he'll regain of his arm is up for debate."

She felt a pang of guilt at that, but only nodded, thanked him for the update. "I'll go see him."

Another silence. He seemed to be gauging her mood. "He told me what happened, his role in it, anyway. I'll need a statement from you."

Like she hadn't already known that. "You'll get it." She was looking past him, her cold reserve a familiar, comfortable suit of armor.

He nodded. "You'll have to go on admin leave. You're aware of that, right? It's protocol. That, and the inquiry."

She jerked her chin once in affirmation, still not looking at him.

"And the psych evaluation, that's mandatory, of course."

She said nothing.

"You've surrendered your gun and badge?"

"At the site," she replied and smiled thinly, humorlessly. "Protocol."

"Will you—do you need some extra time off? For this? I mean, for her?" he added hurriedly.

"I'll let you know," she answered coolly.

She saw him nod.

A brief silence followed.

"Why didn't you call me back?" she asked quietly, still staring down the hall beyond him, feeling her muscles hard and tight beneath her skin. "Why call me, then not return my call?"

He seemed to hesitate, then came out with, "My initial reason for asking you to call me back was to reiterate what I'd spoken with Daina about, so we'd all be on the same page. When I called you later, it was to tell you he was changing his story; they almost always do. He was saying it wasn't him; it was his wife who was after Daina. It sounded ridiculous, especially in light of his confession and his knowledge. And his wife was nowhere to be found; she never answered our calls—"

"So she never showed up at the station?" Emma inquired, mildly curious.

"No, though he said she was in the city, hiding out, he just didn't know where, said that was part of their arrangement. We actually seriously believed he'd killed her and was trying to shift the blame."

Of course. She'd considered the very same thing.

"At any rate, we had nothing to go on, it seemed a flimsy cover-up, so when I got your message, I didn't think it important enough to bother you with."

She finally looked at him, a withering look. "It was important," she said coldly.

He nodded, looked away. He didn't apologize. She was grateful. She might have hit him.

After a moment, he looked back at her. "You'll get your gun and badge back once your admin leave is up. It won't be a problem."

She didn't respond. It didn't matter to her. She'd killed somebody. That *might* have mattered to her, under different circumstances. Right now, nothing mattered, except Daina. She realized that what she had glimpsed, that inescapable change, of herself, of her world, was already happening. *Interesting, how perspective changes.* He'd screwed up, he'd admitted to it. She felt lighter, freer.

"I have to get back," she told him and turned.

"Listen…"

She paused, eyed him narrowly.

"I hope…" He blinked, appeared uncomfortable, unsure beneath her gaze. "I hope she's going to be okay."

"So do I."

"Take care of yourself, okay?"

"Mmm," was all she said, which really wasn't anything at all. And then she walked away.

"We should get going," Daina said, looking up at her.

Emma nodded, tiredly.

"Help me up?" Daina held out her hand.

Emma grasped it, helped her to her feet, rose at the same time. She saw Daina wince, heard the small, painful exhalation.

"Are you okay?" she asked, peering into her eyes, those stunning blue eyes, with concern.

Daina gave her a smile, warm, genuine. "I'm better than okay. I have you, don't I?"

Emma smiled at that. "Yes, you do." And she leaned to kiss her, and marked the desire that flared within her.

Daina smiled at her again, a knowing smile this time. *How does she do that, get inside me like that?* But she knew that some questions just didn't have answers. And she gripped Daina's hand, they interlocked their fingers, and together walked slowly from the room.